SPACESHIPS
IN THE NIGHT

Oisin B

OISÍN BLENNERHASSETT
SPACESHIPS
IN THE NIGHT

LEVANDER PRESS

First published by Levander Press in 2022
Dublin
Ireland
For further details visit levanderpress.com

Paperback	ISBN: 978 1 78846 243 3
eBook – ePub format	ISBN: 978 1 78846 244 0
Amazon paperback edition	ISBN: 978 1 78846 245 7

Produced by Kazoo Independent Publishing Services
222 Beech Park, Lucan, Co. Dublin
kazoopublishing.com

Kazoo Independent Publishing Services is not the publisher of this work. All rights and responsibilities pertaining to this work remain with Levendar Press.

Kazoo offers independent authors a full range of publishing services.
For further details visit kazoopublishing.com

Cover artwork © Lauren O'Hara 2022
Cover design by Andrew Brown
Printed in the EU

PLAYLIST

Chapter 1	*Lovely Day*	9
Chapter 2	*A Night to Remember*	17
Chapter 3	*Lonely Town*	29
Chapter 4	*I'm Coming Out*	38
Chapter 5	*Forget Me Nots*	52
Chapter 6	*One Night Only*	65
Chapter 7	*And the Beat Goes On*	80
Chapter 8	*Stand on the Word*	95
Chapter 9	*Heat You Up (Melt You Down)*	106
Chapter 10	*There's an Angel in the Shower*	119
Chapter 11	*Teardrops*	125
Chapter 12	*Inspector Norse*	136
Chapter 13	*Wolf Like Me*	154
Chapter 14	*Stayin' Alive*	168
Chapter 15	*Get Free*	181
Chapter 16	*Watermelon Man*	195

Chapter 17   *Fists of Fury*   204

Chapter 18   *I Say a Little Prayer*   213

Chapter 19   *Everybody Dance*   224

Chapter 20   *The Hero and the Madman*   239

Chapter 21   *I Wanna Dance with Somebody*   253

Chapter 22   *Down in My Soul*   266

1

LOVELY DAY

Music is a magical thing, as Bernard discovered on the day he met Levander. Before that day, he thought music was nothing more than sweet sounds and background noise. He didn't listen to it, nor did he play any instruments.

Then he met Levander, and Bernard was dropped into the dangers and delights of disco music. For that was the day he first set foot on the Musical Planet.

The adventures began on a sunny Saturday morning. After cereal and cartoons, Bernard got dressed for a skateboarding session. His best friends, the Skater Kids, would be spinning wheels on Monday, and he needed to practise. He combed out the tangles in his Afro, and was ready for the day.

Coming downstairs with a skateboard under his arm, he heard his mum in the kitchen. 'Prepare to be covered in pancakes!' she said.

Shaking his head, Bernard walked in and found her talking to a new canvas on her painting easel. It wasn't always normal, having a modern-art mum. Ealaín was a bubbly African-American and an excellent artist. She'd earned a reputation for making wacky versions of fairytale characters. She'd even won an award for making a Big Bad Wolf out of hundreds of recycled forks.

'Don't tell me you're going to waste our pancakes on art,' he said.

'Good morning!' she said, chewing the tip of her paintbrush. 'No, I'm going to paint Sleeping Beauty's castle surrounded by pancakes rather than thorns.'

'Well, you always make it work,' he said.

She smiled at him, then her eyes flicked to the skateboard. 'Don't think I've forgotten your chore.'

'It's so nice out . . .'

'You promised you'd clean the garage. Get in there and tidy it up. And make sure to be careful with snacking as it will attract the mice!'

'Sounds like paradise. All right, just don't ruin my stuff. I don't want a repeat of that time you turned my socks into ski-masks for snakes.'

'That was one time! And they were for tiny dragons!'

Bernard walked into the garden and stopped by the palm tree planted in memory of Ceol. His father had passed away in a surfing accident when Bernard was tiny. He knew from Ealaín's stories that his dad had been a warm-hearted Hawaiian who loved music and the sea. She insisted that Bernard had inherited his sense of adventure.

He tapped his father's tree for good luck, then strolled into the shadows of the garage. It was a cold, whitewashed space, crammed with forgotten clutter. Pieces of furniture, covered by sheets, sat like forgotten presents. A bicycle without wheels lay barnacled with rust. A cracked old clock read quarter past eight, and probably would forever.

The task, at first, was as boring as he'd feared. He moved boxes out into the garden, tidied up the junk, and tried to ignore the gloomy cobwebs.

After forty minutes he discovered the pyramid of cardboard boxes. Most of the labels promised contents as dull as ditch water. Taxes. Cassettes. Swimming togs. However, he uncovered one at the centre which sparked his interest. Bernard recognized the art on the label; this was the property of Ceol. His dad had painted what seemed like the inside of an enchanting bell tower. Among the golden bells there was a swarm of silver stars. They spelt out 'DISCO RECORDS'.

An hour later, Bernard left the garage holding a single box. He tiptoed back to the house and eased open the back door. His mother was at the computer talking to her agent, Ali, on video call.

'The art world needs new stories!' Ali was saying. 'Fairy tales don't astound like they used to, unless they're packaged in a colourful app.'

'I'm not about to swap out my paintbrushes for a smartphone.'

'Just give us something new, some unfamiliar va-va-voom!'

As Ealaín argued her case, Bernard slipped upstairs unnoticed. He swung by his bedroom for headphones, then entered the spare room. This small space housed stacks of books, art supplies, and old family photos. He found what he was looking for beneath hills of dog-eared paper: an old, forgotten record player. He dug it out, getting excited. The machine was covered in dust bunnies, so he wiped it down and plugged it in.

When the power light winked on, he connected his headphones and turned to the cardboard box. He opened it up and there, as he expected, was a treasure trove of disco records. He slid them out for inspection, one by one. The record sleeves were huge, about twenty times larger than the cover-art images he was used to on their digital music collection. Bernard chuckled to himself. *How did people manage back then?*

The record sleeves showed many different happy scenes. Robots glinted, swimming pools sparkled, spaceships journeyed across star-bright skies. Musicians beamed in dresses and tuxedos, cool cats from another century.

The very last record caught Bernard's attention. It was called *Discopia*, and the cover art showed a pink and blue cityscape. He flipped it over. On the back there was a warning sticker, and above this were words printed in cursive font:

Side A: Levander's Penthouse

He withdrew the twelve-inch vinyl record and placed it on the record player, with Side A facing upwards. *How dated can it be?* he thought. It began to turn, wheeling round and round. He slid his headphones over his Afro and took hold of the needle. He placed it upon the outermost ring of the record. The music began to play.

It started with drums swelling and getting louder. Then suddenly he heard an explosion of trumpets, strings and singing, and he was launched into a place of stars. The spare room vanished and suddenly he was speeding across outer space, riding an invisible roller coaster. Had Ealaín slipped VR goggles onto his head? Was this an art piece? He felt his eyes and ruled that out. The happy music surrounded him as he rocketed past entire galaxies. His initial shock settled, for he was a skateboarder at heart. He couldn't help but enjoy the thrill.

Before long, a gorgeous display of colourful spheres appeared among the stars. There were hundreds of them, suspended and swirling like so many planets in a solar system. They came together to form a gigantic ball pit, into which Bernard crashed. All he saw was colour. All he heard was disco music.

Then he felt gravity again and stood on solid ground. The colours scampered from his vision, leaving him in a confined space. This wasn't the spare room. Music was muffled in the distance. Feeling his ears, he discovered the headphones were gone. He took a breath to steady himself, and ran his hands over the walls. He discovered a door, and swung it open to find a living room unlike any he'd seen before. A mirrorball stood like a globe in the corner, casting light over everything. Modern-art paintings decorated the lilac walls. Beneath the room's candle chandelier, a video screen was built into the floor. Strangest of all, however, was the occupant of a bubble chair by the sound system.

SPACESHIPS IN THE NIGHT

Staring straight at Bernard was a skeleton. It was stylishly dressed in a silver suit, teamed with a piano-key scarf. Bernard wondered why someone would dress up a skeleton. Then the bones began to move. It stood up, and two enormous butterfly wings spread out behind it.

Bernard rubbed his eyes.

The skeleton spoke in a voice that was chilled and sweet. An ice-cream-smooth voice. 'If you're not a ghost, then that's a great entrance. I've never seen anyone stroll in from there!'

Judging by the voice and clothes, the skeleton was clearly male. Bernard didn't know what to say. He turned and saw that he'd just stepped out of a spaceship. It was seven feet tall and covered in hieroglyphics, like an ancient Egyptian coffin. He scanned its empty interior, extremely befuddled. The skeleton was not so tongue-tied.

'That being said, you could be a funkless thief or a tiny paparazzi. Should I be worried?'

Bernard returned his gaze to the tilted skull. 'Dude! I should be the worried one!' he said. 'You're a stranger and a skeleton. Those are major red flags.'

'Hey, you've got a skeleton too. I'll have no bone-shaming in my home.'

Bernard slapped himself to make sure he wasn't dreaming. At least there was a kindness about this spooky host.

'I'm sorry,' he said. 'I . . . didn't know I was in your home. My name's Bernard, and I guess I'm lost.'

'So,' purred that voice from the skull, 'if you're not here to steal my shoes, how did you get here?'.

'Well . . . I came here by star-travel, I guess I'd call it. And 1 ended up . . . here.'

'You breezed in from another planet?'

'I guess I did. It happened while I was checking out some disco records.'

'DISCO?' The skeleton performed a gleeful backflip. 'Why didn't you say so? No wonder you ended up in my penthouse.'

'Oh. So you must be Levander.'

'The very same!' Levander proudly exclaimed, launching into a lavish introduction. 'Some say I arrived fully-formed in a flashy X-ray disco. Others say I was dug up from the ground by miners, and a saxophone solo from their radio jolted me to life. What can I say? I keep it mysterious.' His great wings flickered. 'It's great to meet you, Bernard. I'm the resident Disco Fairy of Discopia.'

This final word hung like perfume in the air.

Bernard raised an eyebrow. 'Discopia?' he asked. 'What exactly is Discopia?'

'My dear child, look outside!' He pointed to stained-glass doors at one side of the room. At his beckoning, Bernard approached them. They were patterned with pineapples and pianos, and opened out onto a balcony.

What visual riches met Bernard in the starlight!

He looked out from the top of a skyscraper. All around him was a marvellous city, like New York revamped in bubblegum. The sprawl of skyscrapers in pink and blue stood in neat formations. Every window flashed with different colours. Far below, the cars were moving like conga lines on wheels, not a traffic jam in sight. On the pavement some kids were playing hopscotch. Bernard thought he saw golden sparks fly from their hands and dancing feet. Everywhere, the city thumped with disco music.

The winged skeleton stood by his side.

'Welcome to Discopia. The greatest city on the Musical Planet.'

2

A NIGHT TO REMEMBER

'Now,' said Levander, turning on his heels. 'Cloud 9 is spinning records down at Pantheon 54. Why don't you come with me? You can tell me about your world and this disco it holds.'

Bernard turned away from the enchanting metropolis. Walking back inside, he considered his options. His mum would be mad if she found him missing. Then again, she'd be painting pancakes until sundown.

'I don't know . . . I'd set aside the afternoon to go skateboarding.'

Levander bowed, while attaching a silvery cape. 'I wouldn't want to keep you from your world. Feel free to head back through the portal. Honestly, I thought it was an antique tanning bed before you showed up. That being said, you're welcome to join me. We can teach each other the quirks of each other's worlds.'

Bernard looked from the spaceship to the front door. There was no hiding his curiosity. He couldn't return to his normal life without a taste of that city below. 'I'll need to borrow a jacket,' he said, and Levander did a cartwheel.

Ding! Out in the hallway, the lift doors opened. A uniformed operator greeted them from within. She was human and would have looked normal were it not for the vivid lion face paint. The Disco Fairy breezed in and Bernard followed in the cartoonish blue jacket he'd borrowed. There were no buttons on the lift wall.

'How low do you wish to go?' the attendant politely inquired.

'Oh you know me, Kimmy, bring us all the way down!'

'Very good,' Kimmy replied and then proceeded to shake her body, dancing passions Bernard had never seen before. She started to groove her way down to the floor, inch by inch, and as she danced, the elevator went down too. They smoothly descended at a great pace. By the time Kimmy had brought her boogie all the way to the floor, the elevator stopped – ding! – and the doors reopened. 'The basement carpark!' she exclaimed, without rising from the floor. Levander thanked her and exited. Bernard, evermore puzzled by Discopia, repeated the thanks and followed.

Through rows of fancy cars, Bernard kept pace with the long-legged skeleton. 'How did she move the elevator by dancing?' he asked.

'Oooh boy, little one, that right there was boomba – energy channelled through the power of dance. Alongside electricity, boomba from dance and music are what powers this city. Observe.' He performed a twirling backflip, and colourful sparks leaped from his bones and wings. 'That's boomba,' said Levander, as he unlocked a car. 'Now hop up into my Diamante!'

SPACESHIPS IN THE NIGHT

Seeing the Diamante, Bernard happily obliged. The car was a beast of old-school luxury. Poised high on white-walled tyres, the outside gleamed black as if had been painted with midnight. Bernard settled into the spacious passenger seat next to the Disco Fairy. With a mighty roar of the car's engine, the pair cruised out into the streets.

The windscreen framed an epic show of wonders. Happy people glided by on roller skates. Neon signs and shopfronts blazed like enchanted fires. Vintage cars weaved in and out as the streetlights twinkled in time to a city-wide symphony. Rainbows arched overhead like bridges, and people strolled across them.

'It must be nice having this on your doorstep,' said Bernard, trying to take it all in.

'The sights are pretty on point,' Levander replied, 'but around here it's all about the sounds.'

He turned on the radio, and a voice squawked from the speakers. 'What's happening, chicklets? Now for Zam FM's hourly partywatch. Mayor Soldavril has moved her gospel fandango from the Garden of Bopalon to Roseland Park. It's the perfect place for sweet beats and harmony. Stay right here for tunes that are fruity and fruitful. Wahoo!'

As disco music filled the car again, Bernard couldn't help but laugh. 'That dude has charisma,' he said.

'That's Flamingo James, a dear friend of mine. Selectors choose what tunes to play, and he's one of our best. I always listen to his show when I'm not vibing to my own mixtapes.'

'He's not actually a flamingo, is he?'

Levander looked over, confusion colouring his skull.

'Of course he is! Discopia welcomes anyone who wants to live by the disco spirit. Humans, talking animals, the soulified . . . We've got them all!' Just then, Bernard spotted a basketball court where ten tigers were playing a game. They dribbled up and down like humans, jerseys swishing. The ball hit the hoop, and the big cats leaped for the rebound.

Bernard peered out at the pavements of Discopia. There were animals sprinkled here and there, from the cuddly to the cool. He saw gazelles going shopping and a walrus flagging a taxi. He even spotted a mermaid in a futuristic wheelchair. Then, when the Diamante stopped at a red light, a giant croissant in a cowboy hat swaggered across the road before them.

'That's . . . a walking pastry,' said Bernard, barely able to articulate the sight.

Levander, lost in a little dance to the music, looked at the crumbly cowboy. 'Him? Probably a tourist from the Wobbly West. He's soulified . . . Don't you have those on Earth – when a soul ends up in an everyday object?'

'No,' said Bernard, watching the soulified croissant go. He looked around at the far-fetched characters, all brought together in one city, unified by the magical grooves of disco.

Levander laughed, happy with his passenger's wonder. 'There's only ever one Disco Fairy. You can think of me as the city's doctor, making sure the heartbeat stays healthy.'

'What kind of doctor dresses like you?' Bernard mischievously replied.

They moved on, and Bernard saw from a signpost that

they were turning onto a ring road. A river dotted with yachts and speedboats rushed through the night alongside them.

'This beautiful drink is the Vamvozio River,' said Levander. 'It winds all the way to an ocean called the Sonorous Deep.'

Bernard's gaze fell to a shadowy forest across the water, removed from the glitzy city. 'What's that place on the other side of the river?'

The Disco Fairy didn't look over. 'Don't even get me started. Every party has grumpy next-door neighbours. Ours live in the Watermelon Wood. It's brimming with monsters and maniacs. Don't give it another thought.' He turned up the music and drove on.

Bernard continued to examine the mysterious trees. He thought he saw burly shadows moving in the gloom. Then the Diamante turned a corner and emerged once again in the party of skyscrapers and sound.

'So what's the catch?' asked Bernard in disbelief. He looked at his skeletal companion, whose silver suit glittered in the darkness of the car. 'This place is like nowhere I've ever been before. Everybody's smiling, the music's all in sync, you give out scoops of magic. The cities I know are grey, loud, and everyone ghosts each other.'

'My city,' said Levander proudly, 'is built around the positivity of disco. Happy music with four beats per bar so that everyone can jam to its goodness. You said you arrived here by listening to this stuff? Then you should know that there's no catch. Discopia stands tall thanks to the message and boomba of disco music.'

Bernard was impressed by the world he was cruising through, but he remained unconvinced. 'What about this whole dancing thing? Isn't that . . . you know . . . a bit stupid?'

Levander slammed the brakes, the car screeched to a halt and he slumped forward over the steering wheel. He appeared suddenly lifeless in the tradition of normal skeletons. Cars behind them started to beep – even the car horns sounded lovely – and Bernard shook Levander's shoulder. 'Are you all right?'

'Woah, sorry, I tend to faint when I hear such sacrilege.' He started the car again.

Bernard raised his eyebrows. 'Should you be driving?'

'Dancing,' he continued, 'is among the healthiest pursuits of the body, mind and disco spirit. How lucky you are to find yourself under my wing! Let me show you the spells and sorcery of dancing feet.' With this enchanting exclamation, which Bernard was starting to recognize as typical, they arrived outside a building.

Pantheon 54 was a classical stunner. A majestic temple with a turquoise dome, it looked like it had arrived here straight from Ancient Rome, getting tangled up in fairy lights on its way. A queue of swanky Discopians trailed up the polished steps, up to the impressive pillars at the entrance. Levander parked the Diamante right outside and unbuckled his seatbelt.

'It seems pretty lax to leave your car here,' said Bernard.

'It lets the people know we're in. Now let's mosey up to the portico and check who's guarding the doors!'

Stepping out, they were met with cheers of devotion.

Levander walked along the line, offering high fives and fist-bumps to everyone. Bernard trailed behind him, looking at all the stylish adults and kids. He started feeling nervous, like there were nettles in his chest. He did not want to dance.

'I don't think this is a good idea,' he said, tugging Levander's cape.

The skeleton turned and smiled, his wings flicking happily. 'Nothing bad awaits within these walls. I just want you to enjoy yourself. Now check out this bouncer!'

Guarding the entrance was a soulified fridge. The lower half was dressed in a cubic tuxedo, the upper half was decorated with alphabet magnets that seemed to jumble about and form sentences.

'That's a strange title,' said Bernard. 'He doesn't seem bouncy at all!'

The Disco Fairy managed to discreetly whisper despite being high above the boy's ears. 'Chilly George is a gem of a bouncer. He never gets butterflies in his stomach because it's too frosty in there.' Levander swaggered up to the bouncer. 'What's the sitch, my favourite fridge?' he said kindly.

The colourful letters slotted into place on the smooth stainless-steel where George's face should be. 'Welcome, Disco Fairy. Who is your companion?' the letters spelt out.

'This is Bernard! He's just arrived and has never danced to disco.'

The letters moved with the urgency of carp at feeding time. 'Get in there immediately!' he said, shimmying aside.

'Nice to meet you, George,' said Bernard, before entering Pantheon 54.

It was a vast, circular space, full of music and laughter. The domed ceiling was capped with a circular opening at the tippy-top.

'You're not gonna tell me,' said Bernard, 'this is meant to be a whale and that's the blowhole?'

Levander gave him a high-five. 'I like your groovy ideas! But no, that's an oculus. It lets the stars shine their spotlights upon us.'

The starlight did indeed illuminate the sea of swaying heads and hands moving at the room's centre. Over the silver waves of this dancefloor, Bernard set eyes upon the stage. Before a sky-blue backdrop, a small cumulus cloud floated. She wore sunglasses, and lorded over her table with a fluffy aura of cool. Upon the table, two vinyl record players flanked a central mixer in the middle, all three connected by wires. Bernard recognized them as turntables, or 'decks', and she was spinning some excellent music.

'I guess that's Cloud 9,' he said.

Levander cried, 'The very same! It appears we've missed her opening tunes.'

Elsewhere, an ice-cream bar ran along the curved wall to the left, offering every flavour imaginable. Everyone who passed Levander greeted him, and he coolly returned their waves and high fives. Bernard, meanwhile, was puzzled by the purpose of Pantheon 54.

'I understand the ice cream,' he said, 'but why is everyone here? It's just music. Everybody's squashed.'

SPACESHIPS IN THE NIGHT

'The dancefloor is a place of healing. These Discopians are liberated from their troubles, floating free in the realm of the Lost Chord.'

'Levander, what are you even saying?'

Like his voice, the Disco Fairy's laugh was chilled and gentle. 'Hop on in there, disconaut. I have to give greetings to one or two swanky peeps, but I'll fetch you some water and we'll rendezvous on the floor.'

With a flurry of his butterfly wings, Levander cavorted away. Bernard inched onto the dancefloor. Although it was crowded, people respectfully slid out of the way, clearing a path. Boomba gently flashed from all the dance moves.

Surrounded by dancers as blissful as they were enthusiastic, Bernard decided to dispense with his notions that it was silly. *Just for a moment*, he thought. He started to nod his head in tiny, uninvolved movements. Soon, however, symptoms of a deep enjoyment began to surface. His feet tapped, his knees loosened, his arms swung. Before he knew it, he was hopping to and fro and beaming along with the rest of the dancers, who all started to cheer. The percussion from golden hi-hats fell upon his soul like raindrops. The bass rumbled through him in benevolent earthquakes. The strings section conjured all sorts of sunshine. And the lyrics! Every verse and chorus soared with messages of hope and belonging, bringing him to happier heights still.

The Disco Fairy reappeared, his wings shining in the starlight. He handed over a plastic cup of water. 'There is no trendier party accessory than this. Stay hydrated!'

'Thanks, dude,' said Bernard, feeling the coolness in

his hand. He truly meant it. What a moment it was!

Suddenly, a hideous shriek filled Pantheon 54. The records scratched to silence, and everyone looked upward. Scuttling in from the oculus was an exotic, whitish flower wearing a beret. As it descended, Bernard saw its eyes, legs, and pincers.

'Holy fajoley,' he said, 'that's a man-sized orchid mantis!' He recognized the insect from a nature documentary. It had given him nightmares.

'Monsieur Le Mantis,' said Levander, putting his skull in his hand. 'An absolute buzz-buster from the Isle of Pollenesia.'

The insect crawled down a pillar and the crowd cleared. 'Levander!' he hissed. 'The same disco spirit that patterns the stars flows also in me. I challenge you to a dance-off!'

'You've hunted me for many weekends, you jitterbuggin' screwball. I absolutely accept.'

The crowd formed into a circle around them. Cloud 9 nodded, consenting to the battle.

'Be careful,' Bernard urged his friend. 'Be sure he doesn't chop off your head!'

'Who's this pipsqueak,' jeered Le Mantis, pacing before them, 'your new coach?'

Levander was cool and composed. 'As a matter of fact, he is! This disconaut flew in from another planet to be here, to give me more tips!'

Those bug eyes flicked hungrily to Bernard. 'Well, get him out of here so we can start.'

Levander glanced at his friend and spoke softly: 'Any advice on taking down this clown?'

Bernard racked his brain, unsure of what could be useful. 'There's a dance move back on Earth called the caterpillar. Bury him with a taste of his own bugginess.'

'I know the move, and I adore the plan.' Levander grinned and stood up. Bernard backed away into the crowd, leaving the two dancers to face off.

The music began, the lights went down, and the challenger began.

The dance of Monsieur Le Mantis was a terror. This glamorous monster used every inch of his exoskeleton to twist and dive into freaky dance moves. He used the full space of the circle, and boomba trailed in the air behind him. At one stage, he stroked Levander's face with his feelers. In a chilling conclusion, he twirled upside-down on his pincers, clicking his fangs to the fading drumbeats. The crowd applauded a dance well danced and turned worried eyes to their champion.

The Disco Fairy had taken in the performance with a calm resolve. He now stepped forward, letting his cape slide to the floor. His wings flicked into an upright position, and he smiled at his fearsome foe. As Bernard was later to learn, Levander was the master of a technique called the semi-quaver bop. This meant that for every beat, he could bust out four dance moves. For every four-on-the-floor, Levander lit up his dancefloor with sixteen moves. A few bars of this and he was all but invincible.

As the music rose up again, Levander exploded into a tornado of colourful boomba. He never faltered, alternating through poses at breakneck speed. He finished with the most complicated and beautiful caterpillar dance

Bernard had ever seen. When his work was done, people fainted and burst into tears. The applause was deafening.

Monsieur Le Mantis bowed in defeat. 'Alas, this is too much for me,' he conceded, and skulked away to the ice-cream bar.

Everyone cheered and Levander ran over to Bernard.

'I need your wisdom more often!' he said. He took a violet envelope from his sleeve. 'Why not come to the parade on Tuesday night? I'd love your company!'

'I'll be there!' said Bernard, accepting the envelope. The happy crowd moved in and pulled the winner away, hoisting him onto their shoulders. In no time, Levander was surfing the crowd before the decks of Cloud 9.

Bernard smiled and a shadow fell over him. He turned to see a strange figure, dressed in grey, with a pineapple for a head. A human hand, ringed with silver, reached out and touched his shoulder.

'Wait,' said Bernard, but everything started to fade. Pantheon 54 disappeared, swirling away like water from a bathtub. The last thing he saw was Levander falling, his skull turned towards Bernard in surprise. Then he was back in the spare room, with the headphones around his neck. Ealaín was calling him for supper.

3

LONELY TOWN

The needle had slipped from the record, which now spun in silence. Bernard switched off the record player, then ran his hands over the room. It was real. He was home.

In his head, he replayed every scene of his strange adventure. The pineapple-headed person had returned him to Earth, and the surprise exit had left Bernard dizzy. Settling himself, he glanced at the clock. For all the hours spent in Discopia, only six minutes had passed in the real world. He also noted that Discopia was four hours ahead of the real world.

Downstairs, Ealaín looked up from a steaming pot of mushroom risotto. 'By Kusama's pumpkins! Where did you get that?'

Bernard froze, realizing he was still wearing Levander's jacket. It had returned with him!

He thought fast. 'What can I say? The garage is full of weird stuff.'

'You did an admirable job in there,' Ealaín said.

The garage! How long ago it seemed!

'Did you find anything else interesting?'

'Oh, not much,' he replied, containing himself. 'I found some of Dad's old records.'

'I didn't know we still had those. Disco, I'd imagine? He was coconuts for that music.'

Bernard felt laughter bubble up but managed to control it.

They sat down to eat, and Ealaín brought her fingers together in a steeple. 'So, I was speaking with Ali today,' she said. 'She's secured me an art show in Dunewright Castle!'

'No way!' Bernard said through a mouthful of rice. 'You've always wanted to throw some paintings up on those walls.'

'It'll open at the start of summer, and I'm calling it *Beach Noises*.'

Bernard liked the name. 'Congratulations, Mum. That's awesome.'

'It should be fun, but it's going to be hard work. My mind is full of big tropical creations. For now, we'll celebrate the victory.'

They finished their meal and Bernard headed for his bedroom.

Bernard thought he had escaped his Discopian adventure without consequence. It surprised him, then, when he went to bed and slept for thirteen hours. When he awoke from his deep sleep (or sleepideep as he liked to call it), it was late on Sunday morning. He felt like he had new bones. He stretched his arms, and his eyes fell to the jacket on the floor. He zipped open the pocket and rummaged for the violet envelope. Opening it, he read the sophisticated handwriting:

> It's time again for the Parade of Superfloats! As Levander's guest, you are cordially invited to view the procession from the VIP stands in Good Times Square. Arrive on Tuesday at 8.30 p.m.

It was only Sunday now. Bernard itched to star-travel to Levander's penthouse straight away but decided it would be rude to appear before he was invited. He would honour the time.

Meanwhile, he vowed to learn about disco in his own world.

He set about his afternoon's tasks, mowing the back garden and studying for a Spanish test. After lunch – pancakes with lemon – he moved to the living room and logged on to the computer. First he searched for Discopia. He couldn't find a scrap of evidence of its existence. Next he searched for Levander. This brought up many links to lavender but nothing about his mischievous friend. The realization dawned that he might be the only person on Earth who knew about this place.

He played some footage of something called *Soul Train* in the corner of the screen and went in search of chat forums. He was bursting to tell someone about his discovery but he didn't want to freak out the other Skater Kids. He found a site called *Disco Discourse*, so he set up an account and wrote a public status.

B: Travelled by soundwaves to a city called Discopia. Message me for my five star review! Also, any disco wisdom for a new kid?

As he waited, his eyes wandered to the terrific dancing show in the corner of the screen. He received one reply.

TuneHog101: Disco is for adults, not for children.

Then he got another one.

DancinMadLad: Disco is the musical expression of Martin Luther King's dream, man!

These comments – probably penned by bored wackos – disappointed him. He soon logged off and walked back to the box of disco records. He decided to check out the other albums in Ceol's collection. He lay on the floor in the spare room listening to disco, holding the Discopian record in his hands. He couldn't wait for Tuesday's parade.

Fairweather School had a zero-skateboarding policy, so naturally, Bernard had entered a secret society of skateboarders. The Skater Kids, as they were known, was made up of his best friends: Kirsten, Bucky and Jay. On Monday morning, Bucky was waiting for him by the playground.

'Look at that new gear!' Bucky said, ogling the jacket. 'I didn't know you were a host on MTV.'

'I took it off a skeleton,' Bernard drily replied. 'Hey, do you know where I can find Kirsten today?' The other two

Skater Kids were in the year above them.

'I don't know, amigo. I know she'll be practising her keytar solos at break.'

The bell rang, and they strolled to class.

In history, he daydreamed through charts on Stone Age cave paintings. Mr Flannelly's music class ('Who wants to hear my Chopin ukulele variations?') was fun as always. A Spanish test blurred by, and then it was break. Taking Bucky's advice, Bernard headed straight for the music room. He felt nettles in his chest as he saw Ricky Rockwell and his hyena pack of followers – the thuggish jocks of Fairweather – in the corridor. They *hated* Bernard. Squelchy dubstep oozed from their boom box. Bernard kept his eyes down.

'That is some outfit!' sneered Ricky. 'It'd go well with make-up and a handbag.'

Bernard kept walking. 'When I need advice from dubstep fans, I'll let you know.'

'This music is class.'

'Maybe for people with brains wrapped in bubble wrap.' He sidestepped their lunges and sprinted away, laughing.

Ricky's threats followed him. 'Talk to me like that again and I'll squash you, FREAK!'

Reaching the music room, Bernard found the Skater Kid he wanted to quiz. Kirsten was nuts about music. She knew everything from Mozart to Japanese pop. She was currently practising scales on a keytar, an electronic piano that looks like a guitar.

She looked up from her instrument. 'What's up, dude? Skateboard much over the weekend?'

'Not much, buddy. I was wondering if you could tell me about disco.'

'Ah. That's pretty retro for a twenty-first-century kid. What do you want to know?'

'What was it like here on Earth?'

'As opposed to where, you spacecake?'

'Just . . . go easy on me and let me know.'

She smiled, consulting the libraries in her brain. 'Well, by the 1970s, African and South American musical traditions were circulating in the United States. Disco was born when things like African rhythms and sassy salsa were mixed in with pop music and church gospel. It was a perfect storm.'

'It's certainly fun to dance to. Did it have something to do with Martin Luther King Jr.?'

'Kind of. I guess once the civil rights movement helped millions, disco was the after-party. Minorities would gather in discotheques to dance and feel accepted. By the end of the seventies, the movement was growing bigger and bigger, like some glitzy snowball rolling down a hill. And then . . .' Here Kirsten trailed off, lost for words.

'What happened to it?' Bernard asked.

'A big, crunchy crash.'

The rest of the day passed without incident. After school, Bernard helped Jay and Bucky film skateboard tricks in the car park. He made sure they all had plastic cups of water. Sadly, this didn't stop them from falling. His two friends headed home to tend to their bruises over a session of *Steampunk Blimp Wars*, a popular online game.

Bernard hung back for a little while, but when he spied Ricky Rockwell smoking by the bike shed, he skated home too.

He motored through his homework in the living room, waiting for Ealaín to finish using the computer. He was itching for Tuesday, when he could step into Levander's Penthouse again.

'For one of my pieces,' said Ealaín, playing with the twist-outs in her hair, 'I'm trying to source a shedload of surfboards. But it's hard to convince surfers to lend me their boards.'

Bernard thought for a moment. 'Have you tried offering them burrito vouchers?'

Ealaín's fingers hammered the keyboard with renewed speed. 'You're a genius!' she said.

When Bernard finally got to log back on to *Disco Discourse*, he had a new message.

> KittyLikeThread: Hi! I assumed myself to be the only kid who liked disco ^_^ Haven't visited any cities like that though. I'd love to hear more about it.

The profile picture showed a young girl at a piano with her back to the camera. She seemed to be playing with great aplomb. Bernard decided to respond.

> B: Hi there! I think you'd like this place. It's pretty much made of disco.

She responded a few minutes later.

> KittyLikeThread: Haha how can a city be made of music?

B: Well, they listen to it but it's built like a normal city with bricks, roadways and parks. Everything is so vivid and colourful that you feel 100% pure disco vibes on every street.

KittyLikeThread: And what does that feel like exactly?

Bernard paused for a moment, to try to summarize the sensations of that fateful Saturday night.

B: Going down a water slide that has no end.

KittyLikeThread: Haha ok. Hey, do you want to ditch this website? There are no kids ☹ I have a good one you can join me on!

She sent him a link to something called *Wacky Werewolves*. Before diving in, he figured he'd run it by the Skater Kids on their messaging app.

Bernard: Anyone down for Wacky Werewolves?

Kirsten: I'd rather be eaten by actual werewolves.

Jaydizzle: Come and join the Steampunk Blimp Wars!

Bernard rolled his eyes and closed the chat. Clicking into the online game, he was greeted by adorable music and teddy-bear werewolves. *Wacky Werewolves* was written in bubble font cracked in two. Polyphonic music played in the background, and Bernard smiled at the silly lyrics ('We are all your friends / where moonlight never ends!'). After a quick sign-up, he designed his werewolf character and was ready to go. A portly werewolf in a waistcoat gave him a tour of a village called Amble Totes, a safe haven for werewolves. It contained twelve cottages built with peach-coloured bricks. One would act as Bernard's 'home' and the others could be allocated to friends. Behind them, a mansion called Headspace House sat on a hill, giggling with a face made of windows and doors.

Once he'd gone over the introduction, labelled Finding Your Paws, he typed KittyLikeThread into the search bar to connect their werewolf characters. One of the little cottages pinged and the letters KLT appeared above it in gold. Bernard clicked on it, and the screen swept in for a close-up of this cottage. The doorway had purple curtains patterned with stars. He selected the fluffy Contact button and his werewolf, kitted with a 1970s outfit, began some cute growling. A red-furred werewolf, also in a 1970s outfit, popped out and growled back.

> KittyLikeThread: Yay! Thanks for joining me ☺ Now we can chat about disco in peace!

> Bernard: Sounds like a plan! Let the games begin!

Bernard spent the best part of an hour on *Wacky Werewolves*, playing its games and gaining 'howlie points'. He told Kitty about his night in Discopia, and she told him her favourite disco bands. Once he said goodbye to his new friend, he left the computer feeling a warmth within.

4

I'M COMING OUT

Bernard emerged from the spaceship and stepped back into the penthouse. Levander was in the centre of the living room, playing a solitary game of Twister. The scene was candlelit and sound-tracked by light disco.

Bernard greeted him, trying not to laugh. 'Em, Levander?'

'You're late, disconaut!' cried the Disco Fairy.

'To be fair, I'm still getting used to the star-travel.' Bernard pointed at the Twister mat and candles. 'What's all this?'

'I tend to get antsy when awaiting delayed guests. Twister helps.' The winged skeleton disentangled himself and stood to his full height. His outfit was reliably exotic, consisting of a salmon-pink blazer, blue skinny jeans and a big woolly scarf.

'You're looking Discopian anyway,' Bernard said.

Levander bowed with a smile. 'Welcome back! That was some exit from Pantheon 54, being zapped out by Wollohy Peels.'

'The pineapple dude?'

'Yeah! That's Discopia's demi-god. Barely ever sighted.'

Bernard ran his hands through his Afro. Why would a demi-god interact with him?

'Well,' he continued, 'this so-called Wollohy Peels teleported me home.'

'You vanished like a funky ghost!' said Levander, shaking his skull. 'In all my years, I've never seen such a surprise.'

'It probably means that I can bounce back to Earth through your spaceship here or by meeting Wollohy Peels.'

'Discopia remains bursting with surprises.' Levander spun his mirrorball globe. 'So let's move! We're in for a fiesta tonight!'

They descended via the lift, but not all the way to the basement. Kimmy was wearing panda face paint this time, and she only danced to knee level. When the doors opened, they breezed into the ground-floor lobby. Bernard noted that the letterboxes were much wider than the ones on Earth.

'How else could we get our vinyls?' Levander explained.

It was night-time again and they walked out onto Sweetbeat Street. In the fresh, musical air, a stretch limo awaited. Bernard had never travelled by limousine, and this one seemed extra special. The driver was a man made of leaves.

'What's up, Uncle Crunch?' said Levander. Then he dropped his voice and said, 'Keep the windows closed, Bernard. Uncle Crunch has a crippling fear of the wind.'

The leafy fellow nodded and tapped his watch. They

climbed into the back. The luxurious interior was crammed with musical instruments, and sitting at the drum kit was an ostrich.

'Bernard, meet Miles,' said Levander, settling in at the keyboards. 'I like to bring along my drummer.'

'You're late,' said the ostrich with a rich voice.

'The whippersnapper got held up.'

Miles winked conspiratorially at Bernard. 'Guessing the Twister board was taken for a spin, then.'

'Less chats, more hi-hats, please!'

'If you're anything like the ostriches on Earth,' said Bernard, 'I'm guessing you keep a pretty fast rhythm.'

Miles answered with a blistering drum solo. Bernard was impressed, and noticed that the city was already cruising by outside the windows. He saw the crinkly outline of Uncle Crunch through the tinted-glass divider. They joined Discopia's traffic, still free-flowing even with a parade presumably blocking off the main roads.

The musicians began to play. Miles drummed in a smooth and professional style. Levander, on the keys, produced quick-fire arpeggios and crispy chords on the downbeats. The volume level accommodated comfortable talking.

'Back when my mum used to take me for drives,' said Bernard, 'she seemed to appreciate my silence when I sat in the back. Is the leafy dude OK?'

'Don't worry,' Miles assured him. 'We don't bother Uncle Crunch. That soulified speeder wears noise-cancelling earphones.'

Bernard nodded. He turned to Levander and focused on the keys being played by skeleton hands. The sound was rhythmical but it seemed to him . . . to be the rhythms of a machine.

'From what I've learned of disco music on Earth,' Bernard said, 'it's created with natural instruments played with funkiness. Big bands, gospel choirs, things like that. Surely a machine doesn't belong there?'

'The synthesizer is absolutely sacred,' Levander said, with a delicate fold of his wings. 'It is a gift from the dance gods themselves.'

'Can you get boomba out of them?' Bernard asked.

'Oh yeah! Synths are instruments just like pianos, but they come with technological firepower! On these plastic keys you can hammer out magnificent tunes.'

Miles was chuckling softly. 'You're right though, Bernard,' he chipped in. 'Nothing beats music that doesn't need a nearby plug socket.'

Levander shook his head, grinning. 'Miles is touchy because of the increasing popularity of drum machines.'

'I know you went low in your dance moves, I didn't know you went low in your insults!'

'The thing is,' continued the Disco Fairy, his skull blushing as he laughed, 'disco tunes are long and energetic. They're marathons of sound, and the synthesizer can keep up with such demands. The dancefloor isn't hurt by the inclusion of synths.'

'Unless the keyboardist is a highly strung numpty!' cried the ostrich, and what ensued was a friendly, sheet-music throwing fight. In the whirl of paper and printed staves, Bernard couldn't help finding the mayhem-on-wheels delightful.

The limousine pulled up outside a building and stopped. Bernard looked out, and his eyes widened. Uncle Crunch had brought them to what must have been the tallest skyscraper in Discopia. A towering edifice that shot up into the skies above, its top floors were so high that they disappeared into the fluffy clouds. As if that wasn't enough to drink in, the base of the skyscraper resembled a Greek temple. Elegant marble steps led up to the entrance. Above it, in the triangular pediment, the words Tower Smooth were proudly carved under a sun-shaped clock. Four pillars seemed to hold up the pediment and the weight of the entire skyscraper itself. They were carved as four giant statues, dressed in shirts and ties by the sculptor's hand. All four stood at podiums, with wires and circuits carved down the stand. The four giants made a potent impression, their serene faces looking down at the residents of the city walking and skating on the pavement below.

'Wow!' said Bernard. 'What is this place?'

'This is Tower Smooth,' Levander replied, 'the city hall where all Discopia's politics goes down.'

'And why are we stopping here?'

'Didn't I mention? This is a government vehicle. We have to pick up the mayor!'

Between the two middle pillars, a figure appeared. She confidently strolled out, followed by an entourage of bodyguards. Her dress was glittering black, and a huge cloak billowed about her.

'Her bodyguards have branched out to give her fabulous cloak some breathing space,' exclaimed Miles.

As the mayor got closer, Bernard beheld her mighty Afro, a friendly dark-skinned face and a flawless smile that would be at home in the dreams of dentists. She wore a gold medallion that brought her whole image into perfect focus. The woman made a beeline down the steps and straight for the limo.

'Mayor Soldavril!' said Levander with a flourishing bow.

She flashed him a stare that was both queenly and playful. 'I send an official car to collect you, I agree to your bizarre request to pick up your drummer – hello, Miles, nice to see you – and yet still you leave me hanging.'

'Apologies! The boy was late.'

'Ah. So Twister and candles it was then!'

Everyone laughed as Levander looked aghast.

The mayor turned to Bernard. 'I've heard all about you! I'm Hazel, and you're very welcome. I'm always charmed to meet visitors to Discopia.'

'It's very nice to meet you too,' replied Bernard happily. 'It's a great place!'

'You are the perfect mix of groovy and gentlemanly.'

'What did you expect from my interdimensional dance protégé?' said Levander.

They were gliding away from Tower Smooth, the mesmerizing pillars still visible through the rear window.

'Who are those giants on the front of your offices?' Bernard asked his newest friend.

'Those,' Hazel said with pride, 'are the Kraftyatids. Gifts from the Electronican Empire. Without their musical technology, disco wouldn't have sprouted and blossomed quite the way it did, and indeed there would be no Discopia.'

'And what,' Levander swept in, 'are those musical heroes playing on their mysterious pedestals? Miles?' His wings spread wide in mischievous delight.

Miles released a pained sigh (which took a while to climb up his ostrich neck). 'I guess they're playing synthesizers, Levander.'

The skeleton gave Bernard a zealous high five. They all laughed, and Hazel polished her gold medallion. Up close, Bernard could see it was designed like a small vinyl record with wings. Onwards they cruised, towards the Parade of Superfloats. Bernard sat among his fashionable friends, convinced that his happiness could never perish.

The limousine parked beside an ice-cream truck, and they laughingly spilled into the night. Uncle Crunch saluted them, turning his attention to a book entitled *Trees With Attitude*. They entered the stripey VIP tent, and Bernard beheld Good Times Square before him. It was a dazzling urban sight, ringed by television screens, jumbotrons and scrolling neon signs. It was filled with Discopians, save for the road along its centre. Bernard had always considered parades overrated. In the swell of the crowd, he never saw anything but the tops of the parade floats. Here, the crowd had arranged itself from the smallest to the tallest, so everyone had a perfect view. Children lined the front, giraffes sporting heart-shaped sunglasses stood at the back. Directly across from him, a giant neon pineapple crowned the entrance to a vinyl record emporium called Feel the Peels.

Bernard turned his attention back to the tent. Miles had gravitated to the candy buffet, and was currently talking to two others.

'Drummers!' said Levander, handing Bernard a drink of Cosmopop cola. 'You can't keep them away from each other. We might have to schmooze with some peeps too. Just follow my lead.' They were approached by a giant bat and a businessman in an Asian-style dragon mask.

'Well, if it isn't Levander and his spaceboy,' said a cold voice from the dragon's mouth.

Levander nodded. 'Bernard, this is Vlad the Bat and Esdragon, two of our most renowned architects.'

The duo rudely kept their attention on Levander.

'Any word on Pilgrim?' asked Vlad the Bat. 'I hope he'll be caught and desist defacing the streets with his graffiti.'

'I haven't heard a thing.'

The bat and dragon-man drifted away, bowing to Mayor Soldavril.

Bernard was happy they left. 'They seem to hate you,' he said to Levander.

'I had a sizeable spat with those boys. They designed a sixty-four-floor discotheque. I thought it was too many floors . . . it got messy. They're masters of glass with class. Anyway, remind me to show you Pilgrim's stuff, because he's a genius. Nobody knows who he is, but he's fixing us all up with toasty street art!'

Hazel now came over with a beautiful woman in a suit of mirrorball armour. 'Bernard, meet Tulsisan, Commander of the Disco Knights. Discopia is well protected by these warriors of boomba.'

Tulsisan bowed. 'It's a pleasure to meet you, Earth child. Hey, Levander.'

The Disco Fairy gave her a fist-bump. 'Any word from the Occupants of the Watermelon Wood?' he asked.

'They keep to themselves, as always. We guard the Bumblebee Bridge well.'

'I'm glad you do,' Levander said. 'And I appreciate the security you give Owlapeño's, my little burrito bar for owls.'

'The Occupants will never attack as long as I'm in charge,' said Hazel. 'I guarantee it.'

Bernard's curiosity was piqued once more. What exactly lurked in the Watermelon Wood? And Levander owned a burrito bar?

For now, he kept his attention on the colourful Discopians around him, and he soon found himself talking to a handsome soulified beach ball.

'The name's Lance Brophy,' said the smooth-faced fellow. 'I'm a reporter for *Grapevine News*. If there's a hot story, I'll be the first to roll towards it.'

'How do you stay so clean?' asked Bernard.

'Pure charisma,' said Lance 'The Bounce' Brophy.

Just then, the show began. The speakers all around Good Times Square rang out with a familiar voice from Zam FM.

'What is up, chicklets?' squawked Flamingo James.

Everyone cheered. 'The Superfloats are just coming through now. From the look of it, we're in for a supersized treat. This is going to be a party for the history books!'

Levander whisked Bernard over to some beanbags

beside Hazel. Getting comfortable, they watched the parade approach.

Flamingo James commentated on each of the wondrous floats as they glided by.

'First up, a float from the Wobbly West, topped by Chuck the Buckalicious himself!'

Astride a float layered with cardboard cowboy saloons, swaying tepees and prancing horses, a real amber minotaur sang with bassy might.

Flamingo James continued, 'I hope nobody's wearing red. We don't want a repeat of the RollerBowl stampede! I'm kidding! It's great to have you, Chuck! Next up we have the float from Pollenesia!'

A giant hive appeared on wheels, yellow and mountainous. Stationed on its balconies were giant bees playing taiko drums and pan flutes. 'These bees are the bee's knees, I can tell you that much. Next up we have the Sonorous Deep!' This float was impressive. From an elaborate web of glass baths, mermaids played elegant rhythms on harps. Bernard saw Vlad the Bat and Esdragon taking notes.

Flamingo James went on, 'Following those folks is the Eighth Cavalry of the Disco Knights.' Twenty knights on horseback, all clad in similar mirrorball armour to Commander Tulsisan, trotted down the street. Tulsisan nodded as they passed her by.

'And now, chicklets, some more Discopian fun! Here's our one and only Disco Fairy, looking a little larger than usual.'

A giant puppet of Levander came shimmying down

the street, to the adoration of the crowd. Behind this, a large wooden horse creaked along slowly. Beyond that, a whirlwind of pretty flags waved. Bernard stalled, rewinding his vision. A wooden horse? It moved along with nobody pushing it. Below its unkind eyes, smoke slithered from its nostrils.

'Something's not right,' said Bernard, tugging Levander's sleeve.

'But I look so suave as a twenty-foot tall marionette!'

'No, the wooden horse behind it.'

Hazel chimed in with political positivity. 'It's a testament to the hard work and creativity of those who built it!'

'Yeah, maybe,' said Bernard as it dawned on him that perhaps the tale of Troy had never reached this place. 'It just reminds me of the hide-and-seek tactics used by the ancient Greeks. They used something exactly like that to hoodwink their enemies.'

Hazel's smile faltered slightly. Over the speakers, Flamingo James sounded equally perplexed. 'I can't find any information for this tall hunk of horse. I can't possibly say why it's stopping!'

The wooden horse creaked to a halt right before the VIP area. The screens all around showed its image and then started to glitch. Ealaín had a saying she liked to drop back on Earth: anyone who finds themselves part of a museum tour twice in one day will learn an awkward truth: history definitely repeats itself.

Bernard thought of his mother's nugget of wisdom as the wooden ribs of the horse peeled away and dozens of ropes dropped out. People started scrambling down the ropes with thuggish cries. Pouring down from the wooden horse came the intruders. Bleak and colourless against the razzle-dazzle of Good Times Square, it was a waterfall of pirates! There was no denying the hallmarks – eyepatches, bandanas and peg legs – and Bernard went pale when he glimpsed cutlasses and knives. They reached the street and fanned out. The crowd, well-accustomed to Discopia's taste for surprise, saw that this was different. The screams began. Revellers fled as the enemy reached the barriers, which the pirates quickly smashed to the ground. This opened the way to the record store across from which Bernard and his friends watched in horror. Feel the Peels was the target of this scurrilous mission.

'Those funkless seadogs!' roared Levander, leaping into action from the stand. Hazel and Commander Tulsisan tried to follow but were blindsided by police, who whisked them away to safety. The Disco Fairy cartwheeled forward in rage, preparing for some mighty dancing.

A horrific, high-pitched sound pierced through the entire square. Everyone covered their ears in anguish. Levander fell to his knees in the shadow of the horse. He held his skull as the final pirate glided down, landing before him. A robotic voice rose above the deafening white noise. 'Seize the records. The music must be burned.'

Bernard had always thought robot voices were quirky and amusing. The one that filled Good Time Square was neither of these things. It was inhuman and disturbing. The pirates all cried in response as they looted the record shop. 'A-I, Captain! A-I, Captain!'

That's when Bernard noticed the figure standing over

Levander. The final pirate. His slender frame was draped in a plum-coloured coat. He wore bronze vambraces on his forearms. They were shaped like catfish. His gloved hands sprang from their mouths. On his head he wore a tricorne, with a red jewel at its peak. The most unnerving feature was the face, or rather what hung where the face should be. The man wore a mask, bearing no features except for two scribbled shapes – one pink and one red – where the eyes should be. He gestured to the people (he was now on the screens all round) and the robot voice spoke once more. 'That oceanic feeling . . . that oceanic feeling. It has been written about disco that it makes you feel like you float in something bigger than yourself. But what of wicked ships, and those depths where krakens prowl?'

As everyone panicked, the pirates had toppled the giant puppet of Levander and were pouring the plundered records on top of it. A pile was forming of sleeves and records, slowly submerging the skeleton. The real Disco Fairy still reeled at the feet of the masked one. Around them, nine tall pirates formed a defensive circle. They had flashing eyes and silver faces.

'Those things are robots!' yelled Bernard.

The robopirates met no resistance; the white noise paralyzed everyone.

The masked pirate continued his monologue: 'I am Captain Vyse. We shall get to know each other very well over the next while. At first you will fear me, which is clever. But soon you will bow before me as Levander does now.' The human pirates had now formed a small hill of records. They began pouring petrol on it, and their dark intentions dawned on the crowd. A pirate with a beard of baseballs approached his captain, offering a flaming torch. The mask turned towards it, devoid of emotion. Captain Vyse took the torch and strode to the records. Above the white noise could be heard the manic, sonorous wails of the Discopian people.

'We shall not sleep,' Captain Vyse continued. 'We watch from the shadows and not a dance move goes unnoticed, nor a tune unrecorded. Soon all of your disco will be ours. Your precious records will burn.'

Unspeakable grief flared through Bernard, as it did through the Discopians, as Vyse lowered the torch to the records. Within seconds, they were swallowed by an inferno. As the flames helped themselves, Vyse turned to regard the VIP area. Chillingly, he stared straight at Bernard. He then moved back towards the Disco Fairy. Levander's skull was shiny with tears as he struggled on. Vyse grabbed him by his scarf and dragged to the edge of the flames. He forced Levander to watch the bonfire as the puppet in his image slowly burned.

5

FORGET ME NOTS

Inside Kitty's cottage in Amble Totes, the werewolves sipped moonbeam milkshakes. Pet birds surrounded them, blinking in looped animations.

KittyLikeThread: Oh my gosh. That sounds frightfully dark!

Bernard: It was literally dark because the place filled with smoke. Once the Disco Knights took control, the pirates disappeared. The Blues captured their robopirates who'd guarded the burning pile till it was toast. Then the pirates self-deactivated. The lights left their eyes.

KittyLikeThread: What are the Blues?

Bernard: Oh, that's what they call the Discopian cops. They're armed with laser guns that stun anyone they hit.

SPACESHIPS IN THE NIGHT

It was Wednesday morning and Bernard felt rotten. He'd once heard that misery followed hot on the heels of disastrous parties. He understood that now. He had messaged Kitty just before school to vent the trauma of the wooden horse.

> KittyLikeThread: Robotic pirates, huh?

> Bernard: Yeah, they're mostly humans, but with some robot minions. I thought Captain Vyse was a robot at first, but he's a man just using a robot voice. Creepy!

> KittyLikeThread: I saw animatronic pirates in a theme park once. Their salty disputes play out again and again. The drunkards drank forever, but the gunners never missed their mark. I can only imagine how lethal they'd be as weapons.

Ealaín's keys rattled from down the hall, and she called Bernard's name. He rubbed his panda-tired eyes, then typed his goodbye.

> Bernard: I have to go to school. Thanks for the milkshakes.

> KittyLikeThread: No worries ^_^ I hear whining from Headspace House anyway. Perhaps it needs some care. TTYL.

On the car journey to school, Bernard replayed the horrors in his head. Was there more he could have done?

SPACESHIPS IN THE NIGHT

Could he have been more than a bystander? Captain Vyse had escaped, following his crew into the smoke. Miles had carried Bernard back to Uncle Crunch's limo, and when Levander returned – his life spared by the enemy – he had sat at the keyboards with his hands around his skull. They'd barely spoken all the way to the penthouse, then Bernard had slipped into the spaceship, and was home.

The next three days galloped by in a blur. Bernard was in his own bubble, spaced out in classes. Mr Flannelly's beaming greetings went unanswered. He didn't skateboard at break, and at lunchtime he didn't eat a crumb. A maths test that had slid out of his mind promptly appeared on his desk. He squeezed his tired mind for the answers, but they would not come.

On top of this, the Skater Kids had entered an ill-timed feud with Ricky Rockwell. It started when Ricky began playing *Steampunk Blimp Wars*. Jay and Bucky gleefully set their fleets on Ricky's starter-level blimp, destroying it instantly. In a rage, Ricky wedgied them both. In retaliation, they slipped into the locker room while Ricky was at training and turned his bag inside out. The next day, Ricky and his goons cornered Bucky with steel rulers, beating him and drawing blood. Kirsten stood up for her boys by spreading a rumour that Ricky had webbed toes. The culmination of these pranks was that Bernard – while walking home on Friday – was ambushed by Ricky's hyena pack of bullies and clobbered with eggs. His week ended in squelchy, sticky misery, and a long shower was required to scrub the mess away.

On Saturday morning, Bernard was listlessly watching

cartoons when Ealaín sat down beside him with coffee.

'Good morning,' she said, turning the volume down. 'I need to ask you something. For my art show *Beach Noises* I need a palm tree. Would you mind if I uprooted the one in our garden?'

Bernard looked over, considering her plan. 'Dad's one? What would you need it for?'

She innocently sipped her coffee, then replied, 'I was going to put it on the body of a giraffe.'

'WHAT?'

'It wouldn't be a real giraffe. Yeesh!'

Bernard wasn't ready for modern-art chats this early in the morning. 'What's the point of a palm-tree giraffe?'

'Well, giraffes are endangered in Africa, so it's good to raise awareness. And secondly, Ceol loved giraffes. I think he'd like if we used his tree to make one.'

Bernard was reminded of the parade, where he'd seen terrified giraffes gallop away from the flames. His face betrayed this grim recollection, and Ealaín noticed.

'What's wrong?' she asked softly.

'It's . . . been a tough few days,' said Bernard. 'There was a maths test on Thursday. I don't think I did that well.'

'That's not like you,' Ealaín said. She interrogated him about the troublesome week, but he gave non-committal answers.

'Listen, one bad day in the classroom isn't going to capsize your future. In order to succeed, you have to be able to relax. That takes work in the downtime. It's the same for adults.'

'I guess so.'

'What are your plans this afternoon?'

The Skater Kids were laying low, planning a counterstrike to the egging. Bernard thought about visiting Levander, but another flashback of the pirates and their bonfire made him reconsider.

'I've no plans,' he said.

'Well, I have just the medicine. Let's head out, but I'll be sure to feed you first! I can practically see the bones in your face.'

They travelled by train to the city. A gallery there was showing the most expensive painting by an American artist ever sold. The painter was Jean-Michel Basquiat, and soon they were settled in a cavernous white room, in front of the $110 million artwork. *Untitled* portrayed a floating head with eyes like floodlights, skin like crushed M&Ms and crazy hair that was spray-painted black.

'He looks a bit frazzled,' Bernard whispered.

Ealaín slowly replied, 'Just coexist with this piece and this little place in the universe.'

He studied the painting, amused at the hypnotic effects it was having on his mother. He couldn't tell if the monumental head was angry, confused or simply grouchy from a bad night's sleepideep. To his surprise, he looked over and saw tears in Ealaín's eyes.

'You're upset?' he asked.

'I'm sorry,' she said, wiping her face. 'The American art world used to shut us out. Basquiat changed all that. He ripped down those walls for the Black community. I . . . just wish he'd lived long enough to enjoy it.'

Bernard, amazed at this reaction, read the exhibition

catalogue. The artist grew up in disco-era New York and had died tragically young. Bernard looked up at the face again. He now decided that it looked wise and forlorn. He imagined what it might say: 'Disco plays and life ends . . . make some art and treasure friends.'

He felt warmed by the thought. His mind began to whirr with disco. A tapping foot began to betray the place he wished to be. They soon departed, mother and son both refreshed by the art in their own ways.

Back home, Ealaín went straight to her studio to work on *Beach Noises*. Bernard hurried to the spare room. He opened the box and set the *Discopia* vinyl on the player. Before playing it, he went downstairs to the computer and checked on *Wacky Werewolves*. His friend had sent him an encouraging message.

> KittyLikeThread: It's Saturday night, Bernard.
> If ever there was a time to get over the bleak
> week, bury the ghosts and rock out, it's right
> now! Consider returning to the city :) You've
> got this.

As if he hadn't encouragement enough already, this was the cherry on top.

> Bernard: Thank you. Now isn't the time to
> turn my back. I star-travel to Discopia tonight.

His werewolf waved goodbye. Giddy with adrenaline, Bernard returned to the record player and crossed over for the third time.

The penthouse was quiet. Black and white footage of

a submarine played on the video-floor. Walking forward, Bernard heard a vintage voiceover: 'Through tropical water we closed in on the creatures we sought. Flickering there before us were the strobe eels . . .'

'It's been too long, disconaut,' said the ice-cream voice of the Disco Fairy. Bernard looked up and saw his friend curled like a dragon around the chandelier. Among the glittering crystals, Levander smiled kindly.

'What are you doing on the ceiling?' asked Bernard.

'This is where I watch my video-floor. I'm checking out footage from the Gothsemane Aquarium archives. Anyway!' He uncoiled himself and dismounted with elegance. He landed silently on the screen. His still wings betrayed his hesitancy. 'I thought you wouldn't return,' he said quietly.

Bernard glanced around, noticing the burnt-out candles and crumpled Twister mat.

He stepped forward and hugged his Discopian companion. 'I'm just glad you're safe. Besides, it's Saturday night! No better time to make an entrance. Do you have anything lined up?'

'DO I?' he boomed ecstatically, wings stretching to full span.

Within minutes they were out of the apartment, buzzing to explore the city of a million dancefloors.

'Nice to see you again,' said Kimmy, with lizard face paint this time, throwing a friendly wave into her elevator boogie.

They reached the car park and jumped into the Diamante. As they drove into the night, Bernard regaled Levander with news of his own world, from KittyLikeThread to Basquiat. His foot tapped along to the bouncy music as the car slotted smoothly down the roads.

'Those computer games sound funky,' said Levander, turning the radio dial.

'Welcome back to *Grapevine News*,' said a smooth voice, which Bernard recognized as Lance Brophy's. 'We have Mayor Hazel here, and I'd just like to ask, who is this Captain Vyse? This man, with his followers and robots, who has declared his wish to burn disco music?'

Bernard was happy to hear Hazel's voice, and noticed it carried a much sterner tone.

'Well, Lance, it's important to remember that Discopia welcomes all. That being said, those who would bring harm to our people and music will be brought to justice. Captain Vyse is a rogue criminal, but a man none the less. We will find him and his cronies.'

They discussed her plans for Disco Knights to patrol the discotheques, and soon the soulified beach ball played a disco song rich with dreamy guitars.

The radio interview forced the two friends to the conversation they'd been avoiding.

'That parade was barbaric,' said Bernard.

'It was one of the worst,' winced Levander. 'I felt ill for two days afterwards. At least no souls were lost. The Blues are investigating the party-crashers, but they left few clues.'

'Do you reckon they'll return?'

Levander's fingers drummed the steering wheel. 'They haven't been spotted since. They've probably gone back to whatever grog-pungent nest they came from.'

'It was my first experience of party-crashing,' said Bernard nervously. 'I felt awful the next day.'

'Ah, my little disconaut, parties get crashed. It was also a Tuesday.'

'What's wrong with Tuesday?' Bernard asked. Then he sensed the approach of another passionate dance lesson. He was correct.

'Some people,' said Levander, 'are of the belief that one should never go out to dance on a Tuesday. It excites the disco spirit too much, too far away from the weekend. Now I usually sidestep politics, but I fear that they were right on this occasion.'

Bernard laughed and looked out at Discopia. He noticed that the people seemed unaffected by the events earlier in the week. It was like the raid on Good Times Square had never happened, like the records had not burned. Was Captain Vyse out there among them? Was he listening to *Grapevine News*, or Zam FM? Was he walking the streets in disguise?

Looking at the happy crowds outside, Bernard shuddered.

The Diamante glided into an empty car park. A tumbleweed with an Afro rolled across the scene.

'Where are we going?' asked Bernard, as they slipped off their seatbelts.

'Oh, I want to show you some art.'

'Art? Come on, Levander, don't you know that I've been drowning in art all day?'

'Now, now, beach your jet skis.' They slipped out of the

car. 'I'm showing you street art! Unprotected by a gallery space, and all the braver for it.'

Levander led him to an elevator (with buttons!) and they shot up to an open-air shopping plaza twenty floors up. As they walked out of the elevator, Bernard spotted a poster on which Levander held up colourful sneakers: 'The Disco Fairy dances with Bungo Millalungos!'

'I do indeed,' Levander said. 'I got freebies when I signed on as a sponsor, but now I'm addicted to those cosy shoes!'

Across a chequered floor and over a rainbow bridge, Levander led the way to a graffiti mural on an east-facing wall. It showed a sunset over the sea, with two human onlookers on a beach in the foreground. The sun had a face and was crying for help, as if it was having swimming issues. In speech bubbles, the humans talked about how beautiful it was.

The graffiti art was very fun, although it had suffered a minor defacement. A black pirate ship had been scrawled onto the horizon.

Levander gasped. 'How could they? And on a Pilgrim piece, no less.'

Bernard looked at it anew. 'Oh, so this is by Pilgrim, the one who Vlad the Bat was grumbling about?'

Levander nodded, trying to remove the pirate ship with a sparkly napkin. Bernard studied the drowning sun. Thinking of Basquiat, he thought it might be worth millions one day. Then he felt the strange sensation of being watched. Innumerable windows and rooftops surrounded them in the pink and blue skyscrapers. Any one of them could host a discreet watcher.

'And who is this Pilgrim again?' said Bernard, moving closer to the Disco Fairy.

'Nobody knows. He's never been seen. Some say he's a chameleon, although the work is unlike that of any reptile I know. Some say he's invisible.'

'Can we go?' said Bernard, tapping Levander's wing. The Disco Fairy looked around, noticing his friend's discomfort.

'Sure thing, disconaut. I guess I'll leave the messiness up.'

Bernard nodded. 'Perhaps there's method in the messiness.'

Levander seemed to approve of this. 'You're beginning to sound like a Discopian!'

After driving around for a bit, they pulled over by a frog-shaped coffee shop.

Levander was talking in a phone booth and Bernard leaned easily outside. He'd liked the Pilgrim piece, but he didn't share his friend's admiration of whoever created it.

Inside the phone booth, trouble was simmering. 'Miles, what do you mean I've been removed from the guestlist?'

Through the violet-tinted windows, Bernard could see the phone pressed to a drooping skull.

'They think I'm a security risk? Ridiculous. So where's our alternative? WHAT? You're staying there to play bongo drums? And Rosco's on the synth?' Bernard could sense the hurt in his voice. 'All right, then, do what you will. See you next time.'

He hung up the phone and placed his head in his

sleeve, sighing a silky sigh. Bernard opened the door. 'What's wrong?'

'The carpet's been pulled from under us by a flaky ostrich. The party's off.'

'Missing one party isn't so bad,' said Bernard. 'When I miss something, it gives me a chance to catch up on something else.'

'I love Miles's bongo-drum solos so much.'

'I can only imagine,' Bernard said thoughtfully.

The Disco Fairy frowned from his curled-up arm.

'Ah forget them, Levander. So what if Plan A is a lost party? Who's to say that anything from Plan B to Plan Z won't be marvellous in different ways?'

This straightened Levander up. 'By groovecats, you're right. This is Discopia! The city will grant us something swell.'

It wasn't long before they found an alternative.

ZZZozzzimus was a sleepover-themed discotheque. A warehouse served as the outer shell and there was a massive pillow fort inside. They passed the snoozy sloth on door duty and entered the sprawling castle of sheets, blankets and bedroom furniture. 'They build it a different way every night,' Levander had explained.

Bernard now sat at its cosy core, enjoying milk and cookies. Because of the low ceiling, the dancers crouched and shuffled in wonderful foxtrots. The turntablist was a beautiful mermaid called Salamis. A selector from the Sonorous Deep, she wore a goldfish bowl around her head to breathe. Her laidback disco lullabies were perfect for the pyjama party.

Levander, who had been chatting with everyone, came and settled by Bernard's side. He said, 'It's pretty cosilicious, don't you agree?'

'It's like a soft, marshmallowy mansion. I love it!'

'True words!' The Disco Fairy was now thoroughly relaxed. 'Pillow forts always make us forget the shadows outside.'

'Until some numbskull mentions them.' Bernard hit him with a pillow.

'I apologise. Listen, I want to keep learning about Earth, and I hope you wish to see more of our city. There's a massive party next week.' He gave Bernard an icy-blue envelope.

'You haven't been scrubbed from the guestlist?'

Now it was Levander's turn to swing a pillow. 'You mischievous messer! Please come along, and you don't need to worry. We'll be guarding the entrances with optimum security. Chilly George will oversee this. Sniffer poodles, metal detectortoises, the *works*!' He clicked his fingers, casting sparks of boomba. 'No pirates will get near it.'

Bernard was curious. 'What kind of party is it?'

The skull glowed in tantalizing excitement. 'You're going to need warm clothes, gloves, and ice skates.'

On the cushioned floor of ZZZozzzimus, the Skater Kid from Earth grew excited. This next adventure sounded excellent. He didn't know then that its security would fail. He didn't know that he'd need much more than ice skates.

The mermaid's soothing disco filled the adorable pillow fort. The shadows, meanwhile, waited patiently outside.

6

ONE NIGHT ONLY

'We dance on holy ice tonight!' cried Levander. Excitement sprinkled his ice-cream voice. Bernard sat on the skeleton's shoulders, drinking in the scenery around them. Roseland Park lay at the heart of Discopia. It was sheltered by a perimeter of cotton-candy trees, sonorous with sugar-rushed birdsong. Beyond these, the pink and blue skyscrapers of the city stood like guardians, and above them the night sky's fresco of stars shined on.

The Disco Fairy continued: 'The ice we'll skate on is the frozen surface of a pool of water, chilly and deep. The dance gods held their pool parties here at the Dawn of Music. Our founding dancers built Discopia around it, and this is the centre of our city.'

'It must have been quite a sight,' said Bernard. 'Big old dance gods, drinking out of coconuts.'

'Laughter filled the lands around,' said the Disco Fairy, wiping a joyful tear from his skull. 'To honour that history, they built this.'

Before them was a gigantic snow globe, several storeys high, with mists and silver lights flashing within. In the style of Saturn, a ring of frost and snowflakes floated around it.

Hovering at the top, written in electric-blue lasers, were four words: 'The Krystal Klear Icecotheque'. The merry crowds – a fuzzy group of disco dancers – gravitated towards this core.

The park was vibrant with excitement as people laughed and danced in their finest winterwear. Levander was dressed in a fetching cherry-coloured coat and a woolly panda hat. Bernard wore a woolly jumper and ski goggles, which had certainly caught Ealaín's attention as he'd climbed the stairs earlier.

'Why are you wearing those indoors, Bern?' she'd asked, glancing up from a seaside scene she was painting.

'You want to put a palm tree on a giraffe,' Bernard cleverly replied. 'Maybe your habits are rubbing off on me.'

They'd both laughed, Ealaín returning to her painting, Bernard to his magical city.

As Bernard and Levander came into the shadow of the Icecotheque, Levander's enormous wings beat happily. The security procedures were as offbeat as he'd had promised. Sniffer poodles checked bags and Disco Knights stood guard. Two enormous tortoises, the kind that might have roamed Earth in prehistoric times, were standing on their hind legs to make an arch with their front legs. Everyone had to pass between these 'detectortoises'.

The family in front of Bernard and Levander had metal

on their person, for the detectortoises made slow beeping noises, and the Disco Knights smoothly boogie-searched them. The duo passed without problems, breezed through sapphire gates and into the Krystal Klear Icecotheque.

Like a sports stadium, the base of the snow globe was ringed with hundreds of seats. The ice rink itself was a vast and silver plain. It was filled with a thousand gliding dancers. It seemed like a ballet school had toppled and spilled all its students out across the ice.

'It's enormous,' said Bernard breathlessly. 'I was browsing through figure-skating videos, and this is easily ten times the size of an Olympic ice rink.'

'Perhaps that's because our ice skaters are ten times as fabulous.'

They popped into a tent to rent ice skates. With the help of a worker in a snowflake suit, they picked up two pairs of 'cute Bungo Millalungo ice skates' (Levander's preference). They buckled up and eased onto the ice. Bernard found it surprisingly easy, using the music as a guide, and soon he was skating as smoothly as anyone else. He had a skateboarder's rhythm, after all. People all around smiled and grooved with him and Levander. He looked up at the enormous glass dome above them, feeling very little but very safe among the Discopians.

'This tune has such a refreshing strings section!' cried Levander, skating with one leg gymnastically arched above him.

'Perhaps it could use some vocals,' said Bernard, who was underwhelmed by the music drifting over them.

'Ah, my disconaut,' said Levander, twisting into another

preposterous dance move, 'human voices sometimes wake us from the mermaid magnificence of a disco jam.'

Bernard was unconvinced. He looked around at the winter dance scene, thinking for a moment of the depths below.

'I've never seen peeps so relaxed to dance on top of an abyss,' he said, feeling the ice beneath his skates.

'Discopians, it is a great privilege to dance with you this evening,' said a sonorous voice over the loudspeaker, perfectly synced with the music. Bernard looked up and saw Hazel Soldavril hovering in a bubble overhead. All her tuxedoed bodyguards trailed behind her, also in bubbles. 'My people, weeks have passed since the attacks on the parade, and we must keep the memories of those lost tunes secure in our hearts. We must cherish our disco music and our city-wide family with strengthened affection. Never shall we succumb to those who wish to harm Discopia, our proud home.'

Everyone cheered with gospel-like unity. They were all leaving the ice rink, and Bernard moved with his graceful skeleton host. The floors were comfortably padded for the passage of bladed feet, and Bernard bought a snow cone from a snowflake mascot in the stands. They found two seats, and Bernard was thankful to rest his feet.

Mayor Soldavril continued her announcement, as she and her entourage floated down. 'To commemorate the music lost in the attack, we have a special performance. This dancer, Andromeda Pokitaru, has been handpicked by the Disco Fairy to perform a special new piece. It has been specially commissioned and requires the full ice rink of the Krystal Klear Icecotheque, which hosts us kindly tonight.'

A beautiful girl, clad in a dress made of feathers, swept onto the now-empty ice rink.

'I'm so proud of her,' whispered Levander, his skeleton hands clicking as they clapped.

Hazel, sinking out of view, finished her introduction as the music faded out. 'We must always have faith in the disco spirit. Now, without further ado, please enjoy Miss Pokitaru's *Phoenix Flight*!'

The lights were lowered, and the fiery dancer stood alone on the ice. The music began and she burst into blazing choreography. Her dancing was swift, causing flame-coloured boomba to trail behind her. She accelerated over the frozen floor, and the spotlight followed her. Her golden ice skates were lightning quick, her body never lost time with the disco, and her face glowed with concentration. She backflipped into the air in time to an eagle's cry, she twirled without tiring, and she performed figure-skating moves that filled up the glistening stage. Such was her speed and mastery that Bernard truly believed she might take flight. In the urgency of *Phoenix Flight*, it was easy to forget how alone she was. She was like a firebird on a skyward-facing mirror, not a performer alone on an ice rink.

Nobody noticed the growing shadow underneath the ice.

As Andromeda's dance reached a flaming crescendo, an explosive boom echoed through the Icecotheque. The whole venue shook. The music scratched off to silence.

Andromeda fell to the ice. Then the sound returned, louder than before, and cracks shot out like snakes across the ice.

The dancer seemed chained to the spot with shock. 'Help me!' she cried from the centre of the ice.

The violent sound came a third and final time as something came smashing upwards through the ice.

Bernard's eyes widened in terror. A giant shark reared its snout above the surface, letting out an unholy shriek. He was looking at a fully-grown megalodon, a sea monster crowned with a headpiece of television aerials. Its bloodshot eyes rolled down and locked onto Andromeda, who rose shakily to her feet and then fled. The shark lowered its head and began crunching through the ice in pursuit. It tore after her, leaving a trail of murky water behind it. Andromeda was dashing for the exit, for safety, but the ice was no longer level enough to skate on. Her chaser was gaining, gaining, gaining. The shark lunged forward and spread its jaws. Its teeth clamped down, sealing Andromeda entirely within. The terrible fish rolled a bloodshot eye over the crowd, and its belly lit up from the phoenix-feathered dress within. Andromeda's outline could be seen tumbling inside. Then the shark slid beneath the surface, its prize secured.

The crowd was left staring, horror-struck, as water lapped where just moments before Andromeda had danced. Now the ice skater was gone.

Pandemonium descended on the Krystal Klear Icecotheque, as the revellers struggled to escape in their ice skates and platform shoes. A couple of soulified robins took flight, circling the snow globe in a frenzy. Bernard felt sick to his stomach, just like he had at the parade. Then a familiar white noise crept into the sound system. The turntablist, whose booth was nestled in the hands of a giant snowman, seemed powerless to stop the intrusion.

'Discopians,' said the digital voice of Captain Vyse, 'it's insulting to see you skate so joyfully. I had to send a megalodon this time.'

Hazel Soldavril had climbed to the turntables, desperately trying to stop the villain's transmission.

'Pokitaru Andromeda can be saved,' Vyse continued. 'Right now the great shark swims downwards, with the glowing prisoner in its belly. She will not be glowing much longer. So, Levander, dare you descend to depths where disco does not dwell? If courage resides in that party skeleton, I will be waiting.'

Levander remained perfectly still. He kept his eyes on the waters with a stern resolve, as if his task was predetermined. In a colourful blur of boomba, he rushed down to the entrance of the ice rink.

'Fear not!' he cried to the people. 'I have training in aqua-boogie hostage situations!'

He stripped off his coat and panda hat, and stretched his mighty wings. His skull was glowing amber. Bernard hurried to his friend as he began to tread on the uneven ice. He could not let him face this danger alone.

'Levander!' he cried.

The Disco Fairy swivelled. 'Dear child, my dancer is about to meet a foul and sharky end. I have no time to lose!'

Bernard ignored the exclamation as he cautiously moved towards his friend. 'If you go down alone, you'll never come up again! Please, don't fall for a trap. Don't play into the pirates' hands.'

Levander made a dramatic arm gesture to the crowd. 'Sizzlesticks, you're right! I need reinforcement!'

A Goth – known in Discopia for their maritime flair – stepped forward with an old-fashioned diving suit.

'Miho Raven!' Levander addressed her. 'You have a suit?'

Miho blushed beneath her black fringe. 'The only diving suit we brought is child-sized. It's good for sneaking in candy.'

'Take me with you,' Bernard said.

Levander massaged his skull.

'All right! Bernard, if you can get into the suit in less than half a minute and prove yourself an outfit-changer of Discopian speed, you can join the dive!'

Bernard did just that. Twenty-seven seconds later he was looking out from inside the brass helmet.

'I never . . .' stuttered Levander.

'Let's just go, dude!' said Bernard, trying to ignore his fear.

The Disco Fairy sighed, then regained his laser-focused cool. The holy ice was broken, and the city needed heroes. Together, they leaped into waters to chase the shark and rescue Andromeda.

They sank into the pool, chilly and deep. The water's silence was a contrast to the sounds in the snow globe above. Bernard felt surprisingly warm and snug inside the diving suit, while Levander swam downwards with no breathing difficulties. Shaped like a giant natural well, the pool offered only one direction to go. Downwards they went, to depths where disco does not dwell.

'I've failed as your guardian,' the Disco Fairy said with a watery voice. 'I brought you here for joy and melodies, not to bop with a ravenous sea monster.'

'It's all right,' Bernard said, as it got darker and deeper. 'Andromeda needs us. And besides, I've heard roller coasters kill more people than sharks every year.'

'Well, at least it's not a roller coaster we're facing down here,' Levander replied.

Their progress was swift, and soon they reached slowing sinking shards of debris from the hijacked party. They swam down and down. Bernard heard an effervescent sound nearby – almost like a xylophone – increasing in volume.

'Levander, I'm sure I hear some strange frequencies.'

'That,' Levander explained, 'is the beating of my golden heart. It's being squeezed by the increasing water pressure, but it will not burst today.'

'You have a golden heart?' Bernard turned to see that his friend was radiant gold, lit up like treasure in old movies. His admiration for Levander swelled. Even with dangers waiting in the dark, he felt safe with the Disco Fairy by his side.

As they reached the deep pool's floor, they slowed down. An ancient colosseum, coated in seaweed and sun-starved coral, stood beneath them. The megalodon circled the arena floor, glowing like a waterlogged sun from the dancer in its belly. The sitting area, encircling the pit, was filled to capacity with a thousand Captain Vyses. This audience of clones all had their strange masks turned upwards, towards the two figures.

'Talk about a frosty reception,' said Levander, shaking his skull. They sank a little bit lower, into the ruins, and Bernard noticed that the figures were flickering slightly.

'Welcome,' boomed Captain Vyse from all around. 'I'm glad that you accepted my invitation.'

Suddenly Bernard realised what was going on. 'He's using holograms! They use them back on Earth to reanimate dead rappers and whatnot. They're optical illusions.'

'Nicely done, little one,' said Levander. 'But the shark is no illusion. Let me deal with it, while you find the deadbeat pirate among the holograms.'

Bernard was reluctant to let his friend face the beast alone but knew that he had a great chance to catch Vyse off guard. The two split up, forking away from each other as Captain Vyse began to laugh like ghostly blizzard winds.

'Don't dance like a wounded seal!' Bernard shouted back to his friend.

Levander swam downwards, and the shark caught sight of its sparkly challenger.

Bernard glided toward the seats, searching for a man among illusions.

The Disco Fairy landed silently on the arena floor, and the battle began. The giant fish surged with a violent hurricane of bubbles. Levander zoned in to his dance moves of musical spells and boomba, unleashed so fiercely against Monsieur Le Mantis all those weekends ago. Yet this was no bug with notions in Pantheon 54, but a rabid sea monster with a home advantage. The jaws came gnashing forward like chainsaws. Levander danced only inches ahead of them. He was driven to the very edge of the pit and seemed trapped against the wall. But in a stroke of inspiration, he directed his dancing downward, in a corkscrew manoeuvre that disrupted the sand and sent it swirling into the face of his enemy. The megalodon bayed in rage and curled its mighty form sideways. Levander saw the outline of Andromeda inside, barely visible now. The shark made a beeline for the other side of the arena, blinking the sand out of its crazed eyes, and turned to face the Disco Fairy once more.

Bernard hopped through the crowd, slowed down by the immense water pressure. Up close he saw the captain's features again and again. The purple coat. The catfish-shaped armour. The pale mask, blank except for the red and pink painted eyes. The holograms seemed to be programmed to watch the pit; none were looking at the boy who bounced through their ranks. There were so many spectral captains, yet the genuine villain remained concealed.

The shark began to charge again. The Disco Fairy stood tall as his wings whisked up a vast flurry of bubbles. He was moving his fingers in slow, zen V's before his eyes. There was no music, and the boomba didn't flow as smoothly. As the megalodon reached him, Levander leaped upwards. He cleared the hungry mouth, but not the snout. One of his ice skates clipped it and his boost turned into a tumble. He slammed into the twisted aerials of the monster's headpiece and then into the huge dorsal fin. The skeleton floated to the ground in a wincing twist, as the shark headed yet again for the other side of the arena. It seemed less furious this time, as Levander lay on the floor of the silent pool. It sensed his agony, and the climax of the hunt.

Bernard saw his fallen friend and panicked. It was really time for a miracle. He wildly scanned the crowd, hoping beyond hope to find the pirate. As his vision blurred with desperate tears, something caught his eye. About four rows back, one of the Vyses had tubes branching out beneath the mask. *Breathing apparatus!* Then the mask turned slowly towards Bernard, as the hundred masks around it stayed still.

The shark glided slowly forward. Levander struggled to his knees, took off his ice skates and roared, 'Andromeda Pokitaru! If I cannot save you, at least I'll be with you in the belly of the shark, and we'll whisper our last songs together.'

He stood to full height, to face the approaching jaws one last time.

Captain Vyse lunged forward, through the shimmering forms of himself. He clutched Bernard like an octopus, and didn't let go. 'This is the moment,' he snarled in a voice only Bernard could hear. 'Levander's destruction will cause tidal waves in the disco's waters.'

Indeed, this seemed a crisis that not even Levander could dance his way out of. The shark was closing in. Vyse took out a walkie-talkie and held it to his mask.

'End him, and your duty is done,' he commanded.

The megalodon stalled for a second, glancing at the horde of holograms. Then it swam faster. Bernard looked at Captain Vyse's mask and saw a human neck, heard a human voice. He then looked at the shark, with the spiky barbed headpiece. *Headphones.* Bernard suddenly saw what needed to be done.

'Levander!' he screamed, fogging the glass of his helmet. 'Destroy the headphones!'

And through the murky expanse, the Disco Fairy heard him. He picked up an ice skate and threw it. It spun forth like a tomahawk and, with the speed of the great shark increasing its impact, the skate shattered the spiky headphones.

But the megalodon did not stop. It took the Disco Fairy in its jaws and closed them. The shark blinked and paused, blinked and paused . . . and then began to smile.

Squashed among the razor-sharp teeth, Levander was unharmed. His golden heart was humming intensely, and the shark immediately spat him out.

'I was bedevilled by transmissions,' said the shark in a friendly female voice. 'My name is Corribus, and I'm so sorry. Now you have freed me. I can return to the tropics and dream of disco undisturbed.'

Captain Vyse's fingers tightened around Bernard, but Bernard could only feel delighted at the sight before him.

Levander bowed to the shark. 'I am honoured you have come to this chord-change,' he said. 'You're a noble and funky being. However, you still have my friend gobbled up inside you, and she must also be freed.'

Captain Vyse held up Bernard. 'I will relieve you of fin and flippers while you live, Corribus! Finish the deed!'

The shark and the winged skeleton turned to where the pirate held Bernard among the now useless holograms. They shared a similar, mischievous smile.

'Looks like your days of enslaving sharks are over,' said Bernard. Levander and the megalodon swam across the arena to meet them.

In the Krystal Klear Icecotheque, Corribus broke up through the surface again. The Discopians saw Levander and Bernard riding sharkback and fell into perplexed silence. Usually a vomiting shark isn't a cause for celebration, but when this one spat up Captain Vyse and Andromeda Pokitaru, everyone burst into applause. The selector seized the moment, and the scene erupted into disco jams.

'You needed me after all,' said Bernard, as he high-fived Levander.

'I'm starting to think I always will.'

A team of Blues handcuffed Vyse, and medical staff eased Andromeda onto a stretcher. The two figures, both covered in ash-grey shark juice, were taken out through opposite sides of the snow globe.

As Bernard and Levander slipped down from the megalodon, Mayor Soldavril walked over with an elegant spear.

'Smoothly done, boys. I sorted out some business up here too.'

Levander grew concerned. 'Oh yes? What did you do?'

'I found the spy that Captain Vyse placed in our party.

The pirate with a beard of baseballs was handing out ice skates all evening. I took him into custody myself.'

Bernard removed his brass helmet. 'I can't believe a pirate was hiding in a snowflake suit.'

'How did you know his disguise?' asked Levander.

'It was easy, really. The real snowflake mascot was serving food in the stalls. I guess no two snowflake mascots are the same.'

They paused for a moment and then burst into laughter. Hazel brought Levander and Bernard into a big hug, while Corribus curled her tail into the air and disappeared into the pool, free to swim her own course at last.

7

AND THE
BEAT GOES ON

As Bernard and Levander strolled back to the penthouse that night, the streets were full of smiles. News had spread swiftly of Andromeda's rescue. The boy who had helped her was now known and adored. Bernard – the disconaut who'd chased a megalodon – became the talk of the town.

A few days later, a ceremony was organized to celebrate the freeing of the megalodon. Levander, wearing a shark costume on *Grapevine News*, had proclaimed Corribus a friend of the city. The apologetic shark was crane-lifted from the ice rink and secured to a super-truck. As she was taken to Robyntime Harbour, Bernard and Andromeda Pokitaru sat beside her great head, whispering comforts.

'I'm so sorry,' she said to the ice skater. 'I was not myself. And I appreciate the help. I would not find my way back to the sea otherwise.'

'I understand,' Andromeda replied. 'I sometimes get

lost in the city. I can't imagine trying to find my way through those underwater caves that got you beneath the Icecotheque.'

'We all get brainwashed sometimes,' said Bernard.

'If you ever need me,' Corribus said, her eye rolling to Bernard, 'just play a song called "High Tide Friends".'

Old-school cameras flashed from the pavements, and the happy group appeared in all the evening papers.

It was not the end of Captain Vyse, though. The pirate had orchestrated a fiendish switcheroo in the megalodon's belly. He'd placed his mask over Andromeda's face and taken her headpiece. In a slimed-up state, they'd both been taken from the Icecotheque by the wrong teams. He had escaped the ambulance, for the drivers were lost in karaoke, and disappeared into the night. The escape was sour cola, but it did not slow the dancing in the streets.

From that point on, Bernard and Levander enjoyed a lion's share of adventures. They scored ringside seats for Enano Gigante's Wrestle House. They boogied on skyscraper rooftops. They walked the blue carpet at Grandad Tom Cinema for the premiere of *Bankhoppers*, a film about frogs robbing banks.

Because of Bernard's newfound fame as the disconaut from Planet Earth, Discopia's fashion world offered to supply him with chic outfits. Soon he had a wardrobe in the penthouse crammed with spacesuits. He saw the kids on the pavements of Sweetbeat Street wearing makeshift space-helmets and playing dance-offs with pretend pirates.

'Ah, my funky one,' said Levander, bidding him farewell one night. 'I fear you're a superstar. Too many heart balloons will float you away!'

Life on Earth smoothened out. The days seemed sunnier, and school was more relaxed. Having moved the record player into his bedroom, Bernard could now transport to the City of Dance whenever he liked. Ealaín's work on *Beach Noises* was blazing forward, and the house was full of sketches, models and happy art activity.

'I'm going to build a statue,' she said, driving him to school one morning. 'A tropical statue of mysteries. I'm calling it *Sweet Mind* . . . and hopefully it'll work.'

'If the dance is right, you'll find your flight,' said Bernard. His new disco philosophy proved popular in Fairweather School. Suddenly they couldn't get enough of this 'disco kid'.

'Bernard,' asked a random kid, 'what should I play at my little sister's birthday?'

'You can't go wrong with Salsoul records,' he replied.

While skateboarding one day, Bucky said, 'I'm getting stuck at this army of smelly trolls in *Steampunk Blimp Wars*. Any help?'

'Forget them,' Bernard replied. 'Dance into new skies and enjoy yourself.'

The Skater Kids supported his newfound devotion to disco. Jay brought portable speakers so they could play tunes while they practised across the playground from the squelchy dubstep of Ricky Rockwell.

Even school assignments were going Bernard's way. He was able to use what he learned from the 1970s and the disco movement for a history project. Music was easier and easier, and he brainstormed ideas with Kirsten. The one person who seemed unhappy was Ricky Rockwell, but Bernard learned to ignore this sourpuss.

Before star-travelling to Levander's penthouse, he often checked in with the virtual town of Amble Totes. *Wacky Werewolves* was an addictive pleasure, and KittyLikeThread was providing great songs and friendship. Their werewolves played chess, fished for cars that swam in the ball pit swamp and dug happy holes. In their messages, they sent each other disco tunes like messages in bottles. It was a relief to discuss Discopia with someone on Earth.

> Bernard: We were at a gig where the selector, Mr Ouroboros, played the same song again and again and again.

> KittyLikeThread: I mean, I guess they didn't clash if they're the same? XD

> Bernard: Well no XD the party was declared dead 23 minutes in, and black balloons were dropped from the ceiling!

> KittyLikeThread: Sounds like a cheeky selector indeed.

His werewolf collected disco furniture, while KittyLikeThread decorated her cottage with birds. The mini games never stopped, and their werewolves boosted their howlie points.

> Bernard: Thank you for being here to listen.

> KittyLikeThread: Aww thank you, my friend
> ☺

And then he'd be back, ready to visit Discopia once more. Levander had a never-ending list of parties and activities. Indeed, these were among the most carefree days Bernard spent in Discopia.

Inevitably, the pirates surfaced again. Even with Captain Vyse defeated at the Icecotheque, he still lurked in the city. It was a crisp night, with stars twinkling in the sky. The Diamante cruised down neon streets as they headed for a mystery gig at the Tower Smooth Fountain.

'So, half the peeps want to turn it into a scuba-diving underwater disco,' said Bernard, considering the future of the Krystal Klear Icecotheque. 'And I get that. The ruins we found are a tasty historical discovery, and dancing down there would be great.'

'I'd be inclined to ice the thang over,' said Levander, bopping his skull to a radio mix from Flamingo James. 'Ice rinks teach us to think on our feet, and I love that snow globe.'

Bernard laughed. 'Discopia has the best and wackiest problems.'

'I know, disconaut. Speaking of wacky problems, I gotta swing by this place.'

A soulful chorus rose up on Zam FM, as the Disco Fairy parallel-parked by a small blockish building.

Bernard looked out at the sign: Sergeant Philly's Jailhouse.

'A police station? Surely there are better vibes to be

found at the party? This place doesn't even have balloons at the door.'

Levander turned off Zam FM. 'You're not wrong. But all our parties are jeopardized by pirate crackpots. We have one cooped up in a cell, and it is time to hear what he has to say.'

As they walked to the doors, an owl swooped down from the sky, sporting a chef's hat and an Owlapeño's apron. She dropped some tacos into Levander's hand and hooted, '*Olé!*'

'I love my little burrito bar,' he said, then carried the snack inside.

The interview room was sparse except for a table, two chairs and a jukebox. The prisoner, Wimbledon, sat alone, patient like a tarantula. Along with handcuffs and an orange jumpsuit, he still wore the beard of baseballs. Bernard watched this enemy from the secret side of a two-way mirror. He was drinking hot cocoa with Sergeant Philly, a deep-voiced boss with a mighty moustache. The observation room – covered in shag carpets – doubled up as a mixing studio for late-night music sessions.

'You let him keep his beard of baseballs?' asked Bernard.

'We're not the fashion police,' said Philly. 'We let our inmates keep their style. But yes, that freaky sports look . . . yikes!'

All the baseballs had Jack o'lantern faces carved on them, a detail only visible up close. A fly touched down on them, yet the pirate did not move.

'Our prisoner there is Vyse's first mate. He has thuggery

and brains, and it's a dangerous mix. He's been silent on details and says he'll only talk to the Disco Fairy.'

'So that's why we're here,' said Bernard. 'Hopefully Levander can shmooze that info out of him.'

Philly sat back in his deeply cushioned chair, and sipped his cocoa. 'That's the objective. If he could get anything out of this stonewalling waste of space, we'd be getting somewhere.'

The Disco Fairy swanned into the interview room with many hat boxes and shopping bags.

'Hello, Baseball Beard!' he said.

Wimbledon finally showed some expression as the winged skeleton approached. Above the baseballs, his pale eyes glinted.

'Levander. You've come.'

'I'll get to you in a sec. Let me just put a 45 on the jukebox.' He leafed through the discs in the machine.

The first mate stirred. 'What endlessly idiotic place has a jukebox in their interrogation room?'

'One you don't seem to understand.' Levander chose a funky beat and smoothly turned to begin. 'Now listen up,' he said, taking his chair with a flourish. 'I want you to regale me with all the info on Vysey.'

Wimbledon ran his fingers through the baseballs. 'You have no idea. You haven't even seen our mothership yet.'

'What's that doobly-doo, now?'

The pirate barely moved, save for his uncanny, wiggling beard. 'The captain's mission is simple. He wants command of the city, to be Discopia's pirate king and mayor.'

'He'd probably struggle to get the votes.'

'The captain will take this city in one of two ways. You convince the mayor to give up her command. Or he'll sail in and hunt her down, and there's nothing in this city to stop him.'

Levander considered the words, calmly stroking his jawbone. 'Mothership or not, the mayor will never lose her golden chain.'

Then he got up with a wink and danced to the jukebox melodies.

Philly leaned back as the skeleton cartwheeled around the room before them. He grumpily sipped his cocoa.

'You know, this Fairy really ripples my pond. I wouldn't mind his playtime, but he barely deals with us Blues. He always goes straight to his private inspector. It's not ideal.'

Bernard was distracted by the thought of Captain Vyse hunting down Hazel. He took a breath, regaining his cool. 'That does sound like a tricky situation,' he said.

Philly seemed unshaken, like he'd always known what the captain was up to.

'I don't appreciate Levander choosing her over us.'

'I don't know anything about her,' Bernard said, as Levander breakdanced on the table in front of the unimpressed Wimbledon. 'This guy lives for music, though, so maybe she played him a swanky guitar symphony and he'll love her forever for it?'

'Whatever it is,' Philly said, 'she has his trust more than we do.'

'You should play him some swanky guitar symphonies.'

Levander slipped back into his swivel chair and started again. 'The Blues know that you pirates have a hideout in the city. If you tell me where it is, I'll let you choose the next tune.'

'Do you have anything that's not disco?'

'How dare you!'

'I can't tell you where they are, but I can give them a message.'

'What? I can barely hear you through the baseballs.'

Wimbledon's handcuffed wrists crept forward, and he dropped a crumbled-up note onto the table. 'A message,' he said.

'Don't take it, Levander!' cried Bernard, banging on the glass. The Disco Fairy looked towards them.

'For once in your life, don't pay attention to the mirror,' Wimbledon growled.

Levander swiped the note, twirled in his chair and unfolded it.

Wimbledon cackled hysterically, making all his baseballs wriggle.

'You're in trouble now,' he said, laughing.

Levander examined the piece of paper as the jukebox music faded. He tried to talk to the prisoner again, but the cackling continued.

'All right, you lunatic, the song is over anyway. I have to pick up the disconaut. I'll see you . . . never, I guess.'

'So you presume!' Wimbledon said, settling down. Two Blues with spiky blue hair entered to take him away.

'Safe travels, Levander. Consider the shadows in the hours spent alone.'

That cute skull tilted mischievously. 'Only if you consider shaving!'

SPACESHIPS IN THE NIGHT

In the observation room, Sergeant Philly sighed as he picked up the retro-brick phone.

'I never got any notes, you know. And Bernard, y'all should never strike two-way glass.'

After the meeting, Philly and Levander conferred alone. Bernard chillaxed in the waiting room, where they had a bouncy castle instead of seats. The Blues at the help desk were enjoying the owl-sized tacos that Levander had given them.

All around the walls, the robopirates confiscated at the parade had been placed. Powered off and hunched forward, they looked like twisted mannequins from the future. They had all been put in chains, as a warning sign and a photo opportunity.

Bernard rolled over and checked out a list of Discopia's most wanted criminals on the noticeboard.

The profiles included Pilgrim, although the picture was just an outline with a question mark. A blurry photo of a goat man was pinned at No. 4: 'The Satyr, wanted for sinister crimes and slaying a Blue.'

No. 3 was a whole gang of hippopotamuses, called the Mango Mafia. They were led by Mobster Moylan and terrorized mango farmers for 'snackums'. Bernard wondered how hippos could be hard to find. No. 2 had a big 'Booyah!' stamped across it, for it was the captured Wimbledon. No. 1 on the list was Captain Vicesimus Vyse, wanted on counts of tune destruction, shark brainwashing, kidnapping, party-crashing and fairy harassment. Bernard didn't need to view the artist's sketch – he knew the mask from memory.

Levander strolled out, and Sergeant Philly walked them to the door.

'Thanks for coming in,' said the policeman. 'We'll keep y'all updated.'

'Hey, kudos for the jukebox selection,' said Levander, as they fist-bumped politely.

'It was nice meeting you,' said Bernard. 'Good luck finding those hippos, and thanks for keeping the city safe.'

Sergeant Philly nodded and smiled. 'Just worry about keeping this silly skeleton safe, my friend.'

Back in the Diamante, Bernard examined Wimbledon's note. His hands began to tremble.

'Yeesh, that pirate was a hippy,' Levander said. 'And that hammy performance! There's nothing worse than a hammy hippy.'

'Oh sizzlesticks,' said Bernard, poring over the note. 'This is bad, bad news.'

Outside on the streets, all was normal. People danced and roller-skated about their business in the City of Dance. But the piece of paper in Bernard's hand changed everything. It was filled with a dark, smudgy circle. 'They gave you the black spot,' he said. 'Do you know how messed up this is?'

Levander sighed as he wove his stylish automobile in and out of traffic. 'You know me, little dancer. All I can do is be me. I dance to the beat and move my feet. Try to relax, and we'll hear what Hazel says.'

They arrived in no time, flying up the steps of Tower Smooth. The Kraftyatids looked powerful in the starlight, standing tall as the pillars to this great building. In the lobby, an outer-space mosaic tiled the floor. At the far wall was a fountain, where a party awaited them.

'Holy fajoley, little dancer,' squeaked Levander, holding his skull. 'It's the Slowgroove Sunflowers!'

Five little sunflowers stood in the fountain's various basins, bouncing from side to side in perfect harmony. There was a crowd around them dancing. Bernard's worries were overpowered by disco joy.

'I've never seen flowers this funky,' he said, smiling to the music.

Suddenly Levander was up on top of the fountain, above the five sunflowers who sang and danced merrily. The Disco Fairy started to bust out moves, shining with boomba, and for a second his slo-mo hands seemed like tower-tops, and the lights he created were a thousand happy windows. He was a city of dance himself, Discopia in living form. The happy crowd went wild, and the fountain spouts sent water to the ceiling.

Then they rocketed up in an elevator, and Mayor Hazel greeted them in a breath-taking office. The tone was tamer at the top.

'My friends,' Mayor Hazel said as she hugged them both, 'welcome to the Garden of Bopalon.'

The top floor of Tower Smooth was a greenhouse. A five-tiered pyramid stood at the centre, covered in ferns, flowers and water features. On one platform, cheetahs lazed in the grass. Disco harpists chillaxed on another. Marble steps ascended to the top, and piano music filled the air. The roof of the greenhouse was a geometric ceiling with hundreds of interlocking columns of glass.

This was, from the outside, a sculpture of Discopia's skyline, designed by Vlad the Bat and Esdragon. Bernard took in the tropical delights, and his eyes returned to the centre.

'What a lovely pyramid,' he said.

'I'll let you in on a secret. It's actually a musical instrument, repurposed from an old bell tower.'

'This bad boy is the Carillon of a Thousand Bells,' said Levander.

Hazel continued, 'It hasn't made a sound in centuries. It's our most sacred instrument, and rests here, blanketed beneath lush gardens.'

'If only all gardens hid musical instruments,' said Bernard.

They all laughed, and Hazel led them outside to a wraparound balcony. At each of the four corners, a giant stone toucan looked out. Discopia lay beneath them like a pink and blue jigsaw puzzle. Placing his hands on the cool stone of the parapet, Bernard looked across at the Watermelon Wood. The sea of jagged treetops stretched eastward to the Musicallian Mountains.

'That's a spooky view you have,' he said, as Hazel came and stood beside him.

She shrugged. 'I really like the view. Did you know I spent some summers there when I was around your age?'

'I can't believe you weren't eaten,' Levander chipped in. 'It's a monster mess over there.'

'They don't understand disco, but the Occupants were kind to me when I was young.'

'We must never forget how dangerous they are. I mean,

that bassist can cause earthquakes with his instrument!'

'I am well aware of Endymion,' said Hazel. 'He honours diplomacy, or "discomacy" as I like to call it. Anyway, it's preferable to have frenemies in view, rather than hidden in the shadows.' She turned to Levander. 'Which brings me to a worrisome report I just received from Sergeant Philly.'

Levander shrugged innocently. 'Wimbledon isn't much of a talker.'

'What does it mean that you were given a black spot?'

'It sounds kind of funky,' said Levander.

'Please listen,' said Bernard. 'In Earth stories, pirates never mean well with this dark gift. It's a death sentence, and Levander will be hunted without rest!'

'That's in line with the report.' Hazel's brown eyes looked pained.

'Look,' said the defensive skeleton, 'we're all casual cats here. I have the document. Look! These trumpets of Jericho might be a little intense but I'm not afraid of intense trumpets.'

'This page is ripped from a Bible,' said Bernard, shaking his head. 'It's a sacred text back on Earth, and they used the bit where the city of Jericho gets raided and bamboozled into the ground.'

'That's also on the one I received,' Hazel said, taking out an envelope addressed to herself in Tower Smooth. Inside was another black spot on a Bible page. A silence descended. All three of them looked down at the city, the cars, the music, the twinkling lights. Captain Vyse could be hiding anywhere.

Hazel spoke at last, 'The people of this fine city are happy. They buzz with renewed sunshine. Each song sounds sweeter, each friend of the dancefloor is like family. I'm safe in Tower Smooth, but if anything were to befall either of you, this happy peacetime would end.'

She placed a hand on both their shoulders, speaking softly to Levander. 'I'm assigning you twenty-four-hour security. You must not be taken by Vyse.'

The Disco Fairy considered this, his wings turning tense.

'All right, then,' he said. 'For the sake of the boy, I'll accept a bodyguard.'

Bernard looked at these two mighty figures. He felt safe standing between them, and sensed the combined strength of their disco spirit. Then the moment passed, and a mysterious force drew him to the garden inside.

'Do you mind if I check out Bopalon?' he said.

'Of course you can explore,' said Hazel. 'There's actually a senate of koalas dancing at the top.' She withdrew a water pistol from her pocket and handed it to him. 'Why don't you say hey?'

Bernard beamed at his friends and went inside. He began to climb the marble stairs, unaware that Wollohy Peels was even now watching him from the ferns. The sound of happy koalas drifted through the piano chords. He paused and looked back once. Levander and Hazel were framed by the doorway, laughing and beginning to dance.

It was the last time he'd see them together.

8

STAND ON THE WORD

Jay's treehouse was kitted out with electronics, old and new. The Skater Kids were flaked out inside, taking turns playing an old skateboarding computer game.

'It's bonkers having so many gadgets up a tree,' said Bernard, as his little skateboarder tumbled down the pixelated ramp.

'Better here than inside.' Jay turned up the volume. 'In the house, Dad yells about the noise. He doesn't bother me up here. This treehouse is my castle.'

Bernard gave up his cushion in the glow of the little screen, and Bucky jumped in. Kirsten passed the popcorn.

'How's your mum's art coming along?' she asked.

Bernard thought about it. Yesterday, Ealaín had dived into a dumpster to rescue a dollhouse. 'She's fine,' he said. 'The same as ever. I was meaning to ask you about something. I've been looking into discotheques here on Earth. From what I can tell, they seem noisy and sweaty.'

'Well, Earth is the only place with discotheques,' she said, bringing laughter from Jay and Bucky. 'But yeah, the "nightclubs" on Earth sound gross. Adults pay fistfuls of cash for drinks that give them headaches. The more they spend, the more they suffer when the sun comes up.'

Bernard shuddered. *I'll stick with the Discopian discotheques!*

'How can I even control this little shape on the screen?' Bucky moaned as his skateboarder failed again. 'Retro games are the worst.'

Jay laughed. 'The old stuff teaches us discipline. Isn't that right, Bernard?'

Bernard looked at the screen, where the character lay unconscious on the ramp. The skateboard was a glitchy shape nearby, and the two shapes reminded him of something.

The realization almost made him fall from the tree.

'I have to go,' he said urgently. He left the bewildered Skater Kids to their session, and bolted down the rope ladder.

Skateboarding home, he grew more convinced of the connection. Last year, Ealaín had shown him a documentary on the paintings of Cy Twombly. This artist represented great classical events in smudges, splats and squiggles. When Bernard got back, he logged in to the computer. He typed in the artist's name and scrolled through images of these paintings. Then he saw it. There, among the abstract marks of red and pink, he saw the eyes of Captain Vyse. He couldn't log onto *Wacky Werewolves* fast enough.

> Bernard: Kitty, I've figured something out about Captain Vyse. His mask isn't just

random shapes. It's copied from an Earth painting called Achilles Mourning the Death of Patroclus.

KittyLikeThread: That's very clever of you. What does it mean?

Bernard: It means that he clearly has a taste for the Trojan War.

KittyLikeThread: Well . . . it also means he's aware of your world. Be careful, Bernard.

Later, as Levander brushed his teeth in the penthouse, Bernard showed him the image he'd printed.

'Hmmm . . .' said Levander, his whole jaw covered in foam. 'This warrior, Achilles, was he tough?'

Bernard nodded, putting on a space captain's jacket. 'The toughest cookie in the jar. This painting shows him at his bestie's funeral. It's the moment he decides to return to battle, dooming the city of Troy.'

Levander spat out foam and twirled to his wardrobe. 'Vysey thinks outside the boom box, I'll give him that.' He withdrew two sets of headphones, accessorized with cat ears. 'Thankfully, our city has some tricks left in it too. The sound labs have been working around the clock since the pirates arrived. Dr Sugarado was able to create these! He made them to counter the noise attacks, while letting music through. These white-noise cancelling headphones are being posted out to everyone, from babies to buffalo.'

Bernard was genuinely relieved. 'That's great. Do you have any without cat ears?'

Thirty minutes later, they sat on the cobblestones of Candlewick Square, wearing the cat-eared headphones. A quiet space on the city's west side, this plaza held the statue of the Disco Child. It showed a child of colourful glass dancing on a mighty pillar of stone. The monument resembled a flame atop a candle.

'The flame is eternal and the wick never shrinks,' Levander had whispered, 'but anyone can cast a stone to smash it.'

They chillaxed among a small handful of people, who sat around on cushions.

Behind them stood Chilly George, who had been assigned as their bodyguard. They were here to watch a play, a weird mix of opera and puppetry called *Crustacean Frustration*. The story followed lobsters, represented by towering spindly puppets, who were gradually going blind. The whole play consisted of them singing about their pain and misfortune. Bernard was struggling to understand both the plot and why they'd ended up in that unfortunate audience. Levander seemed enchanted, wiping away tears every two minutes.

A trio of salsa guitarists shimmied over to them at the interval. 'Hey, chic ones,' one of them said, 'we're going to rocket over to Neptune's Hall for the annual foam party. Would you like a ride?'

'That sounds funkalicious,' Bernard said.

'No way,' said Levander, straining his sweet voice.

'Come on,' said the second guitarist, tuning her

instrument. 'If you haven't been, disconaut, Neptune Hall is a maze of glass where mermaids dance on one side and landlocked groovers dance on the other. It was made by Vlad the Bat and Esdragon!'

'A pompous labyrinth,' whispered Levander with a dismissive wave. 'And foam parties are the worst. Bubble baths are wonderful before or after a discotheque, *not* on the dancefloor. I tell you, Discopia's darkest hour will have a foam party.'

'Come on,' said Bernard, 'I thought Candlewick Square was meant to have shedloads of disco spirit. All I've felt is boredom and back pain.'

'This is heritage,' said Levander, his skull looking cartoonishly shocked. 'Disco-dancing began in the sea . . .'

'With that logic, amigo,' said the third guitarist, 'we'll party with the mermaids.'

They shuffled away in excitement.

Bernard felt a prickling of anger. He looked up at the Disco Child above. The various pieces of glass actually cast starlight on the square below, filling it with splashes of gold and silver light. 'An unworthy scene for the light to fall on,' he muttered, rubbing his temples as the terrible puppet-opera dragged on. Thankfully, in the ninth act, the players made it political by bringing on a lobster-cage wooden horse, referencing the night of the parade. This prompted Levander to agree to a long-overdue walkout.

Chilly George led them to an open-top carriage pulled by a herd of snuffling vacuum cleaners. This was George's second job, when he wasn't guarding the entrances to discotheques.

'If I didn't look after the vacuums, their days would be spent scavenging in the Stalemate Scrapyard,' the fridge explained, with an impressive flourish of his alphabetical magnets.

'Levander,' said Bernard, tugging his tasselled sleeve, 'I don't want to see any more obscure theatre. I get that lobsters are tragic. Back on Earth they walk over a thousand miles just to be pulled up by fishermen in the shallows. But, dude, enough is enough. We haven't danced in weeks! Remember when harmonies and pillow forts filled our hours?'

The carriage trundled along the neon streets, with colourful cars and motorbikes passing them. Levander rubbed his temples. 'I'm obliged to oversee the entire city, Bernard. It'll mean the world to that theatre troupe that an audience gave them their time. Supervising a city filled with disco takes hard work, and it's not all roses.'

They stalled at a traffic light, beside a television store. On the thirteen screens in the display window, an urgent newsflash was playing.

'This just in on *Grapevine News*,' said Lance 'The Bounce' Brophy, as he was playfully tossed around the news studio. 'A pirate has been spotted in an apartment at the South Side! This harrowing footage was captured . . .'

A robopirate with a guitar could be seen through the windows on the second floor of an apartment building. People were running as if the building was going up in flames.

'Witnesses say the perpetrator was hidden in the sofa, emerging with a guitar to drown out the host's disco with "soft indy music". Medics are at the scene to treat those who have escaped, but some are apparently still inside, suffering the guitar of a bughouse crazy pirate.'

Bernard turned to Levander. 'We have to save those people!' he said.

The light went green and they moved on swiftly from the televisions.

'We can't just go wherever the pirates pop up, little one. This isn't a game of whack-a-mole.'

'Didn't you once compare party-crashing to "poisoning the pancakes"?'

'These pancakes will be saved by someone else.' He flapped his wings in agitation. 'And didn't *you* tell me at the Krystal Klear Icecotheque that I shouldn't fall for traps?'

Chilly George turned on his seat – no easy feat for a fridge his size – and announced, 'Don't worry, the Blues can handle it.'

Bernard slumped down in his cushioned chair, feeling anger once more. He leaned back, looking up at the skyscrapers, trying to calm down. He never lost his sense of awe at the size of those skyscrapers. Reaching dizzying heights, with flashing windows and dancing plants decorating the balconies, the towers connected the city and the starry sky above. He looked back at Levander. It seemed wasteful to spend a night at home when he was needed elsewhere.

'You know I only have a limited time among these discotheques and lights,' said Bernard, as they turned onto Sweetbeat Street.

The Disco Fairy looked away from him and bowed his

skull. 'I know you do,' he replied quietly. 'As do I.'

Upon entering the penthouse, Levander made the mistake of tuning into Zam FM on the sound system.

'This foam party at Neptune Hall has been the greatest fun of the year!' squawked Flamingo James. 'If anyone out there missed it, don't worry! You can catch it later, haunting your regretful dreams forever!'

Levander turned it off guiltily.

'We'll put on this record Hazel sent over,' he said. The sound system played a gospel choir, graceful with a funky twist.

Bernard rolled his eyes and slumped to the ground. He started playing *Pong* on the video-floor.

'Sometimes you just have to take your shoes off and vibe out in a hammock,' said Levander, moving out to the balcony. Before flopping into his hammock, he looked through the telescope welded to the railing to observe the Bumblebee Bridge. Bernard knew he was checking on his burrito bar for owls, that passion project so close to his heart. Owlapeño's, no bigger than a chicken coop, was nestled beneath the steel girders at the halfway point.

Bernard played the computer game, which consisted of a square drifting between two rectangles. If this was *Wacky Werewolves*, he could have added a blast of huffy-puffy emojis. His mind drifted to Kitty. Earlier they'd discussed the mystery of Vyse's mask, but they'd been talking less and less. On his end, there were fewer Discopian wonders to report. It seemed strange that it was hard to talk with her about ordinary things, like school and cartoons.

Over the gospel choir, Levander piped up in surprise.

SPACESHIPS IN THE NIGHT

'Come quick, you've got to see this!'

Bernard strolled onto the balcony where he'd first seen Discopia. Levander invited him to the telescope, and he looked into it. The Bumblebee Bridge was a vast bridge that looked American on top, with triangular steel supports, and Roman on the bottom, with arched pillars like an aqueduct. It passed straight into the Watermelon Wood, along the only protected route in and out of the east side of Discopia. On the bridge, something very fast was trailing plumes of dust. As the lens focused, Bernard realized it was Miles the drummer. The great bird was sprinting out of the city, a conga drum beneath each wing. His powerful legs pulled him forth in a rush, talons scrolling over the tarmac, leaving speed tracks behind him. He never looked back. A moment later, he was gone.

'You always did say he was flaky,' said Bernard, and the Disco Fairy shook his head nervously.

'I just hope he gets safely through the Watermelon Wood. It's always a little dodgy. I don't trust the Occupants to stay away from the highway. Let's hope they don't have ostrich-based dinner recipes.' He sighed and waved to the woods in a dramatic, Levander-like gesture. 'Adieu, sweet Miles. You know, I travelled that road past the Bumblebee Bridge last summer. Wanna hear the story?'

'No, thanks. I should get back to Earth.'

'But I'm making lemonade in a while!'

'I need to go,' Bernard insisted. He had no interest in playing any more *Pong*.

'Aw, please wait a while,' said Levander, sinking into his hammock. He looked at Bernard with deep affection, then placed a pair of sunglasses on his skull. 'I wanted to visit the ocean,' he said, and his marvellous voice purred with remembrance. 'I rarely leave Discopia – for it needs my dancing – but even I need a holiday every now and then! Far away I found a golden beach with a tiki bar nearby. The dancers there were bronzed, carefree on the edge of the Sonorous Deep.'

Bernard shook his head, looking out at the city where somewhere a foam party was bubbling without them.

'There were surfboards lined up all around this tiki bar,' continued the Disco Fairy, 'like the most colourful tombstones one could imagine. The place was cool. No video-floors or flashing lights, just sturdy wooden boards and a sound system. Candles began to flicker, to dance all night, melting to the wick. Howler monkeys called out in the sunset, and I was at peace, disconaut.'

Bernard quietly tiptoed into the penthouse, hiding his sadness as the Disco Fairy's story floated through the air.

'The tiki bar's selector played all the classics, as well as local favourites on steel drums. I sat down with folded wings, and the stars spread out their secret maps above me. In the water, surfers rode the waves, gentle shadows in the shallows. As I watched them, the spout of a Soultown whale glistened far away, as a disco chorus blasted from the decks. Music seemed to bond the creature with the dancefloor on shore.'

Bernard crossed the living room as Levander's voice outside grew fainter.

'I must have been lulled to sleep by the tunes and the tide. I woke up as the sun rose above the palm trees behind me. There was endless sand on either side. No tiki bar. No people. Just myself and the sound of footsteps –'

Bernard heard no more, as he closed himself into the spaceship. He returned to his bedroom in a flash, ending that Discopian night of weak puppet-opera, pirates on *Grapevine News* and a beach story never finished. Perhaps he would have cherished these quiet moments more had he known of the cursed times to come.

9

HEAT YOU UP
[MELT YOU DOWN]

Two werewolves stood on the edge of the Ball-Pit Swamp. They were trying to paint a barn red, but it was hopping around on legs, chuckling. The paint cans kept growing legs to make giggling escapes.

Everything on screen seemed to be laughing.

> KittyLikeThread: I wish our real days could be like this.

> Bern: Did you sleep ok last night?

> KittyLikeThread: I didn't really sleep. Dreading the day actually.

Bernard rubbed his own tired panda eyes. The pretty sunshine of *Wacky Werewolves* differed from the grey, raindrop-speckled window of the living room. The barn shook off the red paint like a dog.

> KittyLikeThread: You've been quiet about Discopia recently :p

Bernard sipped his orange juice and sighed. Levander had stopped dancing in the streets and was cooped up like a glamorous hermit in the penthouse. His secret ventures into the city were taken alone, to meditate in the Gothsemane Aquarium. The last time Bernard was with him, they'd had a petty argument.

'People burned disco records on Earth!' he'd snapped. 'We mustn't let pirates burn them here!'

'Maybe you should chillax in your own world for a while,' Levander had said, polishing his video-floor.

> Bern: Yeah . . . I would love some disco adventures. Believe me.

> KittyLikeThread: I'm starting to doubt Discopia is even real. XD

The werewolves continued swishing their paintbrushes. The barn was still 60 per cent unpainted, grinning smugly.

> Bern: I gotta get to school. Ttyl =]

> KittyLikeThread: Yeah sure champ. Talk to you later x

He turned off the computer. *Wacky Werewolves* zapped to black.

Downstairs, the kitchen was nice and cosy. Ealaín was tossing a salad at the counter. She looked tired, with flecks of paint in her frizzy hair.

'Good morning,' she said. 'We have a box of Trix cereal and a bottle of milk. Go wild.'

Bernard started crunching through the cereal, looking

at the rabbit on the box. He was always chasing Trix, but never seemed to eat it. *Rough deal*, thought Bernard.

'Everything smooth with you?' he asked his mother.

'Not really,' she said. 'I've been researching fake giraffes . . .' – Bernard stifled a small laugh in his cereal – 'and it looks like you can only buy the heads. I need the body though, and it's an artistic conundrum.'

'Hmm. It seems the universe can provide the wrong half of what you need.'

'You can learn a lot from the fake giraffe market,' she agreed, and they laughed together.

Outside, the rain was getting heavier.

In Fairweather School, the disco craze had grown. The football team trained to the music of Chic. Disco lyrics popped up on blackboards. On that grey day, though, funkiness seemed absent from the corridors.

In music class, Mr Flannelly was rhapsodizing about Beethoven.

'Now I love playing *Für Elise* on my ukulele, but I'm not the only one who does new things with his music. In the disco movement, the Fifth Symphony was remixed and became a No. 1 hit. The classical can still be cool.'

He nodded kindly at Bernard. The disconaut made a mental note to see if any Beethoveny characters were conducting music in Discopia.

'Disco, disco, disco,' snapped Ricky Rockwell. 'We're not all sappy retro-nerds.'

'It's not for dubstep trolls,' said Bernard.

'Hey, take it easy,' said Mr Flannelly.

'Take it Für Elisey!' yelled Bucky, making everyone

laugh. The mood settled, but as class continued, Ricky's eyes narrowed coldly.

After class, Bucky took Bernard aside for a word.

'Are you playing *Steampunk Blimp Wars*?' he asked.

'I'm afraid not, dude.'

The Skater Kid shuffled on his feet, seeming antsy. 'Are you sure? Let me just ask a basic question. If clowns overran the cargo hold, you wouldn't know how to blast them out of the airlock?'

Bernard was confused. 'I have no idea. I captain no blimps.'

'OK then, discoman. I'll see you around!'

Bernard scratched his head as Bucky dashed away.

At lunch, the music room beckoned. Bernard had recently uncovered a set of turntables in there and had been practising his record-spinning. The school's limited record collection was all over the place, ranging from the Victorian musical *Pirates of Penzance* to electronica from Four Tet. Yet they all had rhythms, and syncing from one to the other was a cool task of timing. Over the sound of operatic pirates fading into crazy beats, he suddenly heard a real-life voice.

'You're all alone now.'

He slipped off the headphones and turned around. Ricky Rockwell stood in the room, his hands balled into fists. His cronies huddled behind him, keeping watch at the door. 'It's time for disco to be squashed out of this school.'

The huge boy slammed a table out of the way, lurching forward. Bernard sighed. He was sick of these threats.

Had he not dealt with pirates, a megalodon, and a giant orchid mantis? What was this mean Earth kid by comparison?

'What are you going to do about it, Ricky?'

The bully seized him by his collar and lifted him from the ground. 'What do you think you're playing at?' he snarled, shaking Bernard. 'Everyone in the school is talking about old music. Kids from other schools think we're shrunken old men. How can we focus on the now when you're forcing us to choke on the past?'

Bernard was defiantly calm. The recent lack of adventure in Discopia had left him keen for action.

'Well then,' he said, 'why don't we settle this properly? A showdown, just you and me.'

'What did you have in mind, scrawny legs?'

'A dance-off. Disco V dubstep. The abandoned pool, after school.'

Ricky's eyes glazed over as he considered a contest where Bernard might best him. His pack of boys hollered from the doorway. 'That kid's got brass, Big Rick! Take him up on it!'

Ricky placed Bernard back on the floor. He smiled like a komodo dragon. 'All right. A dance-off at 4 p.m. I'll see you there.'

During a free period at the end of the day, Bernard slipped into the art room. His mind swam with thoughts of glory and Levander dancing with the speed of a bullet train. It felt only right to paint his face like a skull. When he'd applied the face paint, he decided to use the art room computer. You can never earn enough howlie points on *Wacky Werewolves*. KLT was offline. Her away status read, 'Gone for now, stay happy ^_^.'

He sent her a message.

> Bern: Do you know anywhere I can get a life-sized giraffe?

> Bern: The lower-half specifically =]

He finished painting the barn alone, and steadied himself for the task ahead. The end bell rang, screeching through the halls like a shot-down blimp.

The double doors of the abandoned pool were chained but children could easily slip through them. With his hood up for full effect, Bernard stepped in from the rain. Feeling like a gladiator, he strolled down the stairwell of cracked tiles, down to the pool area.

He remembered a story Andromeda told him, when they'd danced in the loft of Swanbell Supreme.

'One time a crazy soulified chestnut tree challenged Levander to a dance-off. Our guy busted out a dance move that showed a tree in all four seasons. The boomba around him turned from vibrant green to autumn colours, ending in a wintery, frosty gale. He was more of a tree than the opponent! Nobody saw anything like those moves.'

Bernard grinned in his fierce face paint. How could Ricky hope to triumph in a dance-off with the Disco Fairy's bestie?

He arrived at the decrepit, empty pool. Its faded blue tiles were covered in leaves and beer cans. From the rundown changing rooms, squelchy dubstep floated out.

'Ricky,' he called out, 'prepare for a lesson in the combat of Discopia.'

As Ricky approached, five boys with pillowcases over their heads stepped out. Too late, Bernard realized his folly. This was an ambush, and he was beyond the point of escape.

The white-hooded gang surrounded him in seconds. An elbow in the stomach sent him to the floor, gasping from thunderstruck lungs. They kicked and thumped him mercilessly, and through the blows he saw canisters of shaving foam come out. They began to spray him with the stuff, laughing hysterically. He tried to wipe it from his face but received a vicious kick. He was soon covered in shaving foam, resembling an alien sheep as he struggled on all fours.

When this cruel sport was done, all five goons lifted him into the air.

'If I ever hear you talk about disco again,' came Ricky's sharp whisper, 'I won't be so kind next time, freak.'

Then they threw him into a pile of rubbish, and left him there.

Bernard was able to clean himself up in the school showers, wiping away white foam mixed with red blood. He then skateboarded home by the back roads, so nobody he knew would see him. When he got there, Ealaín was in her studio, taking a buzz saw to a wooden structure. She was surrounded by piles of bamboo thatch and didn't see her battered son passing like a phantom. In his bedroom, he slouched to the floor and let the tears come. He was numb with the pain, and furious at himself for being entrapped.

He bowed his head and sobbed in pain and humiliation.

After a while, he crawled downstairs to grab some food. He then limped to the computer, where the Skater Kids had sent him a few messages.

> Jaydizzle: Omg, Ricky's bragging that he beat you up. Is this true?

> Kirsten: We're here for you, pal. Want us to come over?

He ignored them and sought out the comfort of *Wacky Werewolves*. He clicked over to the village of Amble Totes. He decided his werewolf needed a clean, so clicked into his peach-puff cottage and booted up the Groomomatix Shower. His cuddly character, wearing funky swim-shorts, started to dance in the pixelated steam as he sent a chat request to KittyLikeThread. Soon enough, she appeared. Her fox-like werewolf wore a floral dress and a funny wig.

> KittyLikeThread: I found you some giraffe links!

> Bern: That's nice =] but I have other marshmallows on the fire now.

She sent the links anyway, as her werewolf jumped between the black-and-while tiles of the bathroom floor. One of them actually had what Ealaín was looking for, so he emailed it to her.

> KittyLikeThread: Indeed, giraffes are pretty mysterious creatures when you think about

it. It got me researching a thing about sea monsters.

Bern: Oh yeah? Random . . .

KittyLikeThread: There are all these unidentified sounds that have been recorded in the ocean. Bloop is a famous one, but that turned out to be an icequake. There are other ones though that only appear at certain times of the year.

KittyLikeThread: All this calling from the deep, but scientists have no idea what creatures cause it! ^_^ Man, nature is spooky.

She sent the link, and Bernard listened to the eerie noises recorded fathoms below the sea. Although he loved sea monsters as much as the next kid (had he not befriended Corribus?), he was looking for real talk.

Bern: Kitty, I danced off with Ricky Rockwell today.

KittyLikeThread: Oh, he's the bully kid, right??

Bern: Yeah.

KittyLikeThread: How did it go?

He didn't want to lie, yet he found himself unable to describe the sad truth.

Bern: Well we danced off at a bathhouse down by the beach. A crowd gathered, the disco overwhelmed Ricky, and I was champion. It was ideal, and they cheered my name.

KittyLikeThread: That's great! Well then, I'll forgive you for painting the barn without me :p

In spite of the pain, and the fabricated story, Bernard smiled at this.

KittyLikeThread: Hey, forgive me, but isn't this a story to tell your skeleton guardian in Discopia?

He closed his eyes and saw red. There was nothing he'd like more than to visit Levander's penthouse. But he'd been told to stay away.

Bern: Ah it's OK. Besides, Levander's penthouse would be empty anyway.

KittyLikeThread: Yeah? Where is he?

Bern: The Gothsemane Aquarium, which sounds kind of gloomy for my liking.

KittyLikeThread: Why would a party royal take his dancing shoes there?

Bern: So he doesn't have to worry about pirate spies.

Kitty's werewolf stopped hopping. Bernard's was still moving to the rhythms of the shower dance. There was a pause for a while, then Kitty's werewolf threw thirty silver cookies at Bernard's werewolf and left the cottage. This usually meant that a mini game elsewhere was taking up her attention, or perhaps a trip to the werewolf general store.

> Bern: Hey, thanks for talking. Whatever about
> Levander, I know I can always count on you.

A little pair of eyes appeared under the statement, signalling that it had been read. There was no reply. On the internet, such lulls are common; there are always other distractions.

Yet ten minutes passed and KittyLikeThread didn't reply.

> Bern: Kitty, are you there?

> Bern: haha did I do something wrong?

> Bern: I don't understand . . .

He zoomed out to his map of Amble Totes. The away status above KittyLikeThread's cottage had reappeared: 'Gone for now, stay happy ^_^.' She never left him without a goodbye. The bruise on his face began to sting, so he went down the hall to get a bag of frozen peas. Pressing the icy bag to his face, he thought about KittyLikeThread. Perhaps her WiFi had died? No, she had time to activate the away status. Was she mad? In fact, he had no idea to gauge her feelings beyond what she typed. He didn't even know what she looked like, let alone what went on behind those eyes he'd never seen. Who actually was this friend of his? As if the cold touch of frozen peas had brought his mind clarity, he began to realize something. He had divulged everything to KittyLikeThread. He had told this person about the parade, the ice rink and all about his increasing involvement in the city. Bernard had told her . . . or him . . . every place that Levander would be, and about the city's efforts to find the pirates. A dreadful suspicion began to chill his soul. Where had he first met KittyLikeThread? An adults' musical forum . . . *Disco Discourse*. That's where he'd seen her picture. His heartbeat quickening, he clicked over to this website. After a moment he remembered his password and logged on. He followed the threads and found the original message.

> KittyLikeThread: Hi! I assumed myself to be the only kid who liked disco ^_^ Haven't visited any cities like that though. I'd love to hear more about it.

With trembling fingers, he clicked into the profile. Everything was as he remembered it, except for the profile picture. Before, KittyLikeThread's profile photo was a girl playing the piano. Now it was a different photo. It was a man dressed like a pirate, wearing something familiar to obscure his face. A mask without eyeholes. Two scribbles where the eyes should be.

Bernard, holding back a scream, clicked back over to *Wacky Werewolves*, where he'd just revealed Levander's secret location.

'Gone for now, stay happy ^_^.'
KittyLikeThread had logged out forty minutes ago.

10

THERE'S AN ANGEL IN
THE SHOWER

After visiting hours, entrance to the Gothsemane Aquarium was denied to all but one. Little was known of the Goths who lived here, other than their eminence in ocean research. Tales of their candlelit disco parties were whispered throughout the city. These aquarists, draped in elegant black, concealed their subculture from all but the Disco Fairy, for whom they opened their gargoyled gates at any time of night. They liked him, for his skull was adorable and his manners were impeccable. He came to them because he found their place soothing, and his duty was to all dancefloors of the city. Even the ones unknown to all. The ones nobody outside could hear.

Levander sat underwater in Seahorse Sanctuary, a huge freshwater tank in the east wing. Miho Raven was on the night-time rounds, walking the exhibits in a ball gown and bat-shaped headphones. The wispy presence crossed his line of vision every twenty minutes. Levander wore a wetsuit and snorkelling mask, an uncharacteristically low-key ensemble. His butterfly wings curled weightlessly behind him. All around, seahorses playfully swam like individual notes in a wonderful symphony, a living flurry of colour and movement. The room before him, where visitors stood during the day, was dimly lit and unoccupied. The Disco Fairy was at peace.

Half an hour passed and Miho Raven did not appear. Levander's mask turned to the left, then slowly to the right. Suddenly, in contrast with the gentle blue of the tank, the room before him started flashing dark red. The seahorses scurried out of view. He kept watching. Red. Black. Red. Black. Red, and he saw glints of swords. Black. Red, and blurry figures milled into the room before him. Black. Red again, and a dozen pirates now stood beyond the glass, raising their weapons.

The Gothsemane Aquarium had been invaded.

Levander's life had taught him that the conditions of any dancefloor can change in a millisecond, and his reactions were lightning. He launched upwards in a storm of bubbles, as the pirates started to hammer the glass. A feeding bridge hung above Seahorse Sanctuary. The Disco Fairy broke the surface, raised his skeleton hands, and pulled himself up onto the bridge. In a gurgling explosion, the water disappeared beneath him, out through broken glass.

As he tore off his mask, the doors to the feeding area burst open, and even more pirates hurtled through. He immediately snapped into a dancing position, but the slipperiness of the floor, the tightness of his wetsuit and the state of his dripping wings meant that he couldn't dance at all. The pirates stormed onto the bridge in violent excitement. Through his mind ran all the options, yet only one seemed viable. He had to run.

Dodging a hail of harpoons, Levander fled into the exhibits of the aquarium. Along a corridor exhibiting the fashions of little caddisflies, past screens showing microscopic footage of waltzing krill, down a tunnel of glass where mighty salmon glided on the other side, the Disco Fairy ran. The bloodthirsty howls of pirates followed.

Levander turned into the quarantine lab, where two hulking pirates awaited. They closed in, and he backed up against a tank of cuddlypods. These creatures looked like kittens but were in fact highly venomous urchins in kitten costumes. He gently took one out, apologized, and flung it at the first pirate. She caught it in her tattooed hand and immediately crumpled into a deep sleep. The second pirate charged, but Levander ducked to use the momentum against him and sent him flying into a pile of old diving suits. As he moved on, skipping across a tank of sleeping turtles on their shells, he heard the evicted cuddlypod shuffling away with false meows.

In a room called Coral Kingdom, between tanks of beautiful coral, the pirates hunted. Levander crept among them, undetected. Somewhere, a gramophone played the interview the Goths had conducted with Corribus. He listened to the megalodon's words:

> They ensnared me in the Gulf of Grooves.
> I was enticed to their boats by stolen disco
> melodies, ringing out clearly through the
> water. As I approached, harpoons came
> raining down. I was swarmed by humans in
> the turquoise surf. For all my titan strength, I
> was subdued. The splashes shrank and shrank,
> and soon the waters were restful once more,
> with my body stilled in frightful chains . . .

Levander winced with the pressure of remaining unseen. This was a heavy invasion, and the aquarium suddenly felt smaller. Six more pirates entered Coral Kingdom before he slipped out the far door, his passing obscured by a tank of pink tube anemones.

He entered the Darkwave Ballroom. This oval hall bore witness to those great disco Goth parties, cloaked in secrecy. Behind the fossilized jaws of a megalodon, a candlelit turntable booth overlooked the dancefloor. The walls were lined with dioramas of nature behind glass. One scene, recreating icy plains where the Snowy Llamas mooch, caught Levander's eye, for suddenly he saw the Goths. His friends had been tied up and locked inside the exhibit. They cried out in distress, and Levander swerved his course. He had mere seconds before this room too would be breached, but he could not abandon these Discopians. He rushed over and opened the crudely barricaded door of glass. He slipped off the ropes binding Miho Raven, who rose up with black sparks of boomba flaring from her fingertips. She began to untie the others as Levander turned to run again. He'd sacrificed the head start. Pirates came storming from Coral Kingdom, on his trail again.

The chase continued into the Hall of Oceanic Magnificence. There were upper floors ringing the rectangular hall, and a pristine glass ceiling adorned with whale skeletons. The ceiling was his best point of escape. As pirates crowded in, multiplying every minute, the Disco Fairy climbed up a statue of a giant squid and leaped to the upper levels. The pirates thronged up the cobwebbed stairwells after him. His feet never stopped, even when guns began to fire. When he reached the upper levels, his pursuers had arrived at the platform on the other side and were cutting around to outflank him. The Hall of Oceanic Magnificence was now filled with pirates. As he was surrounded, he clasped the mahogany railings and leaped outward. The jump was successful. He found his mark. Levander clasped the ribs of a Soultown whale skeleton and held fast. These lords of the Sonorous Deep were among his favourite animals, so to have made it here brought a glimmer of hope. He climbed up to the spine and looked up. He had imagined bursting through the glass ceiling, but now cloaked robopirates stood on its upper side. They carried the banner of Vyse, and their metal mouths chanted in unison with the crowd below.

This was, perhaps, the moment he realized there would be no escape.

He turned his skull down from the ceiling. He walked along the great spine to the tip of the whale's jawbone as pistol shots rang out. He prepared himself on the creature that had, in life, filled the seas with melody. Then he dived, wrapped in his waterlogged wings, falling in technicolour down to the crowded floor of the hall. With a cacophonous splash, he landed in a tank of Sunset Jellyfish.

Underwater again, he spread wide among the silent beings, so named for their painful stings that darkened the vision of those who touched them. The jellyfish were his final defence, but not even they could hold back this enemy. In an instant, the hammer strokes from outside began. It took just four blows to smash the tank, and its water flooded out. Entwined in the tentacles of Sunsets, Levander spilled onto the cold tiles of the floor, coming to rest at the boots of Captain Vyse.

11

TEARDROPS

Bernard burst into the quiet dark of the penthouse. He looked around like a hunted jaguar. Nobody was home. He quickly turned on the radio, and Flamingo James reported the dreaded news.

'You know, they sometimes say that disco music is too happy, that it doesn't help us when we feel sad. If the reports we're hearing are true, and the pirates have got our Disco Fairy, then all the music in the city won't heal us.'

'No, no, no,' said Bernard, madly rubbing his curls. He switched on the video-floor and pulled up the bubble chair to watch *Grapevine News*. Sergeant Philly was giving a solemn address at a podium before the battered gates of the Gothsemane Aquarium.

'We can confirm that Chilly George was standing guard in the car park, and was suddenly attacked. We found him with his door forced open. He's lost a lot of ice but is being treated. We can also confirm that pirates ransacked the aquarium. We know Levander was here and have no confirmation of his present location.' He paused, eyes downcast as the cameras flashed. 'It is our understanding that the pirates have skeletonnapped him. We are following up every lead we can.'

Bernard curled up in the chair, wincing as the crowd began to scream. His head was filled even now with the polyphonic sounds and cartoonish visuals of *Wacky Werewolves*. He wondered how Captain Vyse had found him. Had he been trawling the internet, seeking anyone who mentioned Discopia? Bernard remembered the cunning pirates of history. They would fly flags of friendship to gain the trust of distant ships. Then they would close the distance across the sea. That's when the flags would come down and cannons come out. KittyLikeThread was like those ships. By the time he recognized the enemy, it was too late.

The phone calls started rolling in. Levander's answering machine went as follows: 'I'm out on the wing, boppin' on Bungo Millalungos. Stay fly and leave a message.' Then the tearful tributes came. Friends, fans and countless Discopians were reaching out with messages of heartbreak, love and support. Bernard listened to them all as he walked around the penthouse, through the kitchen, the bedrooms and the music hall.

He still had no idea where the pirates hid; nobody did. Captain Vyse had left no clues. On the video-floor, Lance Brophy was reporting live from inside the Gothsemane Aquarium.

'The pirates arrived in normal Discopian cars with blurry licence plates, scattering back into the city afterwards. There are still no leads as to their whereabouts.'

Bernard put the beach ball's gloomy news on mute, and walked out onto the balcony. He looked for an answer in the skyscrapers and spires, but Discopia was blank and forlorn. There was neither music nor laughter. He never knew silence could howl like this.

The phone rang again. Levander's chirpy message. Voicemail click. Then a ghostly robot voice filled the space.

'Bernard,' said Captain Vyse, 'go home.'

He sprinted back inside and picked up the phone. 'Let him go, you cyber-stalking psycho!'

'This is your chance to leave the party,' he replied, and the line clicked dead. Bernard performed a furious war dance, and red boomba glowed around him. After a moment he calmed his breathing and lay down on the hard video-floor, currently showing highlights of Levander's life.

The phone rang again. As it went to voicemail, a carefree female voice began to speak.

'Hey, Skullz, it's Affy. I'm doing that mission tonight and could use your help. You know where you dragged me to Okinawa Frostbite? I'll be there at twelve o'clock star-time. Just spare me the disco. Hugs and kisses.'

Bernard sat up straight. This person, Affy, seemed oddly unaware of the capture. He didn't recognize the voice but something about her was familiar. He moved over to Levander's bookshelf and pulled out an impressive tome entitled *Levander's Party Log*. Within the pages was a record of every concert and party the Disco Fairy had ever attended. He flicked through the O section, momentarily smiling at the entries. He found what he was looking for, in Levander's cursive handwriting.

> Okinawa Frostbite and the Yetis: This pop princess, with her backing band of yetis, grooved us in the skatepark of Tuyentown. She sang of dazzling winters, and 'Ski Lodge Boogie' moved me to tears! The crowd danced in artificial snow, and I boogied with the Inspector.

The Inspector! It dawned on him instantly. Philly had told him how Levander rarely consulted the Blues, relying instead on a freelance inspector. This must be her. *Could she be my shot at finding the pirates?*

He looked back at the spaceship. If he left now, he would forever regret letting Levander slip into the pirate's clutches. Going back was not an option. Bernard knew he must travel to Tuyentown.

Given the situation's heat, he decided to wear a disguise. He found a geometric mask of an owl in a sombrero – a promotional item for Owlapeño's. He shrugged and placed it on his head. He slipped out of the penthouse, down the stairwell and onto the city streets, appearing like a hunter in the dusk. Tuyentown was down south. He'd been there once to watch a dance-off between twenty sumo-wrestlers and a T-Rex (it had ended in a draw). As he walked the streets alone, he desperately missed Levander. Without him, Discopia was a cheerless spot-the-difference puzzle. Rollerbladers removed their skates. Traffic clogged the streets. The basketball court was empty.

He didn't have wheels or a ride, so he'd have to take the Koonslite. This was Discopia's subway system, and he often saw the giant unicorn heads that marked an entrance. Two blocks down, he found the nearest station to Levander's place. He walked into the unicorn's mouth and descended into the colourful passageways. Shuffling in between the legs and tails of rushing commuters, he found a neon map of the circuit. Tuyentown was on the Sapphire Line, six stops. He moseyed to the ticket booth, where a bearded man with a Levander plush toy was weeping.

'Em,' said Bernard, peering through the mask. 'A train ticket for the Sapphire Line please?'

The ticket seller regained his composure, and sniffled. 'There ain't no trains, night owl,' he said. 'This here's a city-wide carousel.'

'A carousel . . . like plastic horses going in circles to kitschy music?'

'There ain't no better life lesson,' he said, printing up a ticket with trembling hands.

Bernard followed the signs to the platform. Indeed, there was a carousel flowing by like a river. Happy, bouncy horses glided into view from the left tunnel, only to disappear in darkness on the right. He leaped on, and mounted a plastic mare. The Koonslite rushed forward into the city tunnels. Up and down in rhythmical progress, he glided through the passages so different from the streets above.

An old woman hobbled up with an enormous, mewling hairdo.

'My hair is a hotel for cats,' she informed him. 'Would you like to stick your face in?'

'I'm fine, thanks,' said Bernard, spooked by the invitation.

The woman proceeded to raise biscuits to her hair, where many paws emerged, claimed them and disappeared once more.

'You must keep the cats on your head happy,' she crooned, leaning toward him. 'Otherwise their claws sink deep.'

This walking cat sanctuary moved through the horses, to the edge, and she slipped into the tunnels. Down a tunnel, for a second, he spied a feeble campfire. Bernard thought of the outcasts in the sadder corners of this city. Disco music was made to wash away our worries, but for lonely souls without homes or families, he knew it wasn't enough. He bowed his owl-masked head, his thoughts with all Discopians. Levander brought this city security and hope. Would it collapse without him? He tried not to imagine it, but that campfire flickered on the edge of his mind.

He jumped off the Koonslite at a super-clean station. He climbed upstairs, into the cool night air of Tuyentown. Bernard had been delighted when he'd first heard about Tuyentochi, a distant land on the Musical Planet with striking similarities to Asia. This neighbourhood had been built up by Tuyentochan immigrants, who had travelled to Discopia with dreams of dance.

In lantern-lit streets, disco played from the sushi bars and arcades. Food stalls huddled in the shadow of massive torii gates. Vending machines lined the walls, and the streets were spotless.

The skatepark was easy to find, full of slopes, railings and halfpipes. Beside it, a towering dragon clock showed five minutes to midnight. An ice-cream truck was parked near its feet.

Only in this town could you get popsicles at this hour, Bernard thought with a weak smile, but it didn't cheer him up.

There was a stage at the skatepark's centre, so he went and sat on its edge. The weight of the day pressed down on him and he was exhausted and sick with worry. A billboard nearby caught his attention, as it showed his own face, drinking cola. *The Disconaut drinks Cosmopop!* Seeing himself so happy and chillaxed in the ad made him feel even worse. His fresh wounds stung just as much as they did back home. He wished he had his skateboard, and he could really use some Cosmopop. Closing his bruised eyes, his thoughts turned to Levander, and he remembered the urgency of this mission. The clock struck twelve and let out dragonish plumes of smoke. Rumblings could be heard from the north. Bernard turned his head, beginning to wonder who exactly he was meeting here. Something big was coming down the street towards the skatepark. For the second time that day, he realized he could not escape.

Like torrents from a broken dam, the hippopotamuses flooded in. The thud of their feet hitting the ground quaked the very concrete. Up and over ramps, curling around halfpipes, their blubbery hides filled every space. The place was overrun in seconds, and Bernard recognized the hippos that surrounded him. Tattooed, pierced and oozing thuggery, this was the Mango Mafia from Discopia's Most Wanted List. One fearsome lout crawled onto the stage, and rose up on two legs. With diamond-grilled tusks, Mobster Moylan was the largest, nastiest hippo of the bloat. He looked at Bernard, who shrank under the monstrous glare.

'Take the meeting notes, you feathered fool,' he grunted, evidently mistaking him for an owl in a sombrero. He thrust a dog-eared notebook into Bernard's hands, then turned to address the crowd.

'My hippos, the Disco Fairy's blasted! Credit to the pirates for taking him out! His dancing can't stop us now, and the Blues are gonna be wrapped up with finding him. The Mango Mafia can now go unchecked. The future is juicy with illegal mangos and crime! Our omnomnomish schemes are just getting started.' The words were well received, and the criminals snorted loudly. 'Now, I think this owl was sourced by our intern. He'll just do a fly-over and make sure everyone's here.'

Bernard backed up, as all eyes fell upon him. 'I . . . can't today.'

'You can't? What kind of owl are you?'

'Not a flying one.'

In one quick sweep, Moylan snatched away the owl mask. 'It's a boy!' He grabbed Bernard's hoodie, and held him up to the Cosmopop billboard. 'It's Levander's boy!'

The Mango Mafia erupted in slobbering laughter. Bernard gagged at the leader's warm, fruity breath. He looked out at all those kayak-crunching jaws and was terrified. He tried to hold his nerve.

'I seek only the pirates,' he said. 'Let me go or you'll never dance again.'

The laughter of the crowd intensified, turning hungry. They began to holler and stomp, and that's when everything exploded into bubblegum pink. Mobster Moylan dropped Bernard and turned, blinking and blinded. The hippos were trying to move but only succeeded in piling upon themselves. Bernard climbed onto a railing, watching the scene before him turn into a hurricane of lasers. Shots were raining down on every hippo, stunning them to sleep. Through blue mist and laser beams, he saw the master of this light show. A lithe human figure strode through the chaos, firing two laser blasters. She wore a white coat, a blue visor, and her hair was pink and spiky.

Within seconds, she'd brought down every hippopotamus except the leader. She turned to Mobster Moylan now, holstering her weapons.

'You screwed-up futurist!' he raged, as she took out a slingshot. 'Wait, I'll give you mangos aplenty!'

She fired something pink at the hippo's belly, which immediately expanded into sticky foam that covered him. He fell forward, rolling into the half pipe below, only his head visible above the hardening pink cocoon. The raider walked forward and placed her foot upon him. She started tapping intel into a beeping gadget, deaf to his ranting.

Bernard let out a huge sigh. His hands were pale where they had gripped the railing. Everything had changed so fast. He picked up the notebook and cautiously approached the woman, crawling over unconscious hippos.

'Hi . . . Affy?'

She answered him with the barrel of a laser blaster. 'Wait right there,' she commanded. It was the same voice he'd heard on the phone. 'I have to signal this location to collect my bounty.'

As she continued to tap on her gadget, Bernard held out the notebook. 'This is their ledger. It has details of their operations.'

She stopped tapping, and lowered her weapon. She looked over, taking the notebook. 'Thanks,' she said.

'I came on behalf of Levander.'

'I just heard what happened.' She started walking away.

Bernard hurried after her. 'I know he's your friend too. He needs us right now.' She didn't stop. 'Please! I'm alone in this city otherwise.'

This seemed to strike a chord, and she paused. Turning around, her hard stare softened behind the visor. 'I can't help you, Bernard. Skullz talks highly of you, more than you know.'

'I have no one else,' he said. 'Please. I can't find him on my own.'

She took a deep breath, looking from the conquered hippos to the bruised child before her.

'I guess . . . I owe it to Skullz to drop you home.'

Bernard shook his head. 'I can't go home until he's safe.'

She rolled her eyes, walking to the gate again. 'I'm taking you back to the penthouse. If it makes you happy, we can swing by the aquarium on our way. But know this, if Captain Vyse has him, then he's beyond rescue.'

The sirens of approaching police cars rose from afar. Affy opened the door of an ice-cream truck.

'Hop into my office.'

Although this was a stranger, she was Levander's friend, a cop of sorts, and had just defeated the Mango Mafia. Bernard trusted her. Also, he'd always wanted to travel in an ice-cream truck.

'Thank you,' he said, feeling safe for the first time in hours. 'By the way, I didn't catch your full name?'

A smile breezed across her face. 'It's been a while since somebody's asked me that. I'm Inspector Affogato Norse. Care for some Cosmopop?'

12

INSPECTOR NORSE

It was like boarding a futuristic submarine. The ice-cream truck's kitchen was customized with drum machines, shiny keyboards, laser guns and old-school computers. On the screens, pink font marched across a soft blue background. Everywhere Bernard looked, buttons flashed and dials glowed. Up front, a robot gleamed in the driver's seat. Inspector Norse whispered directions to it.

'Make haste, Momotaro,' she said, and the robot began to drive. The ice-cream truck cruised through Tuyentown and Bernard settled into a seat, still rattled to have come so near to death-by-hippopotamus.

'Welcome to Tastybase,' said Affy, throwing him a can of Cosmopop.

'You have a nice place,' he said, glancing at the flashing surroundings. 'Is that robot, Momotaro . . . soulified?'

'Not really. I custom built her to save myself time. It means I can work in Tastybase without it ever stopping.'

She logged in to a computer and called up some spectrograms. These shapes of sound were chunky and full, which meant her music was loud. Sure enough, an enormous rumble blasted over the sound system, like a grumpy volcano.

'I've been tracking the Mango Mafia for days,' she said, focusing on the screen. 'They avoided detection by hiding in cement-mixer trucks. Once I noticed that the trucks were hollow and going faster than usual, their schemes were doomed.'

Bernard realized she was playing a recording of their footsteps as they'd entered the skatepark. Norse turned it up, smiling briefly. 'Another gang off the streets, a new sample for my beats.'

She switched it off and swivelled to face her new guest. The robot driver had smoothly joined with traffic on busier streets.

'Now,' she said, 'this is my secret workplace. You will not mention me outside of this truck.'

'Of course,' said Bernard. 'I'll keep your secret. I just want to find Levander.'

He proceeded to tell his whole story, including *Wacky Werewolves*, and she listened, occasionally glancing at the dials and screens around her. When he'd finished, they were cruising through Roseland Park.

Affy rubbed her spiky hair, and stretched.

'Honestly, kid, it'll do no good. Disco criminals are as flashy as fireworks, and that's easy to trace. The pirates aren't like that. I've been trying to find them. They leave no clues, and I haven't come close to working out Captain Vyse. My sources in the underworld have no answers either. He appeared out of nowhere with a loyal crew and robots.'

Bernard let out a deep sigh. He was weary and sore from this endless day.

'I hear you,' he said. 'And if Levander couldn't defend himself, it's a terrible force we seek. He must be found though. Hazel said it best: "If the Disco Fairy falls, Discopia goes down with him."'

Affy tapped some intel into another computer, then peered out the food-counter window. Reflections of the city outside glided across her visor, and her face became sad.

'I'd love to bring Skullz home,' she said, 'but we may as well be hunting ghosts.'

After driving across Discopia, Momotaro parked across from the Gothsemane Aquarium.

The grand Gothic building was crawling with Blues. The carpark was webbed with yellow police tape.

Inspector Norse turned to a stripped-down ratchet radio. She put on some headphones and threw a pair to Bernard. He wore them as she turned the dials, and he heard waves of a police broadcast.

'What can I tell ya, chief,' someone was reporting, 'they've acid-washed the CCTV footage, there are no fingerprints, and the Goths were mostly blindfolded. There are no leads.'

'I feared such cluelessness,' Affy said, throwing off her own headphones. She moved back to the window, and peered at the scene with binoculars. Bernard also scanned the building. He shivered at the thought of what had gone down in there.

'Hey, you,' said a crotchety little voice, 'gimme a scoop

SPACESHIPS IN THE NIGHT

of marshmallow mischief, and don't assume I'm paying.'

Affy and Bernard looked over the counter to see a rat in a shabby leather coat squinting up from the pavement. To Bernard's surprise, she turned to the ice-cream machine and prepared a thimbleful of white ice cream. She reached down and gave it to the little fellow.

'What's your name?' she asked.

'They call me Sammy Sharp Eyes, and this needs sprinkles.'

Affy turned to Bernard. 'Please bring me those sprinkles,' she said. Her courtesy puzzled him, until he realized its purpose. An investigation had begun. He placed the jar in her hand.

'Did the police interview you, Sammy?' she asked.

The rat kept his eyes on the sprinkles. 'The police didn't ask me nothing.'

'That's a shame. Did you see anything?'

She hovered the spoon of sugary goods just out of his reach.

'I saw pirates all right,' he said. 'A freaky bunch indeed.'

'That's hardly new information. You mustn't have seen much.'

'Yeah? Well, did you know they were followed?'

Bernard's heart began to hammer. Affy gave Sammy the sprinkles.

'Who followed them?' she asked, her voice impressively calm.

'Well, now,' Sammy said smugly, 'a rat like me knows a dealio when he sees one. That answer's gonna cost you.'

'What does a rat like you need?'

'Vinyl records are everything in this town, Barbielocks. Disco for info.'

'Give us three minutes,' she said, closing the window and turning to Bernard. 'We have to make some music. Can you do a vocal cut?'

He admired this proposal, and jumped up. 'If you lay down some rhythms, I'll freestyle over them.'

Her hands went gliding over drum machines and keyboards, calling up sound files and new rhythms. Her skillset was becoming more apparent by the minute as she invented a wonderful tune. Bernard remembered an old Beatrix Potter story about gangster mice crashing a dollhouse, and thought Sammy Sharp Eyes could relate. He sang what he remembered, and at the end of the quick session they had produced 'The Tune of Two Bad Mice', ready to deliver on a two-inch vinyl to their rodent informant.

'That's fresh vocals from the disconaut,' she said. 'Now tell us what you know.'

Sammy slid the record under his jacket, his whiskers twitching happily. 'All right then. They scattered in their getaway cars. As they left, though, some human bolted down the stairs in that alley. He hopped onto a scooter and tore after them.'

'What did this human look like?'

'I remember people's scents, not their faces. This one stank like crazy paints.'

Inspector Norse thanked him, and Sammy Sharp Eyes scampered away. She swivelled a joystick beneath a screen, pointing a camera on her roof towards the alley. It showed grainy footage of a fire-escape stairwell.

'If our mystery guest was up there,' she said, 'they'd have a perfect view of the aquarium.'

'Let's check it,' said Bernard, and twenty seconds later they were climbing the fire escape.

On the roof they found a water tower. It was ringed by a freshly applied graffiti mural. Its style suggested only one Discopian could be responsible for it.

'This is the work of Pilgrim,' Bernard said. He thought back to that shopping plaza all those weeks ago, where Levander had shown him the drowning sun. This new piece was tricky and incomplete. One half, expertly made, showed astronauts surfing. The other half was manic, little more than a thornbush of squiggles.

'It changed halfway through,' said Affy, touching the spray-painted metal. 'The left side shows care and purpose, but the right side . . . he threw this mess together in seconds, then abandoned it.'

Bernard looked from the mural to the Gothsemane Aquarium, then to the roads by which the pirates scattered.

'He must be trying to tell us something about the attack.'

'Yes,' said Affy. 'He was working on his art, and changed it because of what he witnessed. But why?'

'The messy half has a familiar shape,' said Bernard.

They spotted it at the same time, and voiced it together. 'Pantheon 54!'

The Inspector's eyes sparkled behind her blue visor. 'That discotheque's a few blocks down, on 5th Chord Avenue.'

'I danced there on my first night here,' said Bernard, growing hopeful. 'Could Pilgrim be suggesting . . . it's the pirate hideout?'

Her face slid into cool determination, the same look she'd carried into the skatepark in Tuyentown.

'Let's find out,' she replied.

Tastybase arrived at Pantheon 54 in no time. The party was over, and melancholy dancers were drifting out. Inside the truck, Bernard surveyed the scene through binoculars, while Inspector Norse examined the blueprints she'd called up on a computer screen.

She remarked, 'The place has bogus security, with all respect to Chilly George. But there's not much in the design to suggest a secret purpose. No hidden rooms or tunnels. Plus, it's a well-known place in Discopia.'

That's when Bernard spied the graffiti scrawled on the side of the marble stairwell. 'By the crown of funk!' he cried. 'It's not the hideout, but he's left us another clue.'

Inspector Norse bounced over, taking the binoculars. The graffiti showed a cute little seal.

'You're right!' she said, unable to hide her excitement. 'Pilgrim must have quickly slapped it on and continued the pursuit. Our vigilante has left us an art trail to follow.'

'Let the chase continue,' said Bernard, sitting back down.

Affy stayed standing. 'This is a serious lead,' she said. 'I'll take you home and give chase to Vyse alone.'

'Affy, you can't face this on your own! Levander told me that if parties tailspin, that's when dancing partners are needed the most. I'm going nowhere near the penthouse. If you won't take me with you, I'll follow these clues myself.'

She was unmoved by his words. 'I know where that seal indicates, but I work alone. I've never pursued such wolfish targets, and I'm not about to do so with a kid.' She opened the door, to the city outside. 'If you're not going to accept my lift, take the Koonslite. There's a station around the corner.'

Bernard couldn't believe he was being ushered out onto the pavement. The door slid shut behind him, and Momotaro revved the engine.

'Levander deserves more than this!' he yelled, as the ice-cream truck departed. 'He deserves both of us!'

Tastybase changed lanes, but then began to slow down. Brake lights appeared under the massive pink cone on its rooftop, and it stopped. All around, Discopia continued its mournful silence, and dancers headed home. Affy looked out from her window, sighed in reluctance, and beckoned Bernard back to her.

She didn't pursue conversation once he'd returned. He sat up in the passenger seat as she checked her computers. Music played from the stereo, and it was futuristic by Discopian standards. It sounded like robots playing ping pong. Looking at the robot driver beside him, Bernard guessed it complemented the style of Tastybase.

Above his seat, a Polaroid of a friendly policeman was tucked into the sun visor. It was the only photo in the truck.

They arrived at a little harbour called Dreamboat Dock,

filled with colourful buoys. They walked out and began searching for clues. No graffiti was immediately obvious. A wind was building, and Affy's white coat fluttered against her legs.

Bernard walked to the end of the little stone pier and looked across the Vamvozio River.

There it stood, as always – the Watermelon Wood. With shaggy trees and shadows, its murky expanse couldn't be more different from the extravagance of Discopia.

Bernard asked, 'What exactly lives over there?'

Affy walked to the edge. 'We call them the Occupants. The beasts who make their home under those crazy boughs . . . they worship old, dangerous melodies. Let's just hope you never have to deal with them.'

Bernard nodded, and they turned their attention back to the harbour. That's when he realized the buoys in its waters weren't buoys at all but the heads of skittle-coloured seals. The laidback creatures were facing him, and one sported an unusual hat with five handmade sunflowers.

'Those paper flowers were spray-painted,' said Inspector Norse. 'Now, what could they mean?'

She was puzzled, but Bernard was surer. 'The Slowgroove Sunflowers!' he said.

She cocked her head.

'They're one of the best bands on the circuit.'

'If you say so,' she snapped, rolling her eyes. 'I don't bother with disco bands, but let's see what my system can tell us.'

They ran back to Tastybase. Bernard felt stung, like

he'd accidentally insulted her. She was already on the computers when he stepped in after her. As Momotaro moved on, Affy started drumming the countertop in agitation.

'I'm sorry I was rude,' she said, looking away from the machines. 'You didn't deserve that. You've been swell. It's just . . . I don't like disco. I can't stand the sound.'

Bernard looked at his new friend, beginning to understand her isolation. 'You don't like disco? And you live here? Wow! That must get quite annoying.'

'That's an understatement. I prefer making my own music anyway.'

'It's no problem, Affy. It's actually a bit refreshing.'

'I like what disco could become. I have faith in its future,' she said, glancing at him. 'Now, it seems the Slowgroove Sunflowers are permanently exhibited in the window of Ezio's Recording Studio. Which is . . . further down this riverside road.'

'Pilgrim really is leading us to them.'

'I hope so,' she said as Momotaro picked up speed. 'Otherwise we're following a trail of paintings to nowhere.'

As they neared their next location, rain began to fall. It thrummed on the rooftop and streaked down the food-counter window. The city outside was blurring, and in the flashing space of Tastybase thoughts turned to what awaited them on this wet and sinister night. As they came to a halt, Bernard looked through the drizzle to see the outlines of five sunflowers, obscured behind another pane of glass. Affy headed out with her coat wrapped tightly around her and wiped the far window. The Slowgroove

Sunflowers were asleep, their petalled heads bopping gently from side to side. Even in sleep, they were in sync.

On the glass before the smallest flower's face, Pilgrim had spray-painted a crow's mask.

Affy nodded her head and returned.

Bernard watched the sleeping flowers melt back into the rain. 'It seems unfair that they're constantly on display,' he said.

She ran a towel through her spiky pink hair. 'Discopia is bughouse crazy. The more you look, the more you'll see that. Pilgrim's directing us to the Corvid Pool Hall. We're running out of city, so this one or the next could be the hideout.'

They continued and the downpour intensified.

'It's just my luck to suffer rain in two different galaxies,' said Bernard.

Affy's curiosity came to the surface. 'So how did you get here from your home planet?'

'Star-travel's not too bad. I play this record and it launches me to the penthouse. I can go back through the spaceship, but sometimes Wollohy Peels transports me back.'

'How intriguing. And disco is in your galaxy too, but the movement happened a while ago? Something to do with the seventies?'

'Yeah, the disco era has come and gone in my world.'

'And what came next?'

'Well, in a lot of ways disco mainstreamed into pop music. In dance music, by the 1980s, it transformed into a music called house.'

'House,' she said, looking to her drum machines. She seemed distracted but extremely sharp, like a daydreaming mathematician. 'This is good to know.'

The Corvid Pool Hall was a basement joint in Charmer's Market. This far south, the buildings were more industrial, the whole place haunted by empty lots and warehouses. Before descending the rain-slicked stairwell, Inspector Norse prepared several tubs of ice cream. Inside they found a murder of soulified crows – each one six feet tall – playing snooker in the smoky haze.

'Please accept these free samples of berry-white sublime,' she said, and she began to hand them out. The crows' beaks clicked in gruff approval. After getting brief feedback on the flavour, Bernard asked if any characters had come by or if they had noticed any new graffiti. They had seen nobody, but someone had been heard in the corridor to the bathrooms. Affy went to check it out. The crows went back to their games. Bernard's attention drifted to a television in the corner, where Commander Tulsisan was being interviewed in the Pipelands below the city, a place where the crocodiles boogie. 'Our Disco Knights are searching the whole sewer system,' she said.

Bernard and Affy weren't the only ones searching for Levander, and this gave him a mini-blast of comfort. Just then, a giant wing tapped him on the shoulder.

The crow shyly introduced himself. 'My name's Dylan. You're the disconaut, right?'

'The very same,' said Bernard. 'Nice to meet you.'

'Will Levander be all right?' Dylan asked. His beak was turned towards a black and white photo on the wall. It showed the Disco Fairy with all these crows, laughing in this very room.

Bernard understood the worry in Dylan's eyes. 'I ain't resting till he's found,' he promised.

Inspector Norse returned. She held a fire extinguisher, upon which a message had been scrawled in banana-yellow paint: 'Turrell Factory.'

Bernard recognized the name. 'I know that place. They do lights and props for discotheques.'

'No secrecy from Pilgrim this time,' she noted. 'That could be our place.'

Bernard was keen to leave, but something held his companion back.

Affy addressed the crows once more. 'You're all good with faces. Has anyone seen the Satyr?'

The room fell silent. She was answered by a hunchbacked crow playing pool alone. 'I heard he left town. Ain't seen him.'

Norse stood firm. 'He's in this city. My information's solid.'

Neither the fellow nor anyone else in the room had anything further to contribute. Affy sighed. They thanked the crows and departed the Corvid Pool Hall.

'Who's the Satyr?' asked Bernard in the stairwell.

'Just another villain to cage,' she said, not looking back.

The Turrell Factory was an unassuming place nearby, between the ruins of roller coasters. From a distance they surveyed the windows – neon lit in the building's flaking brickwork.

The Inspector whispered her thoughts. 'I'm in the dark

about Pilgrim's motives. Why didn't he call the Blues directly? If he followed the pirates successfully, past all these locations, why would he hide his work?'

'I hear you,' said Bernard, 'but it's our only thread through the labyrinth. We must follow it.' He lowered the binoculars. 'There's no sign of pirates here.'

Affy glanced at some dials, the pink numbers reflected in her visor. 'No, but I'm getting an intense read on boomba levels. Something's in there.'

She handed him a laser blaster and they stepped out of the truck again. They found a triangular fire escape around the side, and it was unlocked.

Down a fluorescent yellow corridor, across perfectly mopped floors, the Inspector and the disconaut proceeded. They looked right at home in the colours and light.

The entered a large violet space, and the door slid ominously shut behind them. The room held an enormous bug's head fashioned from bronze. Its eyes were perfect triangles, each made up of twenty-eight light bulbs – with one at the top and seven at the base – and from the centre of this piece, out of smoke-machine mists, strode Wollohy Peels.

Bernard stamped his foot. 'No!' he yelled. 'I can't be torn from Discopia, not on this night! Somewhere out in the rain, Levander is suffering. I can't abandon him now.'

Wollohy Peels towered over him in grey robes, his pineapple head like a fruity beacon.

'Whatever you are,' Bernard pleaded, 'whatever

powers you have in that disco trunk of yours, please don't use them today.'

Wollohy's hand arose, but in that moment a sheet of turquoise light fizzed down between them.

'He stays with me,' said Inspector Norse. She was holding a gadget shaped like an ice-cream cone, and it projected a force field that shielded them both.

Wollohy Peels paused, and then he slowly walked back to the bug head, into the mists, and vanished.

Bernard couldn't believe it. 'That was amazing! I didn't know he could be stopped.'

'Let's bolt before the pineapple changes his mind. There's Pilgrim's final clue.'

In the drama of the encounter, he hadn't seen the grim chess-piece knight on the far wall. The graffiti was shiny and wet. It was fresh.

They sprinted back to Tastybase as Affy's force field flickered and disappeared.

'The shielding gadget's still a work in progress and can't be used again tonight. Let's hope I didn't waste it.'

They climbed back into the ice-cream truck.

'You didn't have to save me,' said Bernard. 'You want to keep me on now?'

She cocked her head. 'You're in this now, kid. Besides, I'll need someone to carry the gear, given the amount of laser power I'm bringing. Pilgrim's confirmed my fears about our destination.'

After giving some coordinates to Momotaro, Affy called up an old newspaper article on one of her computer screens. 'Read that,' she said, taking her laser blasters to the passenger's seat. Bernard scanned the article, which had been published many years ago, and penned by a reporter called Medusizzle.

> The Vetruvius Club was shut down today after one of the most heated protest movements in Discopian memory. Leading the charge was Levander, our resident Disco Fairy. Many cite his star power as a significant factor behind the discotheque's closure. Speaking to me and my 31 snakes (which make up one of the hottest haircuts in journalism), Levander commented, 'Vlad the Bat and Esdragon's glass building is admirable, but it's totally unsuitable to pure disco vibes. Sixty-four floors? Distanced turntablist booths? These divide rather than unify, bursting the buzz of all who wish to dance.'

> Rocko Meredith, the discotheque's owner, defended its unusual layout. Meredith pleaded, 'The Vetruvius Club offers fun and disco goodies. It hurts that people think it's a claustrophobic sweatbox!' The final deal-breaker, noted by many, was the total absence of mirrorballs. This is – in some cases – a felony.

Bernard turned away and walked up between Affy and Momotaro. Dead ahead, through the windshield, he laid eyes on an enormous wall crowned with barbed wire. In the centre was a gateway so huge it made the ice-cream truck seem toy-sized. Against lightning-forked skies, the sign above the gates read Stalemate Scrapyard.

'This is where Pilgrim's trail ends,' said Inspector Norse. 'This is where we'll find Skullz.'

Momotaro parked beside the pavement and they proceeded through the gates on foot. The Stalemate Scrapyard took all the city's unwanted rubbish, a wasteland of clutter and trash. The rain beat down, and thunder rolled through the mountainous piles of junk. Affy and Bernard trudged the sludgy shadows, over cars, bathtubs and crushed mirrorballs. They even passed the wooden horse, from whose ribs the pirates had first appeared.

'This land used to be the grounds of the Vetruvius Club,' said Affy. 'The only visitors now are boom-box goblins, junk-fashion foxes and . . . other things . . .'

A rumble sounded nearby. It was not thunder.

Bernard gulped, trying to keep his voice steady. 'So the discotheque wasted away, forgotten?'

Inspector Norse nodded. 'Birds don't even fly overhead. It's a perfect hiding place.' As they journeyed deeper, she became silent and focused.

Bernard felt his mind's eye turn to werewolves. Not the cuddly internet kind but scary ones, ragged puppets to the moon, hunting in packs across moonlit suburbs. The thought quickened his pulse.

After about ten minutes they'd hiked to the crest of a tyre pile, bringing the Vetruvius Club into view.

'Pilgrim did not fail us,' whispered Bernard. There was no doubt they had found – at last – the hideout of Captain Vyse.

13

WOLF LIKE ME

Two giants, their upper halves surging up from the ground, played a game of chess with no pieces.

It took a split second before Bernard realized they were statues, and the massive chessboard between them – a smooth construction of glass and steel – was a building. The Vetruvius Club was ghostly clean in the junk piles that surrounded it. Lights flashed below the chequered glass, and the rock music within was loud even from this distance.

On the side wall, an entrance led into one of the black squares. Three pirates stood guard before it.

'Here it is, exactly as you see it,' whispered Affy, scanning the place with binoculars. 'Each square in the chessboard is a room, sixty-four in all. It follows the same notation, A1 to H8. It's clear that plenty of pirates are home.'

Bernard tried to hide the fear in his voice. 'I think I know why Pilgrim let us follow the trail and didn't call the Blues. This place is better suited to stealth than a siege.'

'Whatever Pilgrim's story is,' said Affy, 'I've set up Momotaro to send a message if we don't return within the hour. They'd take too long to get here now, even with choppers.'

She knew, as Bernard did, that there could be no waiting. Levander could be close to death within the grid. It was up to them.

'Are you sure you want to come with me?' Affy asked. Her voice was a comfort in the cold, dark rain.

Bernard nodded. 'We've got shapes to throw and minds to blow,' he said, praying for courage. His hands shook as the pair crept down the tyre pile and started towards the entrance.

Whether the pirates saw them or not, there was little they could do. Bernard downed the robopirates with Discopian dance moves, while Affy stunned the human guard with a laser beam.

Above the grey doors, someone had painted 'Abandon All Disco Ye Who Enter Here'. Within, they could hear snarling guitar riffs and delirious drums.

'Our friend is in one of these nasty rooms,' said Bernard.

Inspector Norse nodded. 'As is the city's most wanted criminal. We must be careful in this chessboard of the damned.'

They crossed the threshold, into ear-splitting rock music. They entered the H6, a black 'square', and faced a derelict ticket booth with nobody behind the glass. The place was grimy and dark.

'Come on,' yelled Affy, passing into the next room.

Bernard's thoughts were scrambled by the raw noise, but the audio switched as they passed through the doors. In the showers, steam and pipes of white H5, he heard Captain Vyse's voice booming from the speakers, still loud enough to sting their eardrums. ' . . . following the lines. Now that I have you to myself, skeleton, we can have some fun.'

Bernard held his ears, trying not to hear. Peering at the white tiles, he was reminded of the abandoned swimming pool. Now, hours later, he stood in a place of even greater danger. He scrunched up his face, wishing for the day to end.

'It seems he's talking to Skullz,' said Affy. 'We gotta find them pronto.'

The walked through another door into black H4, and the rock music enveloped them again. Bernard had to put his hand to his mouth to stop from screaming. The dark room was filled with pirates, dancing and drooling in a strobe-lit rave. Their eyes were mostly closed, and the exit was on the right, beyond the crowd. Bernard took Inspector Norse by the hand as they tiptoed through the strange assembly. The pirates danced aggressively, lost in a toxic daydream. One of them looked directly at the intruders, making Bernard jolt with fear. However, the pirate did nothing but stand and stare with diluted, empty eyes. He did not raise the alarm, just watched them as they crept away from the horrid dancefloor.

The enemies in white G4 weren't so forgiving. Bunny-eared robopirates with knives glided towards them. Before Bernard could react, Inspector Norse beheaded the animatronics with a flurry of laser beams.

'You don't need boomba for that,' she said, stepping over the destroyed machines.

Bernard gulped, trying to stay cool.

Over the speakers, Captain Vyse continued. 'There are always repetitions, in music and in history. There will always be cities like yours, and there will always be conquerors like me.'

They passed through a photographer's darkroom. Dripping photos hung from strings overhead. They showed Tower Smooth photographed from all sides.

Bernard swiftly acclimatized to the chessboard layout of the Vetruvius Club. The perfectly square rooms changed from black to white to black. But the familiarity of the design brought no comfort. In this modern-art dungeon, every new room was a plunge into the unknown.

Up in white G6, they almost ran onto a glass model of Discopia on the floor. Bernard studied this miniature city, creeped-out by Captain Vyse's voice which again played on the soundsystem: 'Don't take my interest in Discopia personally, Levander. There are many more places in the Musical Planet that I can visit next. But crushing disco is a pleasure.'

'His voice plays in the white squares,' said Bernard, 'And the rock music blares in the black ones.'

Affy nodded, examining blueprints scrolling on the inside of her visor. 'That was how the Vetruvius Club worked, with two separate music streams. The turntablists played from the heads of the statue giants outside, playing to thirty-two squares each. It was one of the reasons the place was unloved. It divided its crowd.'

Bernard glanced at the tiny glass replica of the Vetruvius Club. 'Could Vyse and Levander be in one of the heads, then?'

'He seems to be in everyone's head these days, but no. I checked on our approach. The audio is coming from within.'

They moved deeper into the board, coming upon a shooting range in black F6. A pirate with tattooed arms was shooting harpoons. Paper figurines flitted before her, printed to resemble Discopian greats such as Mayor Soldavril, Cloud 9 and the Slowgroove Sunflowers.

Affy pounced and grappled her from behind. 'Where's Levander?' she hissed, cocking her laser blaster.

'You disco scum will never win.'

The Inspector laughed, turned her gun to the targets and blasted them herself. 'Save it for someone who cares about disco.'

'OK, you maniac!' the pirate hissed. 'The brig is in C7.'

Affy aimed the blaster nozzle at her ribs and shot her to sleep.

'Yikes!' said Bernard.

They stepped over the fallen pirate and continued, sprinting up through white F7 and black F8, a two-room armoury. Old pirate weaponry, such as cutlasses and muskets, hung alongside riot shields and assault rifles. Affy already had stacks of laser power, but a shiny oak slingshot caught Bernard's eye. He plucked it from that wall of weapons and pocketed some paintballs. They arrived in white E8, a dingy bathroom where a freaky pirate played turntables by the sink. The peg-legged man turned his yellowed eyes towards them and turned his music up.

Inspector Norse fired, but whatever this pirate had in his system, lasers didn't hurt him. Bernard called up strong, soulful boomba and danced forward like a tornado of lights. Faced with the disconaut's moves, the selector crashed to the floor, unconscious.

'Wait . . .' said Affy, inspecting the selector's equipment. A chessboard-shaped machine was plugged into the turntables, the black squares dotted with a circuit of lights. 'This lowlife is playing music for the black squares, and it looks like he just turned off the audio for H4.'

'That's the rave we walked through. Without music, those spacecakes will come to check. If they find the bunny robots you took down next door . . .'

'Let's keep moving,' Affy said, with an edge. 'I fear this hour requires strength beyond measure.'

They moved swiftly forward, closing in on the brig. Black D8 had nothing more than a television in the corner, showing an old werewolf movie.

In white C8, pirates lay glassy-eyed across the floor and furniture, boozed up and burnt out. It was the Medusa's Raft of afterparties, twisted bodies and unhealthy faces sprawled everywhere. Inspector Norse shook her head. 'These drunkards will be seasick tomorrow.'

There was no door to the brig of black C7, but there was a metallic vent near the ceiling. Vyse gloated over the sound system: 'Disco will be under my control. I will carve it up and sell it as I see fit. What I don't need, I'll destroy.'

This was followed by an ice-cream-smooth scream.

'He's hurting Levander!' whispered Bernard sharply. 'Let me on your shoulders, Affy. We must hurry!'

Affy readjusted her laser guns and let him climb up. The screws on the vent were easily removed, and the metal sheet clattered down. It didn't wake the pirates. Bernard peered through, but couldn't see anything in the darkness of the chamber.

'Levander?' he said. Over the music he could hear faint, anxious whispering from the opposite corner. He crawled through before Norse could object, and fell down onto the hard ground. He could hear the whispering more clearly now: 'The great scale of sounds . . . planets turning and humming . . .' It wasn't Levander's voice.

Norse climbed through the vent and made a smooth landing. She turned on a torch to illuminate the room.

A burly centaur stood in chains. He wore an American-football helmet and was scribbling equations on a blackboard. He hunched forward, his human spine drooping away from the horse half of his body. He didn't seem to notice the torchlight.

'A centaur should never be caged,' said Norse, her voice cracking with pity. 'They're clever enough to know their situation, but they can't help their animal outbursts.'

The centaur turned, roaring. 'Oh please, torture not poor Chirontë!'

'We're not your enemy,' said Norse. 'We're here on a rescue mission.'

'Get away! I could not teach him . . .'

'Look, Chirontë,' said Bernard, trying to calm him, 'this

is still Discopia. Nobody should be imprisoned without boogie justice. We shall free you from your chains.'

'How can I trust you? Humans have tricked me before.'

'Do not harm us. We shall ride upon your back, to escort you to safety.'

The football helmet nodded. 'O-k-kay. I just want to go home.'

'Great. A little help with the chains, Affy?'

Inspector Norse looked at Bernard, her head tilted. This was an unplanned move and could jeopardize their mission. Still, she smiled at the thought of having a centaur on their side. She blasted the chains free, and soon they were sitting on his back.

Chirontë took off, bursting through the doors like a hellbent quarterback. Bernard and Affy held on to his shoulders. Through a jailer's room, he trampled robopirates beneath his hooves. He crossed a laboratory whose walls were lined with robopirate heads – the jaws of whom gnashed beneath swivelling eyes. The charge continued through a room plastered with blueprints and business papers (in here bone-quaking music blared beyond the right-hand wall), and across a room filled with computer hard drives – towers of data that fell like dominoes. All the while, the riders on his back held on. In white C2, five squares down from the centaur's jail cell, Chirontë stopped. They had arrived in a den of titanium wolves. These robotic beasts were switched off, hanging from the ceiling on tubes, cables and chains. There were twelve in all, locked in a frozen explosion of metal bones, fangs and claws that threw distorted shadows onto the walls. It was the freakiest room yet.

Vyse's laughter continued on the soundsystem, but it was overpowered by the centaur's baritone battle cry. 'Here is where I escape!' he said, bucking his rescuers from his back. He bowed to them, then launched upwards, grabbing the cables with mighty arms. He climbed across the wolf pack, over the swinging heads and spines. With a push of his hind legs, he burst through the glass ceiling and galloped away.

'I guess he's given us a way out,' said Bernard, craning his neck to the broken ceiling. Inspector Norse scrutinized the cyberwolves, stroking their bladed teeth. 'These things are apex predators. Let's hope they're never unleashed.'

Beyond the beasts, there was a door leading right. A sign above it read 'Captain's Quarters'. They walked towards it, drawn by a ghostly calling. Vyse's laughter intensified, and they passed through.

Black B2 had a blacked-out ceiling, causing absolute darkness. Rock music was a typhoon around them, and they blindly stumbled through the cube-shaped darkness, unable to hear their own footsteps. Somewhere in the howling, Bernard found a doorknob, and they slipped into white B3. To the left, the wall was covered in computer screens, and Bernard noticed *Wacky Werewolves* flashing on one. To the right, above a shabby mattress on the floor, hung a single painting of a creepy Gothic house. It was covered in teeth marks, as if chewed by a feral creature.

These were the private quarters of Captain Vyse himself. On the wall dead ahead, thick tinfoil curtains hung over a doorway labelled 'Brig II'.

Affy's hand fell upon Bernard's shoulder. 'We must keep our cool in the enemy's lair,' she said. 'Before we enter, all guns blazing, I must switch off the broadcast. Otherwise everyone will hear us.'

A spectrogram slithered across one screen, showing Vyse's words as they played in all the white squares. She started adjusting the dials below it, figuring out the audio stream. Bernard looked at an old computer at the centre of all the screens and realized that Vyse had the same computer as Ealaín. He moved the cursor around, digging through the user information. He found something interesting in the Privacy section, and tapped some keys before Inspector Norse called his attention.

'We're ready,' she whispered. They both looked back to the tinfoil curtains.

'We're really doing it,' said Bernard. 'I know if our roles were reversed, Levander would rush to our rescue without hesitation.'

'Of course he would. Don't worry. I've got your back, kid.'

Four amplifiers stood against the walls of black B4. At the centre of their blaring noise, the Disco Fairy was bound to a chair, skull bowed in a cone of dim light. He was wrapped in bandages, mummified, with only his face and wings visible. Painted across his chest were the words 'DISCO SUCKS'. Beside him stood a tall, slender figure. He was shirtless, showing pale skin covered in computer-code tattoos. The mask and hat showed that it was, indeed, Captain Vyse. He was whispering to

Levander, his hand on the Disco Fairy's skull.

'You are a balloon animal, and I am a sea of thorns.'

'Hi, Kitty,' said Bernard, with sadness rather than fear. The pirate raised his mask to face them. If he was surprised, it was shielded by the blankness of his mask.

'How can this be?' He then recognized Bernard's companion. 'Ah yes. Inspector Norse. Welcome to the Vetruvius Club.'

He crouched down behind Levander, and Bernard and Affy knew not to approach.

'I did enjoy our times at *Wacky Werewolves*,' he continued, 'but this playtime with Levander has been more . . . up my alley.'

Bernard swallowed the fury he was feeling. 'We get it. You're the champion of creeps. The games are over now.'

'Give us Levander, and we'll show mercy,' Affy declared, cocking her laser gun.

He raised his hand to placate her. 'You are wasted with the Discopian lot, Affogato. I could use your skills and give you power.'

'I'm very happy with my ice-cream business.'

'You're not going to deprive the city of marshmallow mischief,' said Bernard.

Vyse ignored him, staying focused on Inspector Norse. 'What if I told you I could deliver the Satyr?'

Bernard glanced up at Affy. Her face was statuesque, giving nothing away. She paused, feeling the weight of this proposal in her mind.

'That,' she said, 'is not tonight's mission.'

She shot his exposed shoulder, but like the toilet-dwelling selector in white E8, he seemed immune to laser beams. Captain Vyse rose to his full height, laughing hideously. Bernard loaded the slingshot and let a paint bomb fly. Lilac paint exploded all over Vyse's mask and tricorne.

A cry of rage erupted, then crackled with disrupted electrics. Vyse clawed at his ruined headpiece. Inspector Norse freed Levander from his bonds and threw him over her shoulder. His wings hung lifelessly. The trio returned to the captain's quarters as they heard the mask clatter to the ground. They dived back into the room with no light, and they heard footsteps and the furious tap of keyboards behind them. The darkness of black was now filled with people, and Bernard recognized them by their drooling. It was the ravers from black H4, and through this sweaty game of blind man's bluff, with Levander's wings brushing against their enemies in the dark, Affy and Bernard crept to escape again. They arrived beneath the cyberwolves and locked the door behind them. Then sirens rang out across the Vetruvius Club, and the wolves began to move. Twenty-four eyes glowed yellow. Bernard and Affy abandoned their plan to escape through the broken ceiling and dashed straight ahead. The pirates would certainly be hunting them now, and any hope of escape would be dashed if the cyberwolves were released. They sprinted through a flooded cafeteria in black D2, and into white E2, which was filled entirely with sheep. Wading through this bleating flock, they made it halfway to the door when robopirates burst in behind them. Affy turned and threw seven capsules. They swiftly inflated into enormous pink bouncy balls. Crawling over Barbie-pink spheres and nonchalant sheep, the robopirates flumped and slowed down. Affy's trick paid off, and they made it to black E3, a butcher's kitchen. They slammed the door shut and no sooner was it locked than the hammering from the other side began. They realized there were no more doors. They were cornered three rooms deep in the Vetruvius Club.

A transistor radio played tinny, faint disco from the sink. Bernard dragged Levander towards it.

'Come on,' he said. 'We need you to dance one more time.'

'Dance?' said Levander weakly.

'Yeah, dance, funky bones! You never stop waffling about it.'

'Waffles?' he said.

Bernard took Levander's skull in his hands and looked deep into his eye sockets. They were two pools of emptiness.

'Buddy,' he said, 'it's me. I've stared down pirates and terrible lobster operas with you. We're in the darkness of Vyse's nightclub now. Discopia needs you.'

A mechanical wolf began to chomp through the door. Affy fired upon it but to no avail. 'Come on, Skullz!' she pleaded. 'Help us!'

At the sound of her appeal, a spark of boomba went off in Levander's eyes. He rose to full height and ripped at the bandages over his left breast. He tore away the word 'SUCKS', so now 'DISCO' stood beside his beating golden heart. He took hold of Bernard's hand and then Affy's.

As robopirates burst in with their terrible cyberwolves, Levander's wings beat with renewed strength. His night ended as it began, with broken glass, as the three of them launched through the ceiling. Into the night they flew, and the Stalemate Scrapyard shrank beneath them. Bernard shouted in delight. He caught sight of Chirontë, galloping still, sending bats spiralling up from their junkyard homes. Then he looked back at the Vetruvius Club, and his smile faded. The two giants were now joined by a third. An enormous figure, designed like Little Red Riding Hood, was kneeling in the rain. Pirates were running towards it, climbing onto its body. This thing was a robot of some sorts.

The mothership.

He saw two yellow eyes watching him from under the red hood. Then Levander flew them over the barbed-wire walls, and onto the streets outside. Bernard had no time to relay what he saw. Norse hustled them into Tastybase, shouted urgent directions to Momotaro, and the getaway began. Levander collapsed to the floor, unconscious.

'I saw their mothership,' said Bernard, his breathing unsteady. 'And it feels like I have a buzzsaw in my hearing.'

Inspector Norse winced as she started making calls. 'That would be tinnitus. I have it too. You can tell me what you saw later.'

He leaned against the machines, replaying the voice of Captain Vyse in his head. His exhausted mind mixed it into the cheerful music of *Wacky Werewolves*.

'Are you all right?' Affy asked, putting down the phone. Levander had been salvaged. The hideout of the pirates was exposed. No headlights pursued the ice-cream truck.

Even so, tears marched down Bernard's cheeks like pawns.

14

STAYIN' ALIVE

Leading the charge in a cheetah-pulled chariot, Mayor Hazel brought the full force of the Discopian Blues down upon the Stalemate Scrapyard. As the sky above thickened with helicopters, she kicked down the doors of the Vetruvius Club herself.

Captain Vyse and his crew had fled, leaving not a single pirate. Only sheep roamed the rooms within. As more Blues arrived, a set of enormous footprints was found leading away from the discotheque. Thanks to Bernard's sighting, it was clear these were caused by the mothership. They stopped at the southern walls of the compound, beyond which lay the Burrows. The Disco Knights swept into this neighbourhood, and interviews confirmed that something huge had hurried through. Lamentably, the parties had ended by then, so not a living soul had seen it clearly. From her bedroom window, a girl had glimpsed a blood-red blur dash by. That was all.

Soon after, documents from Vlad & Esdragon were found in the chessboard's depths. The architecture firm was stormed by a SWAT team, and Vlad the Bat was torn from his ceiling desk, protesting his innocence. It became clear that the absent partner was more suspicious. Sure enough, letters written by Captain Vyse were found in his desk. Esdragon was found in Neptune Hall, where he refused to come quietly. He battled the police with flare guns but was eventually detained and imprisoned in a glass maze of his own design.

Back on Earth, returning from his marathon of action, Bernard had fallen into a heavy sleepideep. When he awakened, Ealaín was panicking over the bruises on his face and checking his temperature. He was sick, and he stayed away from school for three days. He mostly slept, and he could hear the whirring of Ealaín's buzzsaw as she continued to build her art. When he went downstairs for snacks, he would see her in a wooden frame, surrounded by totem poles.

'I'm just making a bus stop,' she explained, her voice muffled by the welding mask.

The Skater Kids sent Bernard concerned messages. When he told them of his illness, Jay dropped over the retro gaming console along with the skateboarding game.

When he returned to school, word had already spread of the attack in the abandoned pool. Ricky Rockwell and his crew had been suspended, and Fairweather School was full of sympathy for Bernard.

The weeks passed. His bruises faded. The cuts healed.

In Discopia, Levander remained in hospital. Bernard became the new hermit of the penthouse. He never ventured beyond the front door, and stayed updated through Zam FM and *Grapevine News*. From the balcony, he would watch Sweetbeat Street below. On the first nights after the rescue, happy people danced on every streetlight's stage. These dancers waited for someone who never came. No distant wings were seen. No moonlit bones bounced into view. Levander did not appear.

Bernard missed the Disco Fairy as much as they did. To keep himself occupied, he studied the art of dance combat. Levander had once starred in a series of popular training videos and still had the VHS tapes. Bernard played them on the video-floor.

Levander, dressed in sweatbands and fluorescent gym gear, went through many exercises and tips for dancing in self-defence.

'Show patience,' he said, clapping after one tricky routine. 'The rockiest roads have the tastiest marshmallows!'

It hurt Bernard to see his friend on video instead of in person. Nevertheless, he knew Levander would cheer on his efforts of self-improvement. He picked up new tricks fast. The penthouse windows flashed from the boomba of his newly mastered moves.

The investigation at the Vetruvius Club continued. Various robot parts and leftovers had been taken away to be studied. It soon became clear that this technology was far more advanced than anything in Discopia. Dr Alejandro Sugarado, inventor of the headphones that countered the white noise attacks, sat down with Lance Brophy to outline his concerns.

Bernard shuddered at what he told the beach ball. 'We know that the boomba levels in this city neutralize guns and other weapons of hate. However, we do not know the full extent of Captain Vyse's technology. It may well be more powerful than our natural musical defences.'

Where Vyse had sourced these machines, or how he'd conscripted so many, was unclear. The robopirates were machines without souls. The cyberwolves were all missing. To make matters worse, Wimbledon vanished from his cell in Philly's Jailhouse.

On Earth, a silent trouble seemed to have settled over the Skater Kids. Bucky started missing sessions, making it harder to practise together. Bernard's skating was never better due to the dance-training, but the group felt fragmented. Jay's speakers broke, so they couldn't listen to disco. Kirsten became more interested in her keytar.

Bernard gradually withdrew into himself. His nights in the penthouse were making him tired. As another summer approached, Mr Flannelly asked him to work the turntables for their end-of-year party. He declined the offer.

In contrast to her son's quietness, Ealaín was getting frantic as the opening night of *Beach Noises* drew near. The sink was full of dirty paintbrushes. She handled her stress with coffee and boxsets of *Friends*. One of her art ideas required barrels of sand from Caribbean beaches, which apparently had the purity she needed. She was in online discussions with several friendly Jamaicans.

'You probably think I'm going mad,' she said to her son one day.

'You went mad long ago,' he replied, and they laughed.

After three weeks had passed, Bernard decided it was finally time to see the skeleton himself.

SPACESHIPS IN THE NIGHT

When he star-travelled over, sunlight poured through the windows onto a lonely penthouse. The place was scattered with cushions, popcorn boxes, and VHS tapes. He vowed to clean it up, and turned on the radio to hear the soothing voice of Flamingo James.

'Good morning, chicklets! It's devilishly sunny outside, so pack your shades and parasols. There's still no sign of Levander . . . now if any of y'all see that funky fairy, call in at 000-ZAM-24.'

After tidying the place, Bernard walked onto the terrace and was blasted by heat. Discopia looked bleached and lifeless. The sun was like a wasp's nest in the sky, troubling all who walked beneath it.

Flamingo James continued, 'We have another call on the line, from a family of soulified mangos down in Tuyentown. What's your vibe?'

'Hi, James, we'd like to offer our gratitude to the unknown duo who saved our pulp by bringing down Mobster Moylan and his bloat of hippos. If they're listening, thank you so much.'

'That's great. I love my guests fruity and fruitful! Let me jump in and offer a tune to our mystery mango saviours.'

Bernard smiled, walked back in and called up Inspector Norse.

'Spacehopper,' she greeted him. 'You're back.'

'Of course. I had to check up on him.'

'Yeah, he's not doing so well. Let's rendezvous in twenty minutes. Outside Pluto's Snackiwacks.'

Bernard rushed to get ready, and before leaving, he thought of a token to bring their ailing friend.

Twenty-one minutes later, he was fanning himself in the back of a taxi, sitting next to a burly lighthouse keeper in a yellow raincoat.

'Of all the times to abandon your air-conditioned Tastybase, it had to be now.'

'The base is safe,' said Affy, impressively sweat-free in her disguise. 'I can't drive it now though. I'm Kanye Pebblescoop, a weather-beaten lighthouse keeper.'

'The fake beard and peg leg are a nice touch. I've never seen Discopia by day. It's a serious barbecue out there.'

He looked outside as they cruised the sweltering boulevards. In the heatwave, people looked tired, ghoulish even. Not much dancing was going down. Affy regarded the scene too, chewing her plastic pipe.

'The win was fleeting, kid. They've been chased out of their chess club, but the pirates are just getting started. They have a ship of some kind, and look around. Vyse still haunts every street in this town. His mask could appear at any bedroom window.'

She was correct; they were driving through a spooked city. A stegosaurus lay down in the spray of a hydrant, frowning in the puddles. Bernard even saw Uncle Crunch, windswept and clutching a coffee. His leaves had turned orange with age.

The Swamson Hospital could be mistaken for an Earth hospital, were it not for the water slides. Colourful tunnels coiled around the six-storey building. To treat the mentally overwhelmed, this place was both a water park and a hospital. Inside, the Swamson motto hung above the helpdesk: 'Healing with a Passion for Splashin''. Bernard announced himself and was told he'd been expected. They strolled into the central pool area, which smelled of chlorine and perfume. The space offered all sorts of fun activities for visitors and patients. People rafted along a lazy river ride, danced in the shallows or relaxed by an artificial waterfall. Among the gentle fountains of a paddling pool, they spotted Hazel wearing a floral dress and baseball cap. She was chatting with a familiar centaur.

'My jailbreak buddy!' said Chironté, splashing over to hug him. Bernard was happy to see the fellow free.

Mayor Soldavril hugged him then.

'Hazel,' he said, 'such a nice surprise to see you!'

'It's my day off, so I wanted to visit Levander and all those feeling low in the Swamson. The skeleton's not good, but he's in a better place than he was. You and that Inspector must be commended for finding him.'

He bowed respectfully. 'It was Pilgrim who found the hideout. We just followed his trail.'

'Well, you braved the chess game of your lives and emerged with the Disco Fairy. You've done this city a service.' Her brown eyes moved to Inspector Norse. 'Who is your friend?'

'Kanye Pebblescoop,' she announced herself. 'In town for a lighthouse convention.'

'How wonderful! I hope you enjoy it. Chironté here was just regaling us with his stories. He taught Captain Vyse as a child, on the slopes of Hoppipelion. It's the first info we've got on the man beneath the mask.'

Chironté looked down at the waters lapping around

his horse legs. 'I taught him by my piano in the woods. The boy was quiet and gentle. Yet Vicesimus returned as a man, his face hidden, and put me in chains. He buried my piano in the sand at low tide, leaving its lid open. He made me watch as the sea returned to fill it.'

Hazel rose a hand up to the inflatable floatie on his arm. 'There are few things sadder than the loss of a piano. You're in the right place.' She turned back to Bernard. 'Disconaut, can I speak with you a moment?'

She took him aside as Chirontë quizzed 'Kanye Pebblescoop' on the sea.

'My dear Bernard,' said Hazel, 'there is an all-out pirate attack expected. We face dark disco days. Why not leave this place and stay safe in your own time?'

He shook his head. 'I can't. Levander has become like family to me.'

'This is not your fight.'

'If Levander is in it, then it is.'

She bent her kind, friendly face and hugged him tightly. 'You've done this city a great service. We thank you, and we love you. We'd all understand if you left the party now, even our poor Levander.'

'I've been learning lots of new moves, Hazel. You know I want to take the fight to these pirates.'

'You remind me of myself when I was your age. I just want you to grow up in safety.'

They said their goodbyes, and Mayor Hazel departed. Her bodyguards (still in tuxedos!) climbed out of a nearby hot tub to follow. Bernard thought over her words as a doctor came to take them upstairs. A name tag on her swimsuit read 'Rosa', and she filled them in as they walked. Chirontë trotted away, and Affy did her best not to slip on her peg leg.

'Truth be told,' said Rosa, 'our course of recovery is unclear. There are no recorded cases of a Disco Fairy going so long without disco.'

Through windows, Bernard glimpsed patients on lilos in single-room pools, talking to psychiatrist lifeguards.

'He's not the only patient Captain Vyse has put in here. It's a miracle that Levander is alive, but I can't guarantee that he'll ever dance again.'

Among the patients in one pool, Bernard saw Andromeda Pokitaru, her legs dangling over a diving board. She waved at him shyly, and he realized then that anyone could need help from the Swamson Hospital. He decided to send her a card.

They arrived at the Rhythm-Slaved Ward, a marble corridor lined with doors of frosted glass. A statue of a rectangular-headed woman stood at the end.

Rosa led them to one of the doors and invited them to enter the bluey darkness beyond. 'Be gentle in your tone, and try not to upset him.'

It was a steam room. At first, Bernard saw nothing, and wondered how anyone could occupy a steam room in the stickiness of this heatwave. It seemed to be the building's darkest place. Slowly, a blue, sad skull emerged from the steam.

'Who is this that comes to see me?'

'There you are, you wild skeleton! It's me, Bernard!'

'A St Bernard? Look man, I don't have time for your dogs.'

'No, I . . . don't you know me?'

'I keep getting asked that . . . but I don't even know myself anymore.'

A reassuring hand landed on Bernard's shoulder. Affy was beside him, having taken off her beard and hat.

'How are you healing, Skullz?'

'You can't have ice cream in here.'

'So you do know us.'

'If you have ice cream . . . in a steam room' – his voice cracked – 'it will melt away.'

And he started to cry. Bernard was disturbed to see him like this. Levander was always emotional, but as Discopia's prime protector, his strength had never failed. That confidence had been vaporized.

'Get better soon,' Bernard said. 'We need you on the outside.'

'On the outside? There is nothing but wolves, pain and shadowy crooks on the outside. I am safe in here. This steam room is my salvation.'

The skull disappeared back into the steam with an incomprehensible whisper.

They tried to talk to him further but got no response.

'Come on,' said Affy, her spiky hair drooping. 'We cannot stay here.'

It was true, for the heat was too intense to remain. Bernard placed his offering down on the tiled floor. As they were leaving, a hand of bones slipped out from the steam, and curled around the panda hat.

They didn't talk much on the Koonslite home. Somebody's boom box played a song about a Tuyentochan ship lost in a storm. Above the fake beard, Affy's eyes were troubled. Back at Levander's penthouse, Bernard flicked on the video-floor. Affy entered the guest room as Kanye Pebblescoop and emerged as Inspector Norse.

On *Grapevine News*, Lance Brophy was interviewing a grumpy, fuzzy-faced businessman.

'So in conclusion,' said Lance, 'you had no idea you'd handed the keys to pirates.'

'If I'd known the Vetruvius Club would be used as a terrorist base, I probably would have declined their offer.'

'Rocko Meredith, thanks for stopping by. Coming up next: Will we be prepared for a large-scale pirate attack? And who is the mysterious Kanye Pebblescoop?'

'You're just gonna fill your time with television?' asked Affy, muting the news. 'Honestly, you should get out of here. Levander's fate is now beyond us, and Captain Vyse will return.'

'You too, huh? I thought this was a welcoming city.'

Affy started tidying up the room. 'Come on, kid. Through that door you have a whole world away from this. Fly away from this town of disco downers. This isn't the same city you first set foot in.'

He started tidying too. As he cleared the popcorn boxes, a question crossed his mind.

'Affy, can I ask you something?'

'No.'

'Your relationship with disco is . . . frosty to say the least. What makes you stay? Why don't you leave town too?'

'You don't think I'd like to? I'd be on the first boat

out of here, if it weren't for . . .' Her words faded, and she stared at the bookshelves. Perhaps something in those stacks of stories convinced her to share her tale. After a long sigh, she began. 'Back when I worked for the Blues Squad, I was tracking a big Mafia boss who was into all sorts of unsavoury crimes. The Satyr. Well we found his base and I staked it out with my . . . partner. A brilliant dude called Pedro. He told me not to use my drum machines while on lookout, but I did. Little did we know that the Satyr was watching us too. I played on my stupid toy, with headphones on and my back to the door. He snuck into our stakeout and . . .'

She slapped the kitchen counter and bowed her head. Bernard remembered the Polaroid of a kind-looking cop tacked up in Tastybase.

'I resigned after the funeral. I work alone now, the way it should be. I want to get out of this city, but not until I've brought in the Satyr.'

Her hands turned to fists, and her breathing was tense. Bernard put a hand on her shoulder.

'I can only imagine your pain. Pedro may be gone, but Levander lives because of you. And for someone living life solo, you sure were an excellent partner on the night we followed Pilgrim's trail.'

She smiled. 'You were a great partner too. Listen, I've got Tastybase and Momotaro. I'll be fine. But I have work to do and won't be able to help you again.'

Bernard hugged her.

'I hope you find the Satyr,' he said. 'And I hope we meet again.'

'Hope is always good,' she said. After another speedy outfit change, she was a lighthouse keeper once more. Inspector Norse cast a rope over the balcony, intending to climb down to the streets below. She secured the knot and tested its strength.

'Goodbye, Bernard,' she said.

'Goodbye, Kanye Pebblescoop.' He bowed, then laughed at something small he'd remembered. 'We can give Levander ice cream once he gets out of the steam room.'

As Affy disappeared over the edge, Bernard thought he spied a smile beneath the fake beard.

15

GET FREE

Another year at Fairweather School drew to a close. Thoughts turned to summer. Disco music faded from the halls. The students moved on to other trends, and Bernard kept his head down. He finished an art project on Basquiat, never wore his headphones and avoided the music room. Ricky Rockwell troubled him no more, for he no longer listened to disco.

Bucky started ghosting him, skipping class and vanishing at lunch break. Bernard tried calling his friend, but he never answered. He asked the other two about this, but Kirsten and Jay were busy with exams. The Skater Kids were drifting apart like icebergs. They stopped messaging each other. No skate sessions were arranged.

Bernard returned the cardboard box of records – including the Discopia portal – to the garage. Whenever temptation arose to visit Discopia, he recalled the pain he had seen in that steam room. He told himself it was better to leave Levander alone.

All the while, the final preparations of Ealaín's art

show were taking over the house. A team came to take the half-giraffe away, the palm tree was dug up, paintings were blanketed in bubblewrap and carried away, sand got everywhere, surfboards swapped hands. Bernard helped where he could. His spare time was spent playing Jay's skateboarding video game.

On a weekend afternoon, he overheard Ealaín and Ali talking. They ate salads on the living room floor, with the monstrous blob that would be *Sweet Mind* rearing up behind them.

'How is Bernard handling this bonanza of *Beach Noises*?' asked the gallerist.

'Well, he likes to play tunes and watch cartoons. I don't hear a peep out of him for hours. Although the other day, he was beaten up.'

Ali winced in sympathy. 'Some kids can be real terrors.'

'He seems to have some good friends too. I want him to have a good summer, when all this is done.'

One day, after skateboarding home from school, Bernard found his mother rummaging through cupboards and drawers.

'I can't find that red paint anywhere,' she muttered. 'Oh, one of your friends is here. He wanted to borrow a record.'

'Oh?'

'Yes. I told him you had put them down in the garage, and that he was free to take a look.'

Bernard felt a sharpness in his throat. 'Which friend? And what did he want to borrow?'

'Something called *Discopia*? I can't remember his name.'

Bernard stormed across the garden, panic rising in him when he saw the door wide open. Inside, Bucky was slumped on the floor, his head buried in his arms. Vinyls and their sleeves were scattered everywhere, and on the concrete before him was a single record, covered in red paint. It was ruined.

Bucky started sobbing. 'Discoman . . . I'm sorry.'

'What record is that?' asked Bernard, fearing he already knew.

'Someone on *Steampunk Blimp Wars*, they forced me to do it. K-K-KittyLikeThread. They found out where I lived, started naming my family. They said they'd hurt them if I didn't come over here.'

'What record did you destroy?'

'*Discopia*.'

Bernard closed his eyes, feeling a thousand black balloons falling.

'My sister, man. He was threatening to hurt my sister!'

'Go home and call the police, Bucky.'

The class clown wiped his eyes, and rose to his shaky feet. Bernard remembered his own digital folly and placed a hand on his shoulder.

'You should have told me sooner,' he said. 'We look after each other, us Skater Kids. Please make sure you stay safe.'

'Thanks, Bernard. I'm sorry.'

They embraced, and Bucky left. Bernard inspected the damage more closely. *Discopia* was destroyed. He gagged on the acrid smell of paint, and then lashed out at the boxes nearby. In seconds, he had trashed the place.

He tested the record, but it wouldn't play. The portal was broken. He couldn't reach Levander's penthouse ever again. Bernard rubbed his temples, feeling a wave of sadness swallow him. The city – with all the friends he'd made there – was lost to him. The adventures were over. He had vowed not to return, but the loss still stung like jellyfish. He tried to look up KittyLikeThread on *Steampunk Blimp Wars*, but the account was already deleted. He was crestfallen and alone. He went to bed without dinner and fell asleep without hope.

A notification woke him in the dark of night. Downstairs, a polyphonic sound blooped from the computer. *Wacky Werewolves.*

Bernard rubbed his eyes. *What does that maniac want now?*

He tiptoed downstairs to find out. The living room was full of shadows, and the computer was powered on. *Sweet Mind* stood in the corner, a half-finished statue in clay.

The *Wacky Werewolves* window floated on the screen, showing a mini game called 'Changing of the Sheets'. Twelve ghosts – bedsheets with eyeholes – were parading around Amble Totes. Grafted over this mini game was a request box.

'KittyLikeThread would like to share a video! Accept?'

Sitting in the creaky chair, Bernard slid the headphones into place and cautiously clicked the link. A video popped up and filled the screen.

All he could see was fog. All he could hear was footsteps.

A voice crackled in his ear. It was First Mate Wimbledon. 'Bernard! Welcome to the show!'

Geometric shapes began to appear on the screen. Pink, towering shapes. Skyscrapers.

There could be no doubt – he was watching Discopia emerge from the mists. Judging from the point of view, he figured he was seeing it through the eyes of something *gigantic*.

Wimbledon's voice continued, 'I'm speaking to you from the cortex deck of Scylla941. The boss insisted that you witness this.'

An overground Koonslite line appeared through the fog, its horses frozen in place. People became visible on the streets below. Their faces looked upward and started to panic.

'All stories have an endpoint,' said Wimbledon. 'This is Discopia's time to fall.'

Realizing the point of view was from Vyse's mothership, Bernard's face turned pale. He remembered the third giant he'd seen crouched by the chessboard. They passed a sleek, mirrored skyscraper and once more he saw, in the gold reflection, Captain Vyse's mothership.

'Behold Scylla941!' roared Wimbledon. 'Isn't she a beauty?'

It was Little Red Riding Hood built in metal, hundreds of feet tall. Shrouded in a blood-red hood, the face was dark save for a pair of yellow eyes. Under its metal cloak, the steel-plated body was broken at the waist by a snapping belt of cyberwolves. It was the same twelve from the Vetruvius Club.

The yellow camera-eyes turned away, and the livestream returned to its course. Not even Ealaín would make something so crazy, yet Bernard was wise to a hideous truth. This monstrous robot was more advanced than any technology Discopia could produce to stop it.

'Time to pick up the boss,' said Wimbledon, as Scylla941 strode towards a familiar building. All six floors of the Swamson Hospital were flashing red. One of the water slides was broken, pouring water onto the streets. There was clearly a crisis, as police cars and ambulances ringed the entrance. One by one, the Blues and Disco Knights began to turn, realizing that the crisis was about to deepen.

The yellow eyes swept from the tiny Discopians to the rooftop swimming pool. Here, beside burning beach chairs, Captain Vyse stood alone. Seeing him appear in the *Wacky Werewolves* window, Bernard thought of KittyLikeThread. This was the ventriloquist behind that cute creature.

Scylla941's iron hand landed on the roof, the clawed fingers pointing skyward. Captain Vyse stepped onto the palm, and the getaway was quick. He opened a trapdoor and disappeared into the metal of its wrist.

This mission complete, the mothership continued its slow rampage. Discopian laser bullets and confetti cannon were little more than flies bouncing off its body.

Bernard heard Vyse's wintery voice through the headphones. 'Once this is done, find that blasted skeleton.'

'Orders received,' replied Wimbledon. 'Approaching the next target.'

Had Levander escaped? Bernard had no time to dwell on this hint of good news. He was glued to the screen, seeing through the mothership's eyes. It stomped through the streets he loved so dearly. There were no police to call, no way to stop this carnage. Soon Scylla941 stood above the domed roof of Pantheon 54. Hazel's bodyguards stood guard before the discotheque but were scattered by cannonballs from the pirate-crew, who fired from windows in the giant robot's armour.

The gruff voice of Wimbledon returned. 'Second target in place. Demolition approved. Initiate.'

Slowly, the robot raised an enormous foot. Bernard looked away as it stomped downwards. The crunch of stone sickened him to the core. He thought of the terrible foot smashing through the domed ceiling, rubble falling onto the cracking dancefloor. The stomping went on and on and on.

When he looked at the screen again, Scylla941 was standing in ruins. Pantheon 54 was utterly demolished. He despaired to see this discotheque, the first in which he'd danced, meet such a violent end.

'Surely they must have mercy,' said Bernard.

Wimbledon crackled new commands. 'Now on to primary target.'

The head turned towards Tower Smooth.

By now, the helicopters were closing in. Discopia's forces had come to fight the onslaught. Yet as they closed the distance, Scylla941 raised both hands. Red lasers fired out – *ratatatatata* – and took out all choppers as they approached. *Wacky Werewolves* mascots danced in the video's corners, and Bernard doubted they'd ever accompanied such mayhem and destruction. Scylla941 stomped along, squashing tanks and police cars underfoot. Through apartment windows, Bernard spied families huddled together, holding each other in fear. Throughout the city, he could almost hear the sound of disco dying. Watching from Earth, he was utterly powerless to stop it.

Scylla941 walked down Good Times Square, sweeping aside any resistance. It came to Tower Smooth, casting those eyes down to the dwarfed Kraftyatids. Beneath those, the mayor marched out with a cheetah by her side and a spear in her hand. Hazel Soldavril looked up at the robot, and did not tremble.

'Vyse! Painted tyrant, show yourself. I want to talk with a soul, not a circuit board.'

The screen steadied as Scylla941 stood still. Bernard knew what Hazel saw: a giant robot in red, with cruel yellow eyes fixed upon her.

She held her ground, constant and fearless.

Captain Vyse reappeared in the upturned hand.

'Is the boy still online?' he asked.

'I'm here, you dark-web dork,' Bernard said.

Captain Vyse unsheathed his sword. 'Bring me to her.'

Scylla941 bent down. As the view from the camera-eyes shifted, Bernard caught sight of the twelve cyberwolves clinging to the robot's waist. Captain Vyse was placed delicately on the steps below as if he were a tarantula. Hazel lowered her spear to talk, and Scylla941's microphones caught every word.

'This is my home,' she said. 'If you want to talk about what disturbs you, I will try to help. Otherwise, you have no invitation.'

Vyse's mask, as always, was blank. 'Give me the gold chain and you will be unharmed. Fail to stand aside and you will be deleted.'

'Disco will never bend to a psycho's will.'

Vyse took a step forward. 'It will always bend to a pirate with computers. The digital age is not to be denied.'

'This is the disco age,' Hazel declared, and she seemed to hold her hand out in peace. 'We respect music, love and happiness. You'll never be able to put that in a computer.'

He looked at her hand, and paused for a moment. Then he pointed his sword at the cheetah, a shot rang out from Scylla941, and the cheetah fell down dead. Hazel roared and twirled her spear as Captain Vyse lunged forward. They exploded into a swashbuckling battle.

The sound of clashing steel made Bernard's eardrums sting. The sword and the spear clashed and parried with breakneck speed. Vyse emitted curling black smoke, a true disciple of Blackbeard's tricks. Hazel shone with golden boomba, moving with the agility of an R&B dancer, as elegant in combat as in everything she did. It almost seemed like a fair fight; Bernard nearly forgot about the giant robot whose eyes he looked through. The pirate blocked Hazel's spear with his catfish vambraces, but the mayor kept advancing. She landed a blow upon his shoulder, and a splash of red appeared as he dropped his sword. With cursing and blood, Captain Vyse showed he was human. Hazel held her spear defiantly, defending the entrance still.

'Vicesimus,' she cried, 'see reason! There's still time to stop this hurt.'

He picked up his weapon and slunk down the steps. 'Release the cyberwolves,' he growled.

Bernard heard the booming sound of bolts unlocking. The wolves came away from the mothership's waist. As one unholy wolfpack, they sprinted down the legs of Scylla941. They charged up the steps of Tower Smooth, past their retreating master. Hazel only had seconds, and turned her spear to face them. Her cheetahs sprinted out from Smooth Lobby to defend their mistress.

Scylla941's camera-eyes turned upwards. Bernard heard the snarls of the big cats and Hazel's battle cry. The cheetahs soon stopped snarling, and Hazel's voice went silent too.

Bernard, his own eyes streaming with tears, watched through the eyes of Scylla941 as it laid metal hands on Tower Smooth. The robot began to climb, upwards towards the Garden of Bopalon.

Waking up, Bernard felt like bowling pins blasted in a strike. His blurry eyes opened to see who'd thrown the ball.

'What messing is this?' asked Ealaín, standing over him. It was Saturday morning. He had blacked out and now lay on the floor of the computer room. 'The computer is absolutely shipwrecked with viruses. What in the name of Dalí were you looking up?'

'I'm sorry, Mum,' he said, wincing at the stiffness in his spine.

'I'd finally settled on which jars of sand to order. Now what will I do?'

He lifted up his sore head. The computer screen was a riot of glitching mayhem. He remembered what he'd seen there and began to sob. 'I saw . . . some bughouse crazy horrors. I . . . I don't know how to tell you, but it sucked. I let my friends down. I thought I could stop the party getting crashed. I . . . was wrong. I failed.'

His mum knelt down beside him in the quiet room. 'Bernard,' she said soothingly. 'Nobody is immune to screwing up. I fail all the time. I always worry I've made a mistake by supporting you through art sales and commissions. And your father . . . one of his screw-ups cost him his life.' She paused for a moment. 'We can't let mistakes hold us back. I must complete *Beach Noises*, overcome all the setbacks. Had Ceol survived, he would have been back out on a board the next day.' She wiped a tear from her face. 'So don't let mistakes drag you down. Take notes and continue.'

Bernard nodded, wiping his own eyes. She couldn't understand the pain of watching Discopia under attack, or the fall of Hazel, but her words were soothing.

'Now,' Ealaín said. 'No offence, but you look like something that's crawled out of a graveyard. Get some rest in your actual bed.'

After cereal and a long shower, Bernard climbed into fresh sheets.

Thinking of Hazel, he wept in quiet grief, then sank into a dreamless sleepideep.

When he woke up, he briefly enjoyed the slanting light of late afternoon. He then remembered the invaded city, Scylla941 and Hazel's fate. The tears appeared again.

Soon, Ealaín called him downstairs for dinner. She had decided to order in.

After steaming slices of pizza and a feel-good film, he felt a bit better. He helped Ealaín paint the tropical bus stop artwork, which now had a roof of thatch.

'Tiki bars,' she said, more to herself than Bernard. 'They're a hoax, made up by Californians in the 1930s! Ancient tiki cultures didn't hang around bars drinking cocktails. It's a harmless conspiracy to sell fruity drinks. By making a tiki bus stop, hopefully I can play around with that fakeness.'

'Whatever you say.' He was finding comfort in the act of painting. 'I'm sorry about the computer.'

'Oh, Bern,' she said, 'I'm the one who should be sorry. Children your age grow up in threatening times. Every computer is a Pandora's box, ready to burst with downloadable demons. It's hard to see the hope sometimes.'

'At least you could order a wax giraffe from the neck down.'

'Well,' she said with a smile, 'I guess that's the hope at the bottom.'

Then she remembered something and headed for the kitchen. 'I noticed that one of your records is damaged,' she called from down the hall. 'I didn't know your friend would pull a prank like that. He'll have to volunteer for *Beach Noises* to make up for it. At least you have the B-side.'

She brought in the *Discopia* record and showed the side that had been face-down. Untouched by paint.

'Wait, what?' he said. 'The B-side?'

'Yeah, only one side is paint-drowned. The other is still playable.'

Bernard eagerly took it in his hands, and examined the flip side. It was clean.

'Thanks, Mum!' he said, catapulting up from the couch. He ran for the box of records in the garage. Finding the *Discopia* sleeve, he examined the back cover again. A sticker had been placed there, and he peeled it back to reveal more text. The cursive font read:

Side A: Levander's Penthouse

Side B: Watermelon Wood

Was this side . . . a portal to the notorious wood across the Vamvozio River? If he could get to the wood, then perhaps he could get to the city. Vyse had gone to great lengths to prevent his return, meaning there was something the pirate feared. Also, as far as he knew, Levander hadn't been found yet. He had to give this a try.

'Hey,' said Ealaín, standing in the doorway. 'I know we've both been in our own worlds lately. Just know that I'm always here for you.'

Bernard paused, and turned to her. 'I know you are. Thanks for the pizza and the painting.'

She beamed and threw him a bottle of water.

'Don't stay up too late,' she said, then returned to her artworks.

Refreshed and hydrated, Bernard set up the record player in his bedroom. Wasting no time, he flipped the B-side into place. He'd heard many things about those who lived in the Watermelon Wood. These warnings came back to him now as he dropped the needle down. Dangerous though it may be, it was a path back to the Musical Planet. He took a deep breath and slipped on his headphones. New music took flight.

It was the same sensation of star-travel. But different light whizzed by, the music wasn't disco and the rhythm wasn't 4/4. Before he could determine the type of music, a huge forest filled his vision. It resembled a great shaggy beast, galloping forth on a thousand tree-trunk legs. He soared into it, and it gobbled him up.

All was still. He stood in a new spaceship.

He was in the Watermelon Wood.

16

WATERMELON MAN

Bernard raised his hands in the dark and felt stone. A structure enclosed him, and a harsh, buzzing noise reached his ears. Something awaited outside.

He slowed his breathing and sharpened his focus. Once outside, he would need to orientate himself quickly. He'd seek the best route to Discopia, probably over the Bumblebee Bridge. The Occupants, whatever they were, would have to be avoided. He didn't like the idea of getting lost in a forest, especially when it contained monsters. He reminded himself that this was the move he'd chosen.

When he was ready, he pushed forward and an entrance appeared. Instead of the penthouse of a charming skeleton, he now tiptoed into a cold, misty clearing. Four ruined statues flanked him, manacled in ivy, their faces vanished with age. They stood guard around the portal from which he'd stepped. It was another spaceship, identical to Levander's.

Bernard looked around. The noise was deafening, for the air was loud with bees. The clearing was a strange outdoor apiary; rows and rows of beehives surrounded the statues and spaceship. He was beginning to wonder if he was in the Watermelon Wood at all. Then he saw the Occupant.

An enormous beekeeper plodded through the mist, growling in tongues. Among the hives, its face concealed, it had the eerie resemblance of an astronaut patrolling alien eggs.

Bernard bent low, moving forward from hive to hive to avoid the gaze behind that veil. His forearms suffered beestings but he bore the pain silently. Close by, he could hear heavy footsteps and the fury of angry swarms as the Occupant tended to their hives.

Beyond the apiary were the trees and shadows of the Watermelon Wood. Bernard crossed into that sinister thicket, happy to leave the beekeeper behind him. Among the branches of the oaks, a trail of ramshackle lampshades snaked off into the gloom. It created a path of light on the mossy floor. This he followed, keeping to the shadows.

As he went deeper, he began to hear it. The dark forest, musky with the scent of dead leaves and oakwood, swelled and shrank with music. Sounds of wildlife melted together, from every nest and burrow, from distant flutes to cricket calls, creating a sound wildly different from disco. Thousands of musical notes harmonized in a woozy style. Every hoot, howl and crackle had a place in the score. Bernard soon identified the music, for it existed on Earth too.

'Jazz!' said Bernard with a smile. 'The Watermelon Wood is a place of jazz!'

SPACESHIPS IN THE NIGHT

That freewheeling music filled the dark woods, just as surely as disco reigned in Discopia. Jazz was like the modern-art of music. It followed its own rules, coloured outside the lines, and made the wrong notes sound right. He didn't find the improvisations unpleasant at all.

Catching himself, he remembered the warnings. He looked back to the beehives, and the Occupant working there. These creatures might like jazz, but that didn't reduce the danger. He continued forth, flitting through the trees, watchful for snakes or poisonous thorns underfoot. He hoped he was not leaving footprints, but he couldn't be sure in the dirt and music-sheets scattered on the ground.

Progress was slow, and the path was twisty. All around him, jazz hopped up and down the musical scales like frogs. Try as he might, he couldn't predict where the notes were going to land. His mind began to wander in the ever-changing soundscape. He wondered what Inspector Norse thought of jazz. She had disparaged it at Dreamboat Dock, but he sensed she might approve of its topsy-turvy anti-disco. He found himself wishing for Tastybase, missing the sound of her tapping keyboards and the hum of her machines. He hoped she was safe. Daydreaming, he clattered into a metal object. A retro newspaper vending machine stood by the side of the path. Nobody was coming, so he moved to examine what lay beneath the glass. It was copies of *Watermelon Times*, and he read the doom-laden headline: 'DISCOPIA ENTERS ITS SEVENTH WEEK UNDER PIRATE CONTROL.'

Seven weeks? Had so much time passed overnight? He read the article, written by Laviny Featherworth.

The pirate occupation continues across the Vamvozio River. Our correspondents in the sky, rabbits in Spitfire planes, note that another discotheque has fallen to Scylla941. It appears the cyberwolves rushed into ZZZozzzimus, and tore the pillow fort to shreds.

It is understood that Captain Vyse, stationed now in the Garden of Bopalon, oversees the seizure and burning of disco records. On the ground, with neither Levander nor Mayor Soldavril in the game, nobody has answers. The survivors must acquiesce to pirate rule, or face internment in the Stalemate Scrapyard, which has been turned into a mega-prison.

More details on Discopia's crisis, and how it may affect the wood, will follow.

He shook his head and rattled the machine in anger. He couldn't believe that Captain Vyse now controlled the city. He stormed onwards, wincing from the beestings.

The only silver lining was that Vyse had tried to prevent him reaching the Musical Planet. In this he'd failed, but Bernard was struggling to see what difference his presence could make.

After some time, the trail forked into two paths of light. A sign on the left read 'Bumblebee Bridge', and the other path was unmarked. Bernard paused at this divergence. The Watermelon Wood was feared across Discopia, but why? Levander had spoken of a bassist wielding enormous power, with melodies that could shake the very city. Bernard had close to no plan for what he might do upon reaching Discopia. *What if that bass – and the jazz of the Watermelon Wood – came with him?*

He heard movement behind him, and sank back into the brambles. The beekeeper lumbered into view, pushing a wheelbarrow loaded with honeypots. The veil still concealed its face.

It passed the boy's hiding place and took the right-hand path.

Bernard waited two minutes then took the unmarked path, following the Occupant into the unknown.

Deeper into the Watermelon Wood, the trails split more frequently. They diverged and crisscrossed, creating a maze of light-paths. He was amazed by the endless number of lamps, and the staggering work ethic they implied. The architects of these roads had followed one avenue of thought as far as it would go. The Occupants clearly went to extreme lengths in both their music and building.

These paths, like mellow forks of lightning, even sloped upwards into the trees above, where Bernard now saw treehouses and villages. He followed the straight, muddy trail of the wheelbarrow's wheel, and the enormous footsteps escorting it. He knew this trail led to the Occupants, and this was where he must plead his case.

He was never under the illusion that he was alone. The style and tone of the jazz kept shifting. In time, strange things began to appear. He saw two raccoons riding penny-farthings along a light path. Soon after, he had to hide in a tree hollow as a noise approached. It was a living, soulified drum set, harrumphing through the woods with all the messy beats of its snares and hi-hats. It seemed hungry, so Bernard remained hidden until it faded into the distance. His path led him up among the trees, across rope bridges and through treehouse neighbourhoods. Peeking through a window, he saw a room filled with pianos from floor to ceiling. Crossing a rope bridge, he felt snow fall through the leafy canopy. He paused for a moment and caught some flakes in his hand. To his horror, he realized it was ash. He thought of his beloved city nearby and the records going up in flames. He quickened his pace, and kept his eyes peeled for Wollohy Peels. He did not wish to return to Earth early, but somehow he sensed the pineapple would not find him here.

At last, he followed the lampshades down a spiral staircase and back to ground level. The wheelbarrow trail led to the gaping mouth of a cave and disappeared within. Snoring rumbled from its depths, hand-in-hand with eerie violin music. Over the entrance, a crest of crossed saxophones was mounted.

Bernard was terrified. He wished he had Levander by his side. He recalled his friend's encouragement, even in his absence: 'The rockiest roads have the tastiest marshmallows.' He did a little dance, praying for strength, and stepped into the cave. He passed down a cold, sloping passage. Pinball machines lined the walls on either side. They were much bigger than the ones on Earth, designed for much taller beings. They lit the passage and bore strange artworks. One had a single human figure, encircled by vampires on a suburban street. One showed a child-like rabbit falling asleep in a bedroom, with a light bulb as the moon outside. He was not alone. Yet another showed a sphinx over an abandoned highway. The image made him shudder.

The musky smell was getting stronger, and at the end of the passage, he entered a wide chamber. Here, at last, he beheld the Occupants of the Watermelon Wood.

Bears – brown, grizzly and black – thronged the low-ceilinged jazz club. Slumped in moth-eaten booths, perched on little stools and drooping at round tables, each one slumbered where they sat. An enormous gramophone played scratchy lullabies from the stage. Beside it, in a mighty, oak throne, sat the beefiest bear of the lot. A true titan, he wore a bearskin coat over his own fur, and bore a savage majesty even in sleep. His handsome face twitched beneath a fedora, and in his claws he cradled an enormous double bass. Bernard did not doubt the strength of its strings. This was the mythical bassist, and this cave would frighten anyone. Bernard was scared, yet he remembered Discopia burning and the reason he was here. He tiptoed forward. He crossed the floor of orange autumn leaves. He trod through the sleeping bears, with their pungent breath. He continued up onto the stage, and reached the gramophone. He took a deep breath and lifted the phono-needle from the record. The music stopped, and so too did the snoring.

Many eyes flew open. The bears began to speak in a language both gruff and manic. They lumbered to their feet, gnashing fierce jaws to growl fierce jazz.

'Valoopdaskapish?'

'Beelapadopdup!'

'Makapeepasleepa!'

They closed in, curling their claws and taking out trumpets. The bassist awakened, and beneath a furrowed brow, his amber eyes slid to the boy. 'You have the swagger of Mercury, to glide before a raging sun.'

He plucked one of his instrument's strings, and the sheer force of the sound blew Bernard back like a rag doll. He hurtled into the crowd, who held him high in many claws, facing their leader like a prisoner.

'I am the Jazz King Endymion,' said the bear. 'Who dares disturbs me? You should hear the words my friends are scat-singing.'

He rose to his full height, the stage groaning under his weight. Bernard tried to keep his cool, which was difficult under the bear's carnivorous glare. 'I'm sorry to disturb your sleep. I come on behalf of Discopia, seeking your help.'

'A Discopian spy has torn us from hibernation? Listen up, Jazzly Bears, SCRADABAPPY LAPPYTAPPY!'

The bears all bellowed in agreement with whatever Endymion had said. Bernard fought his fear, struggling to speak calmly. 'With all due respect to the slumber party, Discopia burns. The crisis cannot wait. I ask your allegiance.'

Endymion took a step forward. 'We owe nothing to disco, with all its vanity and jewels. Music should express beauty as a mirror to the heavens, not to hairstyles.' The scat-singing intensified. 'Right now, perhaps I can please my Jazzly Bears with breakfast.'

'Discomacy!' screamed Bernard. 'Hazel in the Garden of Bopalon swore you honoured discomacy!'

Endymion raised a paw to calm his audience. He looked down and blinked the sandman's dust from his eyes. Then he erupted in a ferocious jazzy roar, and the crowd followed his lead. The grip on Bernard's limbs was loosened and he was lowered to the ground.

'You want discomacy, well, you'll get it. Accompany me to the Harp, and we'll see the worth of your words.'

The crowd gasped, and somewhere a pair of cymbals clashed. Behind the stage, scarlet curtains parted to reveal a dark passage. Bernard walked on stage, hoping no one noticed him shaking. A paw the size of six baseball gloves came down upon his shoulders, and Endymion took him away from the scat-singing bears and down into the caves below the Watermelon Wood.

17

FISTS OF FURY

The bears who had carved this ancient stone stairwell had clearly been listening to jazz. They must have raised their chisels to the stone in offbeat rhythms, for there was not a straight line to be seen. The steps were crooked, zigzagging down the passage in twisty shapes. Even the candles were curly. Bernard was at constant risk of stumbling, followed as he was by surefooted Endymion.

Mercifully, the stairwell came to an end. They walked into a cave that served as a living room. The furniture was dotted with biscuit tins, sleeping cats and quilts. Here the Jazz King paused and prepared a coffee from an antique kettle.

'This place is . . . cosy,' said Bernard. 'It's like a grandmother's home, if grandmothers lived underground.'

Bear cubs dressed like old-time barbers toddled into the cave, courteously removing their straw hats. Endymion raised his cup to them. 'My Ragtime Rascals, the bees have gone to town on this boy's arms. Please treat him.' The little bears flurried into action, applying spray to Bernard's arms. One blew incense through a harmonica.

'Thank you,' Bernard said, feeling the pain subside. Endymion drained his espresso, and stretched his mighty limbs.

'Your patriotism for Discopia is touching. I will lead you to a secret entrance and you can disappear. You are pardoned from the Harp.'

Bernard stood firm, despite his hammering heartbeat. 'I'm here to negotiate. Not to flee.'

One of the Ragtime Rascals piped up, 'Surely, Dad, you will not imperil yourself down there?'

Bernard hadn't realized the cubs were Endymion's.

The father growled, towering over everyone in the room. 'I have no fear. Earth child, will you take my offer and leave?'

There was no turning back now. Bernard shook his head, and the bear muttered a gravelly scat song. He fetched a rolled-up carpet in the corner and unfurled it.

'You're a foolish egomaniac and a true Discopian. Sit on the carpet!'

Bernard sat down, happy that it at least had straight lines.

'You cubs run along and I'll read to you later,' said Endymion, his voice momentarily gentle. Then he dropped onto the carpet like a rockslide. The Jazz King growled a command and the carpet took flight. As it cruised away from the giddy Ragtime Rascals, Bernard felt the weightless thrill of an ant on a falling leaf. They dipped and dived past stalactites and ravines, navigating down into a labyrinth of caves. The candlelight weakened the deeper they flew, and Bernard decided to continue his case.

'I get that disco doesn't float your boat,' he said over his shoulder, 'but surely you don't want Captain Vyse as a neighbour?'

He felt flecks of spit on the back of his neck, as Endymion answered. 'You talk as if there has been no resistance to him. What of the cowboys sent by the Wobbly West? Riding through the Outer Dance Zone, they were ambushed by the Scylla and scattered like mice. The mermaid nations of the Sonorous Deep launched an attack at Robyntime Harbour. Again, the Scylla was there to chase them away. The civilizations on the Musical Planet hate what's happening, but Vyse is in control now. They no longer move against him.'

'Those cowards.'

'That mothership, those robopirates, his computers – they didn't materialize from nothing. The man is well protected. People are right to fear him.'

Cave paintings flickered past them now, with stick-bears and trees. They reminded Bernard of humankind, and Endymion's first words to him. 'Hey, how does a forest bear know about Mercury and our solar system?'

'When you orientate your life by jazz,' he said, 'it's good to keep an eye on the galaxies that harbour it. Besides, Earth and the Musical Planet are linked, as you know. I've never been to Earth – I'm not one to butter both sides of the toast – but I know it well. Now, prepare to face the Harp of Ososandia.'

The carpet flew along a long, narrow cave. Lamps dotted the walls on either side, and each one illuminated a cave painting. Up ahead, a gate with shiny prison bars ended the passageway.

'We will debate before the Harp,' said the Jazz King, 'and see who survives.'

Bernard realized they weren't bars up ahead. They were *strings*. Gigantic harp strings coming down from floor to ceiling. Endymion steered them closer.

'It's been decades since any Discopian has set eyes upon this . . . Wait.' A figure danced on the floor before the Harp. Clad in black, it grooved by a boom box from which disco played. 'It can't be!' roared Endymion.

The figure looked upwards from beneath a panda hat. Two butterfly wings unfurled behind him. Bernard beamed.

'I hope you brought cookies!' cried Levander, for it was indeed the Disco Fairy, found at last beneath the Watermelon Wood.

Endymion brought the carpet down to land on the floor, and Bernard leaped off, giving his friend an enormous hug. They tripped over each other's happy words.

'Disconaut!'

'I thought you were in hospital!'

'You saved me from the Vetruvius Club!'

'Well, Inspector Norse did most of the work.'

'And you got Affy out of her shell, working with a partner again!'

'DISCO FAIRY!' roared Endymion, his voice a hurricane wind.

Levander straightened up, and faced him. 'Don't snap at me, you scruffy beatnik. Why are you bringing my boy down here?'

'How have you found Ososandia's Harp?'

'Well,' said Levander, ruffling Bernard's Afro. 'I happen to be the founder of Owlapeño's, the number-one burrito bar for owls of the Watermelon Wood. This means that they're too busy eating my meals to hunt the little bats. Those bats were all too happy to help yours truly, their favourite burrito entrepreneur, fly down the cave system until I reached this thang.'

Bernard was flabbergasted to see Levander so healthy and spry.

Endymion was livid. 'ENOUGH! Levander, you are sentenced to debate before the Harp.'

'Great threat, jazz brains, given that I'm already here.'

'Don't talk lightly of this chamber.' Footsteps began to approach from the far-side of the strings.

Bernard stared into the darkness, then to the enormous Harp. 'What's the dealio with this thing?' he asked.

'You step over to the walls, where the music isn't so tricky. It's the skeleton who must join me now.'

Levander tilted his skull. 'And what do you want us to do here? I ain't got no picnic.'

'We take council as it plays the Harp. The longer we remain, the stronger the music becomes. If the jazz spirit is pure, we will not collapse. Otherwise, this place becomes our tomb.'

With a flick of his fur coat, he strolled to the smooth floor just in front of the Harp. As he did, the figure on the other side appeared. In that moment, Bernard realized two things. He figured out how the Watermelon Wood got its name, and also learned Wollohy Peels had a cousin.

Ososandia was very tall, walking forward in a colourful poncho. Its head was a watermelon. It raised two bear paws, and struck two strings. The whole cave resonated with the eerie sound. The demi-god continued, gliding from side to side, hitting strings and playing strange music on the Harp.

'All right then,' said Levander, removing his panda hat.

'Be careful,' Bernard said. 'It would be a shame to find you down here only to watch you get destroyed by jazz.'

'These fruit-headed gods aren't so tough. Dance-offs are my forte. Just stick by the walls where you'll be safe.'

The Disco Fairy winked and cartwheeled away. He closed the distance to Endymion, who had removed his fedora. They glowered at each other as Ososandia played on, getting slightly faster.

Their dance-off began, blazing with boomba. They tried not to be shaken by the music, and each blasphemed the music of the other.

Endymion roared, 'What is your disco empire? A gumball machine, struck and shattered, sending bouncing colourful junk everywhere.'

Levander roared, 'Jazz is nuttier than a squirrel's cookbook!'

Endymion replied, 'The optimism of disco lyrics is false and shallow.'

Levander replied, 'At least we have words! Every time you bears scat-sing, I think you need medical attention.'

Such was the pattern they settled into for their showdown before the Harp. Ososandia kept speeding up. The echoes of its music grew messier and messier. There was not much Bernard could do, and his eyes were soon drawn to the cave paintings. He walked along, running his hand over each one. There was a giant bear that had fallen asleep, and from its back a forest grew. In the next painting, lots of little bears were running around among the trees. Bernard realized he was looking at the history of the Watermelon Wood, richly told upon the stone.

The paintings showed all sorts of bears, picnics, battles and jazz sessions. All the while, the music and its echoes became increasingly jarring to listen to. Bernard looked back at the dance-off, finding it unchanged. So he continued to walk along the cave paintings. In one scene, there seemed to be a mad king shaking a paw at the city rising above the trees, his kingdom dwarfed by skyscrapers. Then, in another, something caught Bernard's eye. It took him a moment to realize what he was seeing. It planted in his mind the seed of an idea.

He stepped before the Harp and approached the Disco Fairy and the Jazz King. The heavy vibrations washed over him, but he did not fall. Levander had mounted Endymion's shoulders, who was swaying to try to topple him.

Endymion roared, 'The disco beat is like a seal with a ball!'

Levander roared, 'There are more people on stage in a jazz gig than in the audience!'

Bernard couldn't believe two adults could be so

childish. 'Oh sizzlesticks, both of you! Shut up!'

They froze, stunned that he'd joined them.

Levander waved him back. 'Bernard! Skedaddle back to the wall!'

Ignoring this, Bernard pointed to the wall. Ososandia had curiously paused in its play.

'Endymion, who is that girl in the painting?'

The panel he pointed to showed a bear crying, with a girl Bernard's age embracing him. The background was filled with vertical lines.

'Why, that's here by the Harp. That is my dearest childhood friend, Hazel Soldavril. She spent her summers here. Somehow she got down here when my father, the mad King Perathus, was raging alone. He had already been brought to his knees by Ososandia's mad melodies, when she came out and calmed him. She stopped him from going to war against Discopia, and he spent his remaining years in sleep. I . . . I hope she has not come to harm.'

'Oh. You didn't know?'

The amber eyes lost their fire. 'What?'

'She . . . fell in battle. She didn't make it.'

Endymion stepped back, Enormous tears fell down his matted fur.

'It can't be,' he said, sinking to his knees. 'I assumed she'd gone into hiding. I prayed she'd save the city. Oh, poor sweet Hazel!'

'Endy,' said Levander, placing a hand on his shoulder. His skull was the saddest Bernard had ever seen it. 'These tears are shared. Hazel showed infinite kindness, and I loved her dearly.'

Endymion wiped his eyes, and looked up into Bernard's face. 'Perhaps . . . perhaps I can honour that lost child of peace by listening to this one.'

Bernard bowed in respect. 'I followed the B-side when hope seemed lost. It led me to you, and it led me to Levander. I just want Discopia safe again.'

'He's always dealing feel-good zingers like that,' said Levander, showing pride through his sorrow. 'There's no better voice to hear.'

Endymion controlled his weeping and stood up. Ososandia watched on, its bear paws frozen in place.

The Jazz King turned and threw one paw on Levander's shoulder and the other on Bernard's.

'We shall avenge her,' he said.

'Now you're talking,' said Bernard.

'From this cave we shall rise to the highest levels of the Garden of Bopalon, and disco shall ring from its heights again.'

Levander smiled and nodded. Bernard cheered. The debate was done. Behind them, Ososandia walked back into the darkness. The Harp was silent once more.

18

I SAY A LITTLE PRAYER

Unlike in the fairy tales, Endymion's big bear chairs were luxuriously comfortable. Bernard sat in deeply cushioned bliss, eating the best honey sandwich he'd ever tasted. Beside him, Levander napped with the boom box in his lap. In an underground dining room, they waited at a long table fit for feasts. Mounted on the walls, woodwind instruments glinted in the candlelight.

On an awkwardly cramped carpet ride, Endymion had flown them through the elaborate cave system. The underground chambers were dotted here and there with living rooms, pantries and snug music venues. Bernard had marvelled at the lack of signposts or maps.

'How do bears not get lost in these twists and turns?' he'd asked.

Endymion had replied, 'You still have much to learn about jazz.'

Upon arriving here, the Jazz King had called the Ragtime Rascals to 'assemble the Jazz Council'. He had also sent for a beaver named Shanebren, with whom he was presently speaking at the doors.

'Let me get this straight,' said the beaver, with an attitude as big as his buck teeth. 'In all my years I've never played disco, and you want me to break that run?'

Endymion regarded this tail-tapping selector who scowled at him from knee height. 'It's a direct order, old friend. We've procured these records from the library. Once this is done, you can take your turntables to the den for when we sleep again.'

Shanebren shrugged and bowed, taking his leave.

Endymion took his seat at the head of the table. He turned to look at the sleeping Disco Fairy. 'I prefer him when he's like this,' he said, making Bernard laugh.

Just then, echoes of footsteps and grumpy moans could be heard in the distance. Bears began to shuffle into the room, some wearing nightgowns. They scat-sang in distrust, glowering at the two outsiders. They took their seats with much muttering and creaking of chairs.

Once they were settled, Endymion stood to his full height.

'I wish the Jazz Council to proceed without arcane scat song, for the sake of our guests.'

One sleepy bear spoke up. 'Surely these intruders are prisoners, not guests?'

Endymion remained cool in the swell of grumblings. 'Their cause was validated before the Harp.' The candlelight threw shadows on the woodwinds behind them, as they turned left and right in astonishment.

'Therefore,' he continued, 'we must hear the woes that have befallen Discopia.'

Levander, now awake, uncurled from his boom box and stood to attention. 'I can read a room,' he said, 'so I won't waste your time glorifying disco. What I will tell you is that Scylla941, the giant robot mothership, destroys a different discotheque every night. It overthrew our police force and cast aside the Disco Knights. These pirates are enslaving our people and burning our culture. Discopia won't survive much longer.'

An old grizzly piped up from the end of the table. 'We have heard reports of the Blank One. You tell us he has dethroned Hazel Soldavril?'

'He executed her,' said the skeleton sadly, bowing a skull of solemn pink. A loaded silence fell upon the room. He continued, 'Records are burning on every floor of Tower Smooth. Soon there will be no disco left.'

'What is it you would ask of the Jazz Council?' asked another bear.

'We ask you to help us storm the city,' said Bernard. He was the smallest person present, but his voice carried. 'We ask you to cross the Bumblebee Bridge and help us bring Captain Vyse to justice.'

'Where possible, we intend to avoid evil pirates,' said one bear.

'And that dance-crazed city!' cried another. They erupted into nonsensical scat-singing.

Endymion brought his paws together in a thunderclap. His amber eyes glinted, and no one dared speak. He addressed the Jazz Council. 'What shall we tell our cubs if Discopia falls? When asked of our legacy, will we point across the Vamvozio to ruins and broken skyscrapers? No. I see only one righteous option. We must burst out of the Watermelon Wood as cavalry.'

Fearful whispers swirled through the room. Endymion waited until one of the bears, a grizzly with curlers in her hair, spoke. 'You would send us to fight Captain Vyse?' she asked. 'Discopia's infrastructure and population surpass our own in every way. They stood a greater chance of resisting, yet still they failed. You stopped building war machines after your father's death. Why would we attack such a force?'

'Marielle,' said Endymion, 'you've answered your own question. The Watermelon Wood has fewer defences. We're responsible for the well-being of the woods above, and the survival of jazz. My father, Perathus, was destroying the forest to make those machines. The trees now face a different threat. Should the Blank One's mask turn towards us, the Watermelon Wood will burn.'

'I've seen the inside of this psycho's hideout,' said Bernard. 'He's organized, and he won't stop at disco. Jazz spirit, disco spirit – I'm telling you they're two sides of the same vinyl. You are loyal to *musical* spirit.'

They seemed to consider this, settling into hush.

'Would Ososandia come to fight?' asked Bernard.

The Jazz King shook his head. 'The Harp is its only calling.'

Levander held out his arms. 'Your king's eyes are open, his hibernation is broken. Please. I'm begging the rest of you to see this danger too.'

Endymion stood by him, shoulder to shoulder. 'There has been little love between Discopia and the Watermelon Wood, yet we are all musicians. We cannot allow Discopia to be reduced to ruins. Now I ask you, upon our honour as Jazz Bears and our devotion to heavenly tunes, to support this motion to march against Captain Vyse, a most tuneless villain.' This was met by a roar of approval from the baritone voices. He continued, 'I do not ask for much. I will personally lead fifty Jazz Knights, enough to man the siege tower built by my father. I vowed never to use it, but we are bears of destiny, and the hour has come to leave our mark.'

The Jazz Council rose to their feet, scat-singing. For the first time, it sounded kind and sonorous. Bernard knew their support was sealed.

Levander leaned over to whisper in his ear. 'You funky little revolutionary, don't let it get to your head! Revolutions have to work first.'

'One setback remains,' said the bear called Marielle. 'This Scylla941 that can demolish buildings in a flash. There is no force in the forest or the city that could stop it.'

Bernard regarded the assembly and winked at Endymion. 'That might not be a problem,' he said.

It was decided that the battle would be brought to the Bumblebee Bridge at sundown. Preparations were swift. Flutes were polished, strategies were crafted, and more bears were awakened.

The jazz of the forest lost its laidback lustre, intensifying into something sharper. The trees swelled with songs of sadness that mourned the hour of war upon them. In a distant glade, the Jazz Knights selected for the mission began their training. These fearsome warriors ran their laps and completed their drills, all while improvising on clarinets.

Bernard and Levander watched the preparations from a treehouse. The Jazzly Bears, like their music, lived all over the place, from the caves below to the branches above. The Discopian visitors had been granted this treehouse for the night. It contained bunkbeds, an old upright piano, and a stove to keep them toasty.

Bernard now lay on the floorboards, and looked through the skylight as dawn snuggled the stars into invisibility. He knew that when those stars came out again, they'd do so over battle. Shuddering, he turned his head to Levander, thankful to be with him again.

'So I know you smooth-talked the bats to show you through the caves,' said Bernard. 'But how did you know we'd be down there? How did you know about the Harp?'

The Disco Fairy shrugged. 'It's all thanks to Hazel, really. She was over at my penthouse months ago, and we were checking out the spaceship. She told me that she'd seen another in the Watermelon Wood. Sure enough, we found hieroglyphics that showed Wollohy Peels and Ososandia together. I thought nothing of it, until yesterday. I was down by Robyntime Harbour, and suddenly Wollohy Peels was standing in front of me. Your fruity friend simply pointed across to the Watermelon Wood, and that's when it clicked. I guessed that you'd crossed over through the other portal. I also guessed that if the Occupants caught you, they'd bring you to that stupid Harp.'

Bernard paused, taking it all in. 'Well, I'm happy you came to find me. Who knows what would have happened if I had to debate or dance-off with Endymion? But dude, the city's in pirate lockdown. Why were you chillaxing at the Harbour?'

Before Levander could answer, they were greeted from outside. Endymion arrived on his flying carpet, and stepped into their lodgings. Bernard was still amazed by his enormity. The paws that walked towards them easily supported more than eight hundred pounds of brawn.

'It is done,' said the Jazz King. 'I tore the sheets off Perathus's siege tower myself. We're ready to march on Discopia.'

'I never thought I'd be happy to hear that,' said Levander.

'These are strange times, Disco Fairy. The Jazz Knights will be ready for the fight.'

'By the way,' said Bernard, 'I never got a chance to thank you for not eating me.'

Something close to a grin formed on the bear's furry snout. 'I have no taste for soulified things. I am no killer. This fur coat I wear is fake; it's just for show."

'What do you eat then?'

'Honey sandwiches. Although I have a weakness for sushi.' He eased into a seat by the stove, gazing into its flames.

Bernard wondered if he found solace in their random, jumpy rhythm so similar to his beloved jazz. He let out a deep, exhausted growl. Even his breathing belied tremendous strength; Levander had quipped by the Harp that he had 'lungs the size of beanbags'.

'The news of Hazel still pains my soul. I mourn for Discopia tonight. But tell me, Levander, how did you escape the place?'

Bernard had been burning to hear this too. 'Yeah, how did you escape the Swamson Hospital if Vyse party-crashed it?'

The Disco Fairy looked to the fading stars. He began, 'Before the attack, I was moved from the Swamson to Hazel's house. The doctors froze me in a coffin of ice made from the tears of Cloud 9 herself. I was listening to deep-freeze funk, and my mind came back to me like music long forgotten. I woke up as my icy lid was removed, and I saw the glowing red eyes of a robopirate.' Here, his wings flicked in anger. 'Naturally, I dance-tornadoed him into a sleepideep. I tried listening to the radio, but all the stations were gone. The only broadcasts were instructions on where to bring disco records, and how to be of service to the new Pirate King Vyse.

'That's when I spotted a note on the side table. It was from Hazel. It simply said: "Don't be afraid, Levander. Discopia will need you when you awaken, and you must stay strong." That's when I knew she was gone.'

His voice cracked, and he bowed his skull. Bernard felt tears in his own eyes.

After a moment, Levander continued. 'After that, I hit the apocalyptic streets, which were empty apart from patrolling pirates. In Candlewick Square, by the shards of the broken Disco Child, Monsieur Le Mantis was crying inside a cardboard box. I did some yo-yo tricks to calm him, and he explained what happened. I told him not to worry and to stop sleeping rough because I know he has a good apartment. He told me it had been taken because he'd refused to give up his vinyls. He's a good bug, really.

'I thought all hope was lost as I walked down to the Bungo Millalungo store at Robyntime Harbour, and found it shuttered with the lights out. No new shoes were on offer and I slumped on the steps, wondering how to cope.'

Bernard pitched in here, knowing his friend had got derailed when sneakers were mentioned. 'Then you remembered I had another spaceship, right? Another portal to the Musical Planet?'

Levander grinned and clicked back into focus. 'For sure! I knew where to mosey. I managed to slink down into the Koonslite, which was hoppin' with the enemy. I got through them, finding my groove with every takedown. I came back up at the Dreamboat Dock and found my emergency jet ski. I cast off, rode to the trees and headed to the caves. I knew my bats would treat me well.'

Endymion shook his head, stroking his chin in the fireside glow. After a minute, he stood again.

'Such unpleasant tidings,' he said. 'It hurts me to think of your people trapped inside their own city. Hopefully tomorrow we can help to save them. For now, I must depart. Hibernation separates us from the beauty of the forest. I will take this opportunity to ramble with my cubs and take them to our favourite places.' He shook Levander's hand in his mighty paw. 'I know your heart is with the synths, but tomorrow you must prove yourself on a grand piano.'

'Prepare to have your jazzy mind blown.'

'And Bernard,' he said, smiling at the boy. 'Thank you for bringing our musical cultures together. We shall call this union the Funk Alliance.'

'Thanks, Endy,' said Bernard, as he bowed goodbye. 'When this is all through, I'll try to get you as much jazz as possible from Planet Earth.'

'I'll look forward to that,' he said. 'And I hope your plan works.' He stepped onto his flying carpet and vanished into the forest.

Bernard and Levander walked to the balcony, listening to the sounds of Jazz Knights in the pale morning light. Across the treetops, they saw the distant city. Discopia was lit in red, and they could see the shape of Scylla941 perched atop Tower Smooth.

'I have something to confess,' said Bernard, his voice turning quiet. Levander turned to listen. 'I was the one who told Captain Vyse your location.'

He explained all that had gone down on Earth: *Wacky Werewolves*, KittyLikeThread, Bucky coming under Vyse's corrupting influence, the broken record and the livestream of Scylla941's murderous arrival.

Levander absorbed this story with many emotions crossing his face. The skull showed no sense of feeling betrayed. 'Oh my groovecats,' he said. 'It sounds like there's chaos in your world too. I never would have guessed.'

Bernard was puzzled. 'What makes you say that?'

Levander tilted his skull. 'This Earth planet sent you. I just assumed it was awesome.'

'So you're not furious?'

'Of course not, disconaut. You were tricked and you responded by saving my life.'

Bernard could barely speak. This forgiveness warmed his worried heart. 'Thank you,' he said, his voice cracking. They continued surveying the distant city, and the sky grew lighter.

Levander flitted his hands in an arc, and a tiny boomba rainbow formed in their wake. For a second, through the colours, Discopia seemed like itself again.

'We'll get it back to that,' said Bernard. 'We just have work to do first.'

He thought of his life back on Earth. Would he ever see his room again? Would he ever see *Beach Noises*? He didn't want to die a soldier's death, leaving Ealaín sonless and never seeing the Skater Kids again.

'I don't want to die,' he said, 'but I have to see this battle through.'

Levander stood up straight, and his voice was ice-cream-smooth again. 'You, Bernard, I will protect at all costs. As for myself, I should not be rushing into such mayhem. I'm still healing. Yet Discopia calls to me, and I must answer. If this is my last boogie, let it be written about in glittering scrolls in the Library of Dance where confetti falls! With the dance gods as our witness, we shall bring back Disco.'

With that, he strolled back into the treehouse, sat at the piano and began to practise.

19

EVERYBODY DANCE

The winds stilled. The shadows thickened. In small stirrings, the Watermelon Wood made it known that its great bears had awoken.

As the pale noon broke, the Bumblebee Bridge was visited by hundreds of squirrels. Under the reign of Mayor Soldavril, the Disco Knights guarding the bridge had been trained to handle any creature from the forest. The pirates who had replaced them, however, were entirely unprepared as the bushy-tailed raiders scampered across the girders overhead. One shot was fired, and the sound reverberated through city and forest alike. The squirrels withdrew to the trees as quickly as they'd come. Five minutes later, the pirates realized that the flags of Vyse had been stolen from above, replaced by the flag of Discopia and the flag of Endymion.

The response in Discopia was immediate. Pirates appeared on rooftops and in windows. Through this heightened surveillance, another anomaly was noted. By the root-gnarled riverbanks of the Watermelon Wood, a beaver's hut had been built. This was no place for such a creature to set up shop. A radio antenna poked out from its twigs.

Uptown, on the roof of the Garden of Bopalon, Scylla941's yellow eyes switched on. She crawled head-first down Tower Smooth and disappeared into the city.

As the sun crept down to the west, the sky over the Watermelon Wood thickened with birdlife. Tree by tree, the birds took flight, closer and closer to the city. Something enormous was on the move below.

After sunset, loud and menacing jazz rumbled from the woods, growing in volume. Robopirates now held position on the Bumblebee Bridge, their swords sharpened, their batteries charged.

Two jet skis quietly headed upstream towards Dreamboat Dock. Bernard wore a stylish tweed suit Endymion had given him and he steered his watercraft with skill. He smiled, knowing Ealaín would never let him near one back on Earth. Levander, riding the other, wore a hooded cloak he'd sewn together from disused maps of Discopia and a scarf of bluebells.

'At least we won't get lost with that outfit!' said Bernard, over the jet-ski drone.

'On days like this,' Levander replied, 'always get dressed in what you love best!'

The city rose up to meet them. It was like a dear friend weak with illness – quiet and faded in the pirate's red lights. Bernard turned to observe the scene unfolding to their right.

An enormous siege tower, ringed by fearsome bears,

emerged onto the Bumblebee Bridge. It was a fearsome machine, made of trees that had been twisted and chained together. The outer walls were fortified with giant thorns. On the top floor Endymion stood tall, patiently tuning his double bass.

Down on the river, the jet skis passed the halfway point. Bernard was starting to think their voyage had escaped detection, when Scylla941 stepped out from the skyscrapers above the little harbour. The cloaked body was shining blood red, and the spotlights from its yellow eyes swept down upon them.

'Hold!' said Levander, and they both hit the brakes.

Scylla941 was a nightmarish sight. Well they knew its crimes: stomping Pantheon 54 into ruins, slaying many good Discopians and terrorizing the city as the mothership to Captain Vyse's devilish crew.

It now stepped over Dreamboat Dock and waded into the river to conquer these enemies of its master. Bernard steered left and placed a steadying hand on the Disco Fairy's watercraft.

Levander revealed a bow and arrow. The arrow was rigged with glittery explosives. He was a fabulous sight as he drew back the bowstring and aimed at the robot that had terrorized his city. The shot sailed up and into the darkness of the red hood. A flaring, glittery explosion signalled the headshot.

'I'm a dancer, not a fighter,' said Levander with unrestrained satisfaction. 'But surely I can be permitted this fun.'

Scylla941, far from felled, let out a deafening shriek.

The tinted glass of its face had shattered, showing an empty control room. It lurched deeper into the water, until it was up to its waist.

'It didn't work!' cried Levander. Bernard's face went pale, knowing they were alone. The Jazz Knights marched onwards, but the robopirates rallied around their barbed-wire barricades on the Discopian half of the bridge. There was nothing the bears could do for the two-man army that had attempted to sneak by on jet skis.

Scylla941 towered over them, its metal hands arcing downwards. It appeared the battle was lost before it had even begun.

Eight hundred metres behind them, Shanebren furiously worked his turntables inside the beaver's hut. For hours, he'd been playing a song by the mermaid superstar Bizzy Bubblekiss on repeat. 'High Tide Friends' was playing on whale-range speakers beneath the waterline. The soundwaves travelled thousands of miles.

As the fingers closed in to cage them, a smile crossed the skull of the Disco Fairy. Bernard looked to the north and saw it too. Slicing up the river was an enormous fin. It was true that there was no force in the city or the forest that could defeat Scylla941. Corribus, however, was from the Sonorous Deep and had returned to pay her debt.

The giant jaws opened wide. Scylla941 didn't even have time to register the bite, before it was dragged under by the megalodon. Corribus shook it from side to side and curled to the north again. She winked as they passed, and with the red-hooded colossus clamped in her jaws, she swam downstream with the same speed with which she had appeared. Corribus carried her prey beneath the Bumblebee Bridge, upon which Endymion and his knights now slammed through the robopirates, and above that, the new flags flew together.

In the takedown's wavy aftermath, their boosted jet skis blasted into Dreamboat Dock. The seals raised their scared faces above the water and smiled when they saw who was coming into town. Levander and Bernard beached their jet skis and allowed themselves a six-second happy dance.

'You were right!' cried the Disco Fairy, doing a handstand. 'Vyse sent that hunk of metal to us rather than the bridge! That was a trap for the history books!'

Bernard smiled, remembering the fury with which Captain Vyse had called for that 'blasted skeleton' over the livestream on *Wacky Werewolves*.

Levander activated special wheels on his jet ski, making it fit for the roads, and withdrew a skateboard from under the seat. With Bernard cruising by his side on the board, they raced down the promenade.

'The last time we were happy on these streets,' cried Bernard over the wind, 'you took me to that groove-forsaken *Crustacean Frustration*.'

'Ah, yes,' said Levander. 'A painful night! We'll have to launch a sequel, and get them playing steel drums.'

'*Crustacean Celebration* sounds way better. Let's hope we'll have something to celebrate!'

They rendezvoused with the Jazz Knights, who had successfully crossed the Bumblebee Bridge. The robopirates had been blasted by ancient, gnarly jazz and now lay strewn about the ground. The Jazz Knights, in massive suits of armour, marched onto the roads of the city.

Endymion looked down with regal grace over his enormous double bass, from the top of the siege tower.

'Disco Fairy,' he called, 'your grand piano is ready on the middle floor.'

Bernard turned to Levander, knowing they must part. 'Show this city that their Disco Fairy is back.'

'Be sure to dance like a disconaut,' the skeleton warmly replied. He swivelled and entered the siege tower, as they all knew time was short.

On his skateboard, Bernard moved to the frontline of brawny, scat-singing Jazz Knights. Tower Smooth seemed very distant over the dulled skyscrapers. All the lights were off except for the top floor. Captain Vyse was undoubtedly there now, furious and tapping out commands to his army. The road ahead would be hard, and the Funk Alliance was outnumbered.

Yet Corribus had taken out Scylla941, so all bets were off.

'Let's move,' said Bernard, putting on sunglasses.

They moved along the six-lane roadway lined by shuttered shops and burnt-out discotheques. Bernard led the way on his skateboard. The formation of Jazz Knights followed. The siege tower rumbled along behind them, on four wheels powered by boomba. The music was sublime, as Levander's silver-winged piano notes flitted around Endymion's galloping bass. Bernard glanced down the corridors of skyscrapers as they passed. Although these

Discopian streets were deserted, lights seemed to be twinkling back on in the windows.

In time, they passed beneath the torii gate into Tuyentown. The siege tower just about slotted through. Awaiting them there was First Mate Wimbledon, who stood before a burning automobile.

'Baseball Beard!' cried Levander. 'I'd forgotten about you.'

Bernard winced, for he recognized the car engulfed in flames.

'Surrender now,' said Wimbledon, 'and you will be deleted with mercy.'

'What arrogant hogwash!' roared Endymion. 'Stand aside or I'll tear that beard from your chin!'

'Very well,' said Wimbledon. He reached into the flames and blasted the car-horn. If Levander hadn't already realized it, the sound surely revealed that it was the Diamante.

The pirates lay in wait in the Koonslite, and came now to the surface like floodwater. They charged the Jazz Knights, who unleashed their melodies and bear hugs. There was a reason the Occupants of the Watermelon Wood were feared. Bernard saw them swipe their enemies away like flies, swoop them into bear hugs and bring the pirates to their knees with mind-blowing oboe solos. The combat was vicious, and fireworks filled the air above them. Through an orange haze of boomba, Levander's piano melody was volcanic with anger and pain.

'A message from Vyse: you will drownnn–' said a robopirate as Bernard moonwalked him into a system failure. As the minion fell, Wimbledon suddenly leaped forth and grabbed Bernard by the curls of his Afro. With his other hand, he took up the skateboard and threw it into the burning Diamante.

'You should have stayed on Earth,' he spat.

Bernard decided to abandon dance combat and tugged at the baseballs. 'Groom your beard!' he said, and Wimbledon let go.

The first mate reeled away, trying to fix the beard. He then promptly disappeared under a body slam from Endymion, who had dived from the top of the siege tower. Bernard gave the Jazz King a hearty slap on the shoulder, and leaped back into dance moves. Soon the pirates were either unconscious, shut down or fleeing the scene. This wave of enemies had been defeated.

On the tree-lined avenue up to Roseland Park, they were met by another group. A band of runaways stood before them. They were wearing armour made of bits of broken mirrorball, torn clothes and war paint. At their head walked Tulsisan, bruised, with her arm in a sling. 'The Disco Knights remain loyal,' she said, bowing to the army. 'We have waged an underground rebellion, suffering greatly and shrinking in number. Those of us who remain are here to fight.'

These warriors had clearly weathered a dangerous few weeks. Their faces were shadowed and gaunt.

Bernard bowed before them. 'We would be honoured to boogie with you now.'

The rebels cheered and joined the Jazz Knights.

Whatever small joy this camaraderie brought was

swiftly extinguished in Roseland Park. Levander had been adamant that here lay the best route to Tower Smooth, for on any of the major roads they would be easily outmanoeuvred. They walked across the uncut, trash-strewn grass, with the Krystal Klear Icecotheque dark and empty before them. Suddenly, they were pummelled by a volley of arrows.

'Retreat!' roared Endymion. They awkwardly fell back to the treeline as the siege tower took damage.

Bernard glanced around for the source of this attack. Five figures stood upon the Icecotheque. They seemed strangely flat and wore spiky armour. Although the range was impossible and they shot far more arrows than their numbers should allow, they were indeed the archers.

Bears and Discopians fell as they retreated to the park's edge. Endymion roared for his fallen brothers to be fetched, but there was no going out into the arrow storm.

Bernard turned to the siege tower. 'We must go around! Those five freaks have us pinned down!'

'If we cut across to the narrower roads,' yelled Levander, 'we risk getting outflanked and blasted for good.'

'If we stay here,' cried Tulsisan, 'they'll sweep in behind us.'

Endymion, enraged, played his bass with force. It shook the very ground, yet still the arrows came.

Just as Bernard started to panic, something in the sky caught his attention. A majestic creature dived down from the clouds. A pink, feathery missile, it nosedived straight to the snow globe, unseen by the enemy.

Bernard's first sighting of Flamingo James did not

disappoint. Zam FM's top selector curled at the dip of his fall, whooped in triumph, and wing-slapped the five archers. They tumbled down the glass and fell into the piles of trash below. Bernard charged forward, and the troops wasted no time in following.

The archers weren't immediately found, so a Jazz Knight and two Discopians agreed to stay back and make sure they were neutralized. As the injured were treated, Bernard watched the siege tower trundle across the grass, proud of the music that played from it. Endymion was playing the session of his life. A hero risking everything in an unfamiliar city, the Jazz King wielded that bass for his own people and those of Discopia, and for his dear Ragtime Rascals. He nodded gruffly at Bernard, and the boy returned the gesture. At that moment, Flamingo James landed beside him.

'You were amazing!' Bernard greeted him.

'Anytime, disconaut! I was wondering when we'd meet. Word of your Funk Alliance has moved faster than ice-cold smoothies in a heatwave. The city's waking up, and we're all rooting for you. Travel on, and you chicklets be careful!' He took off again, with a spring in his wings.

They passed through the northern gates of Roseland, into the flashy thoroughfare up to Good Times Square. Usually a river of traffic, 5th Chord Avenue was now deserted.

All around Discopia, the gloom was fading like a fever. Dancers were starting to appear. The smog was clearing. Bernard was tired and thirsty but he knew every step brought him closer to victory. He turned around to the siege tower, where Levander was working the keyboard like a sushi chef. On the floor above, sweat poured from Endymion. The bear's smooth bassline continued.

Good Times Square was eerily silent. The video screens flickered with werewolf movies, images of Vyse and scrolling digital commands. They came to Feel the Peels, and Bernard was sickened to see it had been ransacked again. The windows were smashed and vultures perched on the pineapple's leaves. As he stood before the record store, Captain Vyse launched his next attack.

White noise screamed from speakers. Pirates appeared down every road; huge, snaking crowds of them. The Funk Alliance beheld the numbers they faced, right before the power was cut and they were plunged into darkness.

As their eyes adjusted to starlight, enemies swung down on ropes. The siege tower was quickly swarmed by pirates. They shook it with the ferocity of starving baboons, and its monumental frame began to totter.

Melodic chords still streamed from Levander's piano, but he was struggling for balance. The bassline that filled the air developed a rage, as Endymion tried to withstand the turbulence.

Bernard had to turn away, for the enemy on the streets was upon them. He braced himself and then began to dance like a disconaut alongside Jazzlys and Disco Knights. They unleashed fierce dance moves upon the pirates, and Bernard saw many of them fall. It felt good to hold back the hordes using the power of disco. Despite their valiant defence, the siege tower was overrun. The old wood groaned as it finally gave way, and the structure fell with a mighty crash. Endymion and Levander were spilled into Good Times Square. The pirates snarled in victory and pushed in close around the Funk Alliance. Dance moves could not hold back this number, nor could the bear hugs of the Jazz Knights. Even with the historic duet of Endymion's rumbling double bass and the Disco Fairy's piano power, it was not enough. They were getting wiped out.

Bernard climbed the broken siege tower. A memory stabbed through his panicked mind. Ealaín had once taken him to an exhibition of Roman frescoes. These artworks, painted on plastered walls, tried to squeeze a huge story into a small picture. Good Times Square was like that now, with so much happening in one place. A robopirate was taking a sledgehammer to Levander's piano. Endymion was jumped from all sides and struggled to swat away his attackers. The beleaguered bears and Disco Knights were surrounded. The music was amazing and their talents were true, but there were too many pirates smothering them with their sheer numbers.

Before Bernard's eyes was a fight for the very soul of Discopia. He looked down and despaired. The pirates would triumph, echoing the parade's chaos on this very street all those nights ago.

Even now, booming drums approached, coming up 5th Chord Avenue, signalling the arrival of new forces. The source of this sound had surely been summoned to finish off the Funk Alliance. Bernard listened to the menacing beats, but then his musical ear detected something. The drums were machine-made. Not only that; as they joined the battle, they played in time with the piano and bass. Pirates turned in confusion, and Bernard stared down 5th Chord Avenue, too. In the distance, the pirate army was splitting in two, stampeding on the pavements. Beyond them, like Moses parting the Red Sea, was an ice-cream truck.

Tastybase had returned.

Miraculously, Levander and Endymion's band was now a trio. Inspector Norse had come to grant her rhythms to the Funk Alliance.

The pirates stalled and cursed, astounded that such a force could be emerging from within the captured city. They were punished for their pause.

Bernard sprang to the road and danced again, sending nearby enemies into retreat. He strung together vintage dance combinations, and felt unstoppable.

Endymion cranked up into new gears of musical power, emboldened by Affy's booming beats. Levander, even as his instrument crumbled under his hands, played his heart out, and filled his space with boomba glow.

The music entirely overpowered the white noise, and Captain Vyse's troops were scattered.

The balance of power now swung in favour of the Funk Alliance, as pirates threw down their weapons and fled.

The lights came back on, and the story in the fresco had changed. Jazz Knights took Endymion's bass as he walked among them, and Levander was rallying the troops. Bernard smiled to see Tastybase approach, with Momotaro in the driver's seat. The vehicle swerved, and a spiky pink haircut popped out from the window.

'I can't believe you marched without a drummer,' Affy said, rolling her eyes.

The Funk Alliance cheered her appearance.

'I've never been happier to see you, kid,' said Levander. 'Alas, my piano has been irrevocably smashed up.'

She twirled a keytar into view, glossy in the brightening lights. 'You might need this, then.'

Endymion turned to his soldiers. 'This is the wildest concert I've experienced in years! Now, the Blank One must pay for harming my Jazz Knights. I cannot wait to introduce myself.'

'We must not delay,' said Affy. 'Hop into my ride. This isn't the only action happening in the city right now.'

Endymion, Levander and Bernard climbed up into Tastybase.

'Humble apologies,' muttered the Jazz King as he made a beeline for the ice cream and used his massive paws as a scoop.

As Bernard came on-board, Affy gave him a huge hug. 'I'm glad to see you again, spacehopper.'

'I'm glad to be here. Aren't you worried about revealing your secret office?'

She winked through her blue visor. 'Today is bigger than my secrets.'

'Well, after we're done, you'll have to deep clean the place for bear fur.'

'Oh the ice cream's ruined for sure.'

She turned and spoke to Momotaro, who pointed the truck towards Tower Smooth. Tulsisan led the army behind them, a new parade of disco revolution.

In the truck, the police radio crackled with Sergeant Philly's voice: 'Funk Alliance, come in. Over.'

Levander grabbed the receiver. 'This is Tastybase and we are open for busineeeess!'

'We're with you. We're all with you.'

Affy smiled. 'While the pirates have been focused on you and your army, the inmates of the Stalemate Scrapyard decided to stage a jailbreak.'

She pressed a button that switched all the screens to the rear-view camera. Following them from Roseland was a huge crowd of Blues, selectors and Discopian citizens of all stripes and sizes. Flamingo James soared through the air above them.

Now Tower Smooth rose up to meet them. Bernard and Levander sat upfront by Momotaro, and observed the skyscraper. A lone figure stared down from the balcony of the Gardens of Bopalon.

'For better or worse,' said Levander. 'That punk pirate must be faced.'

The Funk Alliance continued onwards. Bernard took a deep breath.

Captain Vyse turned and withdrew into the tower.

20

THE HERO AND THE MADMAN

Tower Smooth was covered in the handprints of Scylla941. From its walls and windows, broken robopirates jutted out like gargoyles. Bernard reeled with vertigo as he beheld these wicked things, which trailed from the Garden of Bopalon down to the graffiti-covered Kraftyatids. All over the skyscraper, Captain Vyse had left his mark.

'We'll clean this place up,' said Levander, pained to see the vandalized landmark. The steps to Tower Smooth were occupied by the Mango Mafia. Fatter than ever and inked with fresh tattoos, the hippos had joined Captain Vyse and guarded the entrance to his lair. Their beady eyes now fell upon the ice-cream truck. In spite of the dominance they must have enjoyed under pirate rule, Bernard knew they'd not forgotten that night in Tuyentown. They began to shuffle and squirm.

Affy grinned and walked over to a microphone. Her

voice carried over the marvellous music being played from the amplifiers. 'You boys want to go for round two?'

Upon hearing their capturer, they scrambled away, falling over each other as they abandoned their post. Only Mobster Moylan remained, standing alone. He showed his diamond-grilled tusks. 'I have no fear of pink-haired pipsqueaks!' he roared.

The door to Tastybase opened, and out stepped Endymion. 'And I fear no disco fools,' he said, charging forward.

Bernard watched Mobster Moylan and the Jazz King go to war, and grabbed some popcorn from Affy's supplies. Tastybase parked across from the steps.

'Allow me to lay down some atmosphere,' said Levander, jumping out. At the mouth of 5th Chord Avenue he awaited the troops, wings spread wide and arms resting on the keytar.

'The dude never misses a photo opportunity,' said Bernard.

Affy smiled, checking one of the radars. 'According to the body heat readings, the only living things in Tower Smooth are rats and the captain.' She shrugged, handing Bernard a can of Cosmopop. 'Maybe we'll get help from Sammy Sharp Eyes. For now, I must prepare for battle.'

'I'll leave you to it,' he said. It was nice to get a moment's rest, and the cola tasted great. He departed and sat on the steps to Tower Smooth, where Endymion now carried the defeated and dazed Mobster Moylan away.

In the distance, the Discopian reinforcements were arriving. Levander turned to his disconaut friend and smiled under his cloaked hood of maps. 'I guess it's too late to ask you to stay on the sidelines,' he remarked.

Bernard nodded. 'If I'd stayed on the sidelines, you'd still be in that cave with the harpstrings.'

That ice-cream laughter escaped, just as Sergeant Philly rode up on a brown horse. The policeman had grown a big, bushy beard, courtesy of time spent confined in the Stalemate Scrapyard.

'Good to see you boys! We have Vyse on the backfoot now! Let us kickstart the helicopters, and take him from the air.'

Levander shook his skull. 'No. It has to be Bernard and me. You must stay down here and defend against any surprises he might still have up his sleeve for the ground.'

Philly glanced at the ice-cream truck. 'All right. Just keep Affogato safe.'

'I can assure you, Sarge,' said Bernard, 'she's keeping us safe.'

The sergeant bowed and led his steed away, talking into a walkie-talkie.

Levander motioned to Flamingo James, who was circling overhead.

'What can I do for my favourite pile of bones?' squawked the selector, landing beside him.

'I need you to spread a message to the Discopian people. Tell them to listen for the carillon's bells. Once melodies ring down like stardust upon the city, they'll know we have passed our tests.'

'Sweet stuff!' the flamingo replied. 'The lights are coming back on, for disco returns!'

The flamingo sashayed back to the crowd, and Levander came and sat beside Bernard. A heavy clang announced that Endymion had dropped his blubbery foe into a dumpster.

'We've come a long way,' said Bernard.

Levander nodded, adjusting the keytar's dials. 'I haven't taken this many steps since my twenty-hour charity dance on *Grapevine News*.'

They watched the crowd grow before them. Tulsisan was now on horseback too, working with the Disco Knights to create a barrier. The ragged Jazzly Bears were handing out cups of water. Bernard was happy to be there.

Affy emerged from Tastybase, wearing space-age armour. Bernard recognized the ice-cream cone on her helmet: the forcefield maker.

'You look like a gladiator from a far-flung moon!' he remarked.

'Now, now, I don't want you in danger,' cried Levander.

'You're stuck with us now, Skullz.' Affy threw him a royal-blue cape. 'Wear this. I made it from the blueprints of Tower Smooth.'

Levander put it over his old, torn cloak of maps. 'Stop giving me things I love,' he said.

After checking on his officers, the Jazz King approached them. 'Is this a Discopian strategy, sitting around doing nothing?'

Bernard looked up at him. 'To be fair, that's what you were doing when I found you.'

The bear chuckled heartily. He gestured to the Kraftyatid pillars. 'The entry is open. Are we going in?'

'You've already done enough,' said Levander, poking his hairy chest.

A bear-paw slapped his hand away. 'What did I tell you in the Harp of Ososandia? We're going straight to the top of this tower. That's what I intend to do.'

Bernard stood up, and finished his Cosmopop. 'Let's get this funkless party-crasher.'

The four heroes walked up the steps, to a mighty cheer from the forming crowd. A familiar fridge emerged from the ranks. Chilly George stationed himself at the foot of the steps, thrilled to be on door duty again.

Beyond the damaged Kraftyatids, the doors to Smooth Lobby had been ripped from their hinges. Total darkness reigned inside. Before they crossed the threshold, Endymion suddenly held them back. His amber eyes narrowed as he scanned the void within.

'Thirty robopirates lie in ambush,' he whispered, baring his fangs. Bernard could not see them, but had come to trust the bear entirely.

'Let's light this lobby up,' said Levander. Bernard prepared dance moves, and Inspector Norse withdrew her laser blaster. They entered.

Robopirates drew their swords in sync, and closed in from all sides. They marched in vain. Inspector Norse pummelled them with laser beams. Endymion tore through their ranks without mercy. Bernard and Levander unleashed fireworks of dance-destruction. The Funk Alliance was not to be stopped in Smooth Lobby. Screws and bolts flew as one by one the robopirates crashed to the outer-space mosaic on the floor, eyes winking out upon its galaxy.

Standing over the horde of fallen robots, Bernard allowed himself a moment to relax. His eyes adjusted to the dark.

'These are the tin cans that have caused you such trouble?' grinned Endymion, kicking one aside.

'The main bee in our bonnet was the mothership,' said Levander. Inspector Norse approached him with a torch, and started consulting the blueprint cape.

'This homecoming won't do,' she said. 'We need light. There's a fuse station in the basement.'

Bernard froze. Since their journey across Vamvozio River, a vague unease had burdened him under the adrenaline. It now became clear.

'The wolves,' he said. 'Scylla941 went down without her wolves.'

Inspector Norse went pale. 'Those things are still in the game?'

'Wolves!' cried Endymion. 'I'll have no problem ousting those jazzless howlers.'

Bernard shook his head. 'Try massive metal ones with a jet-fuelled bite force.'

'He's right,' said Affy, gesturing to the fallen robopirates. 'These guys are factory-produced; cheap and disposable. The cyberwolves, however, are custom-made killing machines.'

A chilled silence followed, as they all looked to the ceiling. Captain Vyse lurked 120 floors up, and now they knew he wasn't alone. Levander thoughtfully stroked his jawbone as this talk went down.

'A tricky dancefloor indeed,' he said, with a playful lilt to his voice. 'Let's make it trickier. Affy, when you're down fixing the lights, can you turn on the sprinkler system?'

She looked confused, but nodded. 'I'll get started. I'll need some cover down there though. How about you, Papa Bear?'

Endymion bowed his head, and joined her as they hurried for the basement.

By the sound of laser beams and bearish roars, many more robopirates met their doom downstairs.

Behind the reception desk, Levander rummaged through the *Fountain Party Supply Closet*. Bernard couldn't help but smile when he learned the object of his search.

'I thought I'd never see the day,' he said.

'You know what I say,' said Levander. 'You can't save a party without getting arty.'

Bernard dodged an inflatable palm tree as it arced from the doorway.

'Hey,' he said, 'do you remember what Vyse said about the sea of thorns?'

Levander paused, and turned from the clutter. 'He said I was a balloon animal,' he quietly replied. 'And he was a sea of thorns.'

'Yes, he did. I just wanted to remind you that you've proven yourself a balloon animal made of steel.'

The skeleton's smile was small, but spoke volumes. The lights flared back on, and the sprinklers unleashed an indoor downpour. Levander walked out with a small plastic box of blue powder. Endymion and Inspector

Norse returned, laughing like long-lost friends. Once they'd all combed over their strategy, they were drenched but ready to go.

The elevator opened, containing no menace. Inspector Norse checked it for booby-traps, and found none. They all squeezed in, and Bernard was comforted to find himself surrounded by three musicians who embodied the past, present and future of dance music. The long ascent through Smooth Tower began.

'I remember,' said Levander, 'when one of the soulified lifts in here snuck out to a party for an evening. He was sick the next day, vomming people out on wrong floors. A florist arrived with a bunch of soothing herbs for Bopalon, and the lift kept it trapped there for an hour to help him.'

They laughed. Scratchy jazz played from the sound system.

Endymion heard it, and gasped. 'You listen to jazz as you rocket up these towers?'

Levander shrugged. 'We honour our roots in strange ways.'

The numbers on the display panel ticked closer and closer to 120. Below her space helmet, Affy gave Bernard a reassuring smile. As they reached the upper floors, the team bent their heads close, discussing their plan of action one last time. Then the doors opened wide, revealing the Garden of Bopalon.

In the rain, the captain waited.

He stood beside computer screens on top of the

pyramid, and the cyberwolves prowled below him. The plants had all been burnt away. The ceiling's glass city was cracked, and water poured down through sprinklers and leaky pipes.

Bernard walked into this wasteland, flanked by Endymion and Inspector Norse.

'Hydration is important,' Bernard said, pointing to the sprinklers.

The dripping mask turned from face to face. 'Look how far you've come,' said Captain Vyse. 'Endymion, I'll be sure to visit your woods once we're through here.'

The Jazz King growled. 'You'll answer for your crimes, Blank One.'

Vyse pressed a button and the cyberwolves all snarled. 'And Inspector Norse? How you ruined my fun in the Vetruvius. I look forward to handing you over to the Satyr.'

Her eyes were free of fear behind her blue visor. She switched on her forcefield.

'The only thing you have to look forward to,' said Bernard, 'is a long funkless stretch in prison.'

'I've always liked you, Bernard. Our chats brought me joy.'

'I enjoyed them too, before I knew you were evil.'

A series of husky screeches rose up, meant to be laughter. 'Good. Evil. These are pre-digital concepts. There is only information. It can be collected and stored as the true wealth.' His hand moved to the handle of his sword. 'Now, where is Levander?'

'Here's the truth about Discopia's darkest hour,' said the Disco Fairy, emerging from the brass vents on top of the lift shaft. 'I always said it would feature a foam party!'

Vyse turned and began tapping at his keyboards with spider-fast fingers.

Levander threw the blue powder into the downpour, and the whole place exploded with pink and white foam. The cyberwolves came snapping forward, but they were blinded and lost in the gloopy bubble bath that consumed the Garden of Bopalon.

Endymion and Affogato Norse charged into the foam to meet them. The Jazz King moved in absolute wrath, smashing the cyberwolves in a rampage. Affogato shot laser beams and tasered them with electronic precision. The crunch of broken metal filled the bubbly battlefield.

Bernard sprinted left, through the bubbles and blindly up the pyramid. When he emerged from the great bubble bath – churned and swollen by the sprinklers – Captain Vyse was gone. The pirate had scurried down the pyramid's other side, and out onto the wraparound balcony. There, he now ran straight into Levander, who had cut across from the doors behind the lift. The Disco Fairy switched his keytar on.

'You must have known, when you set your cracked heart on Discopia, that one day you'd have to face me. Properly, this time.'

Captain Vyse took out his sword. 'I knew. Your dance moves are praised all over the Musical Planet. What a message it will send to defeat you in battle.'

Levander let his cape slip to the floor. Captain Vyse lunged. Whatever preparations the man had made for this encounter, he called upon them now. His cutlass slashed forward with the speed of cobras.

Levander began to play exquisite melodies on his keytar, while flowing into a classic semi-quaver bop, dodging the sword swipes in twists and dips.

Their showdown had begun.

Bernard changed his point of focus to the computer screens. Vyse had logged off, and the screen demanded a password to proceed. He grinned. As advanced as the computers were for the seventies-style of Discopia, Bernard was a Skater Kid from the digital age. He had installed an overdrive security question back in Vyse's headquarters in the Vetruvius Club. He sat where his enemy had sat and hacked into the computer with ease. Through the speakers, the voices of Levander and Captain Vyse could be heard.

'I could have taken any form. A dark lord. An alien. Even Satan himself. Yet I chose a pirate.'

'I can offer some fashion tips,' replied Levander from the whirl of his dance moves. 'The saddest thing about you is that you're creative. You could have thrived in Discopia. Too bad you're a lunatic.'

Bernard laughed, but then heard Endymion roar in pain. The foam, weakened by the relentless sprinkled torrents above, was slowly washing away. The cyberwolves could see again. Endymion bayed as robot jaws found their mark. Inspector Norse's forcefield was beginning to flicker, and claws found their way in. She looked utterly terrified.

Neither of them were holding out against the cyberwolves.

Out on the balcony, Levander and Captain Vyse swirled and swayed, neither having the upper hand. The Disco Fairy shone with rainbow boomba from the purest disco-dancing, whereas his enemy now plumed with artificial smoke.

'It all comes back to the computers,' Vyse said in his cold robot voice. 'Music can be stored and it can be deleted. Even cities can be swept away by a programmer's hand.'

'Not this one, Vysey,' said Levander.

Their mighty duel whirled across all four sides of the wraparound balcony.

Bernard desperately dug around the computer, trying to ignore that the background image was from *Wacky Werewolves*. He couldn't find much, as everything was encrypted, confusing and virus-slow. Yet it was still a computer of his own world, a device he was familiar with. He went into 'programs running', and saw an icon of a wolf. He clicked into it and was thrilled to see it was called Wolf Controls.

Endymion's roar redoubled as he felt the fangs of another cyberwolf.

'Get away from Papa Bear!' cried Affy, who was running out of laser ammunition. The bear fell to his knees and she tried to protect him. All twelve cyberwolves frenzied around them.

Bernard tried to stay calm. Back on the computer screens, twelve video feeds popped up. These were sourced from the cameras in the wolfpack's eyes, and showed high-definition footage of Affy and Endymion being attacked from all angles. He focused on Wolf Controls and noticed there were twelve different sections, one for each cyberwolf. They all had the same command: 'Attack the bear and the girl. Do not harm the boy.'

He started deleting the command and miraculously the wolves below stopped their attacks. He breathed a sigh of relief as they turned their steel snouts upwards, awaiting new instructions.

The battle outside raged on, but Levander was now pinned against the east-side toucan statue. His leg had become caught in coils of barbed wire used to string robopirates over the edge. Captain Vyse sensed he was winning. His attack grew more ferocious.

'You are nothing to me,' he said. 'You and your music are nothing but information.'

One of the monitors showed the captain's point of view, and Bernard realized the camera had been at the tip of his tricorne hat all along, allowing the man inside the mask to see. This footage showed the Disco Fairy's skull up close, defiant even as it was scratched and head-butted.

'We're all points of light,' said Levander, suddenly twisting into a dance move full of boomba. 'Even you.'

Captain Vyse was blasted backwards. He rose up shaking, and came forward again.

'All we are is points of data!' he snarled, his voice deepened by a dying microphone.

Inside, Inspector Norse was suddenly by Bernard's side, hugging him.

'The wolves are controlled here,' he stressed, 'but I don't know how to save Levander.'

'You've already saved the day,' she said, studying the software of Wolf Controls. She typed in a command to the wolfpack.

'Capture your master.'

The cyberwolves snapped into their mechanized hunt.

They left the fallen Jazz King. They departed the Garden of Bopalon. They charged along the balcony, straight for the great endgame at the tippy-top of Discopia, where even now Captain Vyse still spoke.

'Data is the only truth, Levander. All we leave behind are legacies.'

They pounced. He was too close to the parapet. The mask turned, blankly concealing whatever emotion lay beneath. Then Captain Vyse tumbled over the edge, and the cyberwolves poured after him. Levander dived to save him, but the barbed wire at his ankle held him back.

All thirteen screens – from the captain and his cyberwolves – showed a tumbling freefall down the outside of Tower Smooth. Then they all went blank.

When the broken wolfpack was later discovered, strewn across an alley behind Tower Smooth, Captain Vyse was found among them. The Blues removed his mask, showing a plain human face beneath. The man was dead. They covered him in a blanket, and Sergeant Philly went to find Chirontë. The centaur was easy to spot in the crowd. Since his arrival, Captain Vyse had kept himself mysterious. Now, at the end of his cruel reign, his body was lifted up by Chirontë. He was carried away by his teacher, the only one who'd known him before he wore the mask.

21

I WANNA DANCE WITH SOMEBODY

The downpour softened as the pipes ran out of water. Soon, it was nothing but drips and drops. Such was the sound in the Garden of Bopalon.

Bernard stared in disbelief at the disconnected videos on the computer screens. He turned to Affy, who wrapped him up in a consoling hug. Her armour was cold and jagged, but he put his arms around her.

'Don't think about it, spacehopper,' she said quietly. 'I didn't know that would happen.'

'His fall is not your fault. He brought it on himself. The battle is over.'

Through the greenhouse walls, Levander could be seen on his knees, holding something golden in his hands. To the night sky he cried, 'You silly smoky pirate! I could have saved you!'

Affy pulled back, and looked down at Bernard.

'You and I end up in crazy places,' she said.

Bernard wiped his eyes, and a tiny smile appeared. 'You're right. We should choose somewhere normal next time.'

'Good luck finding normal in this town,' she said. Then she turned to the computers, and her eyes sharpened. 'Now go and check on Papa Bear. I need to browse these files for intel on the Satyr.'

Leaving her in the ghostly glow of the screens, he hurried down the marble steps, careful not to slip. He glanced at Levander, who sat with his wings to the glass and his skull in his hands. This fight had shaken them all.

On the floor below, among dollops of foam sliding to the drains, Endymion lay, bruised and wounded. His belly rose and fell like a blacksmith's bellows, his breaths long and ragged.

'You lived up to your legend today.' Bernard knelt beside him.

Endymion wheezed and looked at him. 'You have so many friends here. We would have lost without them. And with all your improvisations . . . you did jazz proud.'

'Don't speak. Just rest.'

'It was better you came for us . . . before the Blank One did. The Jazz Bears thank you.'

'You didn't eat me. That's enough for now.'

Endymion's amber eyes closed, and he sank into a troubled slumber. Bernard stayed by his side, holding his immense paw in two hands. A splish-splash of footsteps drew near.

'Under all that jazz and grumpiness,' said Levander, 'a great soul lies within.' The skeleton held up his blueprint cape, and threw it over the bear as a blanket.

'We should babysit bears more often,' said Bernard, trying to cheer him up.

Levander's face remained severe. He swivelled, casting a quizzical glance to Inspector Norse. 'Affogato! I'm about to blast these bells. Climb down!'

She held up a hand to silence him.

'She seeks word of the Satyr,' said Bernard. He imagined that even the dance gods would fail to rip her from the task.

Levander sighed and shook his head. 'I hope she finds what she's looking for,' he whispered, turning his attention to the item in his fingers. It was Hazel's medallion, the winged vinyl in gold. It must have fallen from Captain Vyse's neck in the showdown. He slotted it into a secret shape in the pyramid's carvings. It turned a clockwork switch, and a doorway appeared. A stone seat rose up from the floor, and a console of iron levers lay within. Above them, golden chains webbed up to where the concealed bells awaited. Bernard was excited to hear them ring.

Levander took a seat and his fingers fluttered above the levers. 'What should I play?'

'You know better than anyone what this city wants to hear. Play the heaviest grooves you can.'

The disco music took flight like a thousand winged things. The unseen system of bell-beams arced and swung within, creating heavenly harmonies. From the brawny bass bells to their bright high-octave sisters, the carillon provided a massive symphony of song.

The soundwaves rippled out from Tower Smooth

and into the city, spreading the message that the reign of Captain Vyse had ended. As Levander got lost in his rhythms, bopping righteously, Endymion stirred again. 'This music is atrocious,' he gruffly declared.

Bernard smiled. He looked up at Affy, who was also showing irritation as the music shook the computers. The screens were coming loose from their frames. He addressed the disgruntled bear. 'If you feel up to it, why not walk outside? There's something you might want to see.'

Endymion considered this and nodded his head. With trembling limbs, he pushed himself to his feet and gripped Bernard's shoulder for support. Bernard led him outside, where the Jazz King slouched against the curved back of a toucan and beheld the sprawl of the Watermelon Wood.

'My sweet forest!' he said. As he stared lovingly upon the trees he ruled, Bernard surveyed Discopia. The red lighting of Captain Vyse was gone. The skyscrapers were regaining their bubblegum glow, becoming blue and pink again. The crowd below was rippling with new dance moves. The city was awakening from its dark enchantment. He looked back inside, where the pyramidal carillon was shaking like jelly. At the top, he saw the screens of Captain Vyse come crashing down, one by one. Affy walked away, sliding off her helmet. Whether she'd found insights or another dead end, her work – for now – was finished. She sat by Levander, who still played the bells with gusto, and laid her head on his shoulder. One of his butterfly wings curled around her. Bernard smiled at the sight. Despite all they'd been through, the pain and loss, the danger and destruction, he felt at peace. He wished the Skater Kids were here with him, and a tear arose as he wished the same of Hazel Soldavril. He would never forget her.

For now, he was surrounded by the Funk Alliance. They were some of the finest friends he'd ever known. Here they were, by his side at the battle's end. For this he was thankful.

Within the hour, all of Discopia had erupted in celebration. The city became a fountain of disco music, where sparkling grooves poured from every window. Shops and parks reopened. Neon signs glowed again. The happy sounds of diggers and builders rang out from all quarters, as rebuilding began. The Disco Knights hunted down the pirates that remained. From skyscraper rooftops down to the Pipelands below the Koonslite, Discopia started to heal.

'Welcome back,' said Kimmy, beaming under smudged reptile face paint.

'Delightful to see you,' said Bernard, as Levander gave her a huge hug. Affy followed them into the elevator, and Kimmy took them to the penthouse.

'Pirates were watching this place like dogs around a dinner table,' Kimmy explained. 'They lay in wait for Levander's return.'

'Thankfully,' he said, 'I was gliding around caves beneath the Watermelon Wood.'

The penthouse was coated in dust, but was otherwise untouched. Chilly George, reliable as ever, had sent help in advance. His team of semi-soulified vacuum cleaners arrived shortly after they did, and after a deep clean, the place looked spruce. Once they'd finished up, Affy set up turntables in the living room, and the Disco Fairy got on the phone.

Levander threw one of the greatest parties the city had ever seen. Word spread fast, and within half an hour the place was hopping. Discopia's noblest selectors stepped forward for turntable duty. Flamingo James played back to back with Cloud 9. Okinawa Frostbite, with blizzard-silver hair, showcased her stuff. Dr Alejandro Sugarado played long, elaborate floor-fillers. Even Monsieur Le Mantis got up on the decks, and his tunes were excellent.

The video-floor became a classic grid of rainbow-coloured squares, upon which the party-guests danced. All over the penthouse were familiar faces. The Slowgroove Sunflowers drank from watering cans out on the balcony. Vlad the Bat showed up with a basket of muffins as an apologetic offering. Koalas scampered through the rooms with super-soakers. Bernard even met some new peeps and was particularly fond of Okinawa Frostbite and her yeti guitarist. A reinflated Lance Brophy showed up on crutches, but the beach ball abandoned them for a jive soon enough. To the host's delight, it was discovered that Pilgrim had dropped by, for he had painted a mural of bells on the music studio's ceiling.

Everyone played the party game of looking out for Wollohy Peels, making sure Bernard wouldn't be zapped away too early. The sentiment warmed his heart. The demi-god with a pineapple head did not appear in the penthouse that night.

In the kitchen, halfway through the party, Bernard and Affy regaled Andromeda Pokitaru with their story of the Vetruvius Club.

'The kid showed moxie with that slingshot,' said the Inspector. 'Who would have thought that a playground knick-knack would win the day?'

'Wow!' said Pokitaru. 'And how did you get past the Lurcher?'

'The what now?' Bernard inquired, as Affy blushed behind her yoghurt.

'The Lurcher,' said Pokitaru with a growing smile, 'is a soulified creature made of bits of garbage. It's the size of an elephant, with broken mirrorballs for eyes. It roves the Stalemate Scrapyard to feast on intruders. The prisoners were fighting it off for weeks!'

'I didn't tell him about that. He would have freaked out.'

'The betrayal!' Bernard cried playfully. 'Good thing it didn't gobble us up!'

As they all laughed together, Levander dashed in, dressed in a dapper tuxedo. 'I've got a sight for you to see!'

He ushered them past the dancefloor and party games, out onto the balcony. Down on Sweetbeat Street, the Jazzly Bears marched in a lantern-lit procession. Though they seemed battered from the fight, they walked tall and proud towards a hibernation richly earned.

Endymion lay upon his double bass, carried by Disco

Knights. From this restful position, he saluted those on the balcony.

Levander nudged Affy and handed her a loudhailer.

'You still down to trade for honey and ice cream?' she asked through the hailer.

The bear replied with an enthusiastic thumbs up. The amber eyes then turned to Bernard.

'Thank you for the tweed suit!' called Bernard.

Endymion boomed his reply: 'The gratitude is mine, dear friend!'

From windows, hundreds of Discopians threw roses, as the heroes of the Watermelon Wood headed home.

The party in Levander's penthouse was truly epic. Every guest knew they were bopping through a history-maker.

Lance Brophy recorded his report for *Grapevine News*, moving in circles atop a spinning record. 'There's already talk that this will be written about in glittered scrolls, to be studied for centuries to come in the Library of Dance. It truly marks the beginning of a disco renaissance following the end of pirate rule.' After the beachball dismounted and rolled away, Levander jumped up on decks. When he unleashed his record collection, there wasn't a happier dancefloor in all of Discopia.

As is the fate of all parties, it eventually started to fade out. Balloons began to droop. The bunting fell down. Taxis were called.

As people started to leave, Sergeant Philly appeared.

'I hope you're not shutting us down,' said Bernard.

A smile spread within the bushy beard. 'You have the

right to remain dancing,' he said, handing him a hamper of cookies.

Bernard heard a voice behind him.

'Hey, Sarge,' said Affy.

'Inspector! I was hoping to see you. We're having a ceremony to commemorate the services of the Blues during the time of Vyse. There's a medal with your name on it.'

She nodded curtly. 'Thanks. I'll check my diary.'

As the sergeant walked away, Affy whispered to Bernard, 'I'll send Momotaro to collect it.'

Sergeant Philly withdrew a VHS tape, and handed it to the host. 'This was recovered from Vyse's hard drives. It's the only video feed still live.'

Levander strolled over and slotted it into the VCR. On the video-floor, a deep blue scene appeared. A light shimmered far, far away.

'What is this freaky-deaky blueness?' asked Levander.

'This is the livestream from Scylla941. It's broadcasting from whatever part of the seafloor the megalodon dragged it to.'

Eating a cookie, Bernard looked down at the footage coming from a giant robot at the bottom of the sea. Would the video remain live as the head became crowned in coral, and lobsters tapped across the yellow eyes? What whales and submarines would cross the vision of this drowned robot? He thought of unidentified sounds, droning in the ocean. The Sonorous Deep would be Scylla941's deathbed, watery and blue, for evermore.

Soon, there were but a few dancers left. Salamis worked the turntables, her face serene within the goldfish bowl. She soothed the scene with lullaby funk. Kimmy, exhausted from a long night of elevator boogieing, flaked out in a beanbag above the Scylla941 footage.

Bernard played Twister with Andromeda Pokitaru and Flamingo James. By the mirrorball globe, Levander discussed public art commissions with Sister Peachy – a gospel nun in charge of public statues – and Vlad the Bat. They brainstormed a memorial to honour Mayor Soldavril. It would stand in place of the shattered Disco Child. She would be sculpted in bronze, and from her upturned palms, a miniature version of the Disco Child would spring. Bernard, from his wobbly upside-down position on the Twister mat, could overhear the talk.

'If she is not remembered,' said Levander, 'then all this will have been in vain.'

Bernard was struck by sadness. Hazel would never be back. She would never see Discopia regained. As a Discopian, she'd shown how pleasant and fierce this city was. As a friend, she was among the best he'd known. At the very least, a statue was called for.

Then his elbow slipped and he crashed out of the Twister game.

Eventually just three or four guests remained. Affy emerged from the kitchen and handed out bowls of her bubblegum bopathon ice cream.

'You wanna hear about the new public art?' asked Levander.

She shot him a scorching glance, making Bernard laugh. 'I don't give a didgeridoo what crass disco art I'll be forced to behold!'

'Well,' Levander continued, 'I'll just tell you about the Philly Jailhouse one. As a quiet acknowledgement to your contribution . . .'

She cringed, holding up a hand. 'Skullz, whatever it is I don't want to hear it.'

'We're putting up a memorial plaque to Pedro Alvarez, your lost partner.'

She fell silent. Her face, usually smooth as glass, trembled for a moment. 'That sounds very nice,' she said.

The three of them came together in a group hug.

'Alright,' Affy said. 'I'm going to sneak in a nap in the guest room, then I better get back to Tastybase.'

'Rest well,' said Levander. 'The drums you played today will rumble through my dreams forever.'

Bernard nodded. 'Samesies. And thank you. For everything. The city is lucky to have you.'

She smiled. 'Spacehopper, I've worked here for years. I've endured the disco. Skullz helps me, but often . . . I've hated my life here. Since you came along, I don't feel that any more. It's you I should be thanking.'

'Listen, I've never met someone more multitalented, on Earth or the Musical Planet. Never forget we love you, Affy.'

She stood up straight and bowed. 'Goodnight, boys.'

In the end, Bernard and Levander were the last ones standing. Taking some fresh air on the balcony, they watched the sun rise over the city. They drank juice from coconut cups.

'This is the longest I've been on the Musical Planet,' said Bernard.

'Wow!' said Levander, shaking his head. 'Will the portal still work?'

'I'll find out. It's too long a walk to the one in the Watermelon Wood.' He yawned. 'You should try coming to Earth sometime. Maybe at Halloween so you don't frighten the neighbours.'

'Hmm. From what you've told me of the disco era in your dimension, I've missed my opening.'

Bernard looked at the blue sky forming over Discopia. 'Back at my school, they say disco's becoming cool again. I think they're wrong. Disco's always been cool. You'd fit into my world anytime.'

They walked back inside. Levander curled up and used his wings as a blanket.

'Don't tell your mum about the jet skis,' he said.

They drained their coconut cups. Inevitably, their attention turned to the spaceship.

'Where did you even get that thing?' asked Bernard.

'A few years ago,' said Levander slowly, 'I visited a fortune-telling magic 8 ball. I was feeling lonely, and wanted help.'

'You? Lonely? The most popular skeleton in Discopia?'

'I was. Everyone gets under rainclouds from time to time. Even those who always smile.'

Bernard was astounded. 'What did this psychic say to you?'

'She simply told me to buy the first thing I saw. At first, I thought this was baloney. Then I passed the window of an antique shop and saw this.' He smiled and gestured to the spaceship. 'It took a while but it worked. You came along.'

'You spooky softie,' said Bernard. He hugged his best friend and heard the golden heart beating within the tuxedo. Their goodbye hug was short and simple. Two days beforehand, their mighty missions had started with a hug before the Harp. Now, their mission was complete.

'I have to go,' said Bernard, breaking away. 'Get some rest, you hear? No pillow fights or bubble baths.'

'I'll be fine. I sleep under kinder stars tonight.'

'I'll see you soon?'

The Disco Fairy bowed. 'Of course, disconaut. Of course.'

Bernard walked to the spaceship. He opened the door and looked back.

Levander had eased into the bubble chair by the sound system. The sight of his smiling skull was the perfect way to end the party.

22

DOWN IN MY SOUL

After his return to Earth, Bernard logged in to *Wacky Werewolves* just once more.

Because he no longer played it, Amble Totes had become a ghost town. The peach-puff cottages were turning into ruins. Headspace House sat weeping on its hill, encircled by rainclouds.

Bernard clicked into the KLT cottage, hoping to feed the birds. They had vanished into digital air. Upon further exploration, he found KittyLikeThread's werewolf, alone in a bare room. She was draped in a blanket, with the same childish smile on the cuddly face. She was unresponsive and did not growl back when Bernard greeted her. Whatever had been there before was gone. Bernard looked at this empty werewolf for a long time. Then he deleted his account.

Sunshine blessed the last week of term at Fairweather School. Bernard had one more goal to achieve before the gates closed for the summer. He spent Monday evening up in Jay's treehouse. Here, his friend kept a computer that could transfer music onto blank CDs.

He made mixtapes inspired by the sets he'd heard in Levander's penthouse, and the disco was immense.

'I never knew you were an evil genius,' said Jay. Bernard sipped his lemonade.

The next day, the four Skater Kids slipped the CDs into the lockers of Ricky Rockwell's goons. By Friday they were hooked. Disco was all they wanted to listen to. It blasted from their boom box in the playground. Ricky sat crossly among them, arms folded and face scowling. In a matter of days, he had lost his squad to disco music. He now faced into a long summer listening to the stuff.

Bernard skateboarded by with a friendly wave.

It was the cherry on top of a stylish revenge.

The good weather continued, and *Beach Noises* opened on a fine summer's evening. In the courtyard of Dunewright Castle, visitors were greeted by Ealaín's *Giraffe with a Palm Tree for its Neck and Head*. They passed beneath it with a mixture of reactions: raised eyebrows, laughter and thoughtful reflection.

At the doors, Ali handed out exhibition catalogues. Beside her, Bucky handed out buckets and spades.

The catalogue's introduction was straight to the point:

> 'Dunewright Castle is delighted to open its doors to *Beach Noises*, which brings the seaside indoors. We hope you enjoy your time in the sun!'

In the entrance-hall, Bernard had the best view in the

house. He spun records at the turntables, as the night's selector. He wore his tweed suit from the Watermelon Wood and a black shirt patterned with skulls.

The gallery floor was covered in sand, and already a jumble of footprints had been left. People stood about with smiles and drinks. To the side, *Tiki Bus Stop* was displayed. Under the bamboo thatch, totem-pole passengers waited for a bus that would never come.

It wasn't quite the extravaganza of Pantheon 54 on a Saturday night, but Bernard was happy to be playing the tunes his father had once collected. He looked down at the Discopia record. Upon returning from Levander's penthouse, he had found it flipped. The red paint had miraculously vanished from Side A. What had reversed the damage on Earth was unclear, but he was deeply thankful for it.

Ealaín soon came and stood beside him. She wore a flower necklace over her formal dress.

'A sandbox for adults.' He pointed at the sandy floor. 'Nice.'

'Some people will never see the playfulness. I just heard an art critic over by the bus stop talk about how it perfectly captures "bus-stoppiness". Imagine! At least your friends are getting into the creative spirit.'

Bernard had been surprised to see his class arrive in suits and dresses, supervised by Mr Flannelly. They were now dancing and using the buckets and spades. Being kids, their sandcastles were the best in the building.

Bernard turned to her. 'Congratulations, Mum. This is all amazing.'

'Thanks for playing the songs!' she said. 'I haven't heard music like that in a long time.'

'It's no trouble at all. In ways, I've been getting into disco just as long as you've been working on *Beach Noises*. I jam to your triumph.'

Ealaín smiled at her son, her pride shining. 'The triumph is shared,' she said, and moved back into the crowd.

After a while, Kirsten and Jay approached.

'This exhibition is great. That piece over there has perfect bus-stoppiness.'

'Thanks, Jay. It's nice to see the finished product. When Bucky and I are free, let's all get a selfie with the giraffe.'

'Sounds like a plan,' said Kirsten. 'Those are quality tunes, by the way.'

'I had a lot of help learning the ways of the disco spirit.'

She chuckled. 'OK, discoman. You'll have to listen to my early house records sometime. You know, the dance music that came after disco.'

'I'd dig that,' he said. He remembered Tastybase, with its synthesized drumlines and musical machines. Affy would encourage him to accept the invitation.

'By the way,' said Jay, 'that *Sweet Mind* sculpture is off the chain. Tell your mum we approve.'

Sweet Mind? Bernard still hadn't seen it.

He vowed to correct this. Using a trick he'd picked up from Levander – a secret of the selectors – he played a super-long track, which gave him time to leave the decks for a bit.

He explored the gallery rooms, crossing their sandy floors. His footsteps trailed between surfboards that stood like pop art tombstones. He passed the dollhouse covered in slivers of bamboo, now an artwork called *Tiny Beach Bar*. He winked at Bucky, who was giving a guided tour and had led his group to a slow-motion surfing video.

'You know,' he addressed them, 'surfing is a lot like life. You roll with the waves, get back up when you fall, and it's more fun in Hawaiian shorts.'

At last Bernard reached the far wing, the end of *Beach Noises*. Evening sunlight filled the circular room. Through a window to the left, he saw the top of the palm tree giraffe. The leafy head bounced in the wind. In a painting on the right, a woman ran by the water's edge. One of her sandals had slipped off.

Sweet Mind stood at the centre of the room. It was infinitely better than the messy lump of clay that had first appeared in the living room. Ealaín had sculpted a person, tall and broad. The figure wore robes with many folds. Its arms were outstretched.

Bernard ran his hands through his Afro and shook his head in wonder. He could barely believe his eyes.

'How did you end up here?' he said. The disco music swelled.

Sweet Mind had been cast in bronze, except for its head. A pineapple served that purpose.

ACKNOWLEDGEMENTS

In some form or another, Levander and co. have been bopping on the Musical Planet since 2015. A great deal of time and effort has gone into the making of *Spaceships in the Night*, and it wouldn't have been possible without amazing help along the way.

Firstly, huge thanks to the team at Kazoo Independent Publishing Services that produced the book you're holding. Chenile Keogh does great work in bringing hidden stories to light, and I'm grateful she accepted mine. She has been tireless in helping me through the process, and I couldn't have asked for a better project manager. I was blessed to have Robert Doran as an editor, and his work improved this story in every way. It was amazing to watch the manuscript transform under his guiding hand. Thanks to Natasha Mac a'Bháird for her brilliant proofreading. Andrew Brown showed admirable patience, and his cover designs were smashing. Thanks are also due to Jackie Burke, who gave me advice and guidance during the whole process. Her books are quality, if you need something to read after *Spaceships*!

Next, a huge thank you to Lauren O'Hara for taking a chance on this little project. She brought Bernard and friends to life with her gorgeous cover illustrations. Seeing them on the rooftop, bathed in neon light, still gives me chills. Thanks also to her agent Angharad Kowal Stannus, who was a kind and welcoming business associate from the start. If you're looking for great children's books, the O'Hara Sisters are not to be missed.

Next up, big thanks are due to Dubray. As a children's bookseller, I was nervous to unveil this disco city to my colleagues, and they've been nothing but supportive of it. I am grateful to my manager, Nicola Kennedy, who has shown enormous encouragement for *Spaceships*. Thanks to Caoilfhionn Fay for accepting me as a small supplier, and giving advice on invoicing. Thanks are also due to my fellow children's booksellers: you guys inspire me and have brightened up the lives of children across this country. I don't have enough room for all of the Dubrayers who have helped me in this process, but special mention must be given to my co-workers on the bookshop floor. Big love to the best of Bray.

Also, cheers to Morteza for the hundreds of coffees, which I always enjoyed while scribbling stories in his Little Coffee Shop.

My journey as a children's bookseller began in Tales for Tadpoles, so a special thanks goes to Caroline O'Sullivan for welcoming me onto the Tadpole team back in the day.

As to my friends, I am blessed to have an excellent selection. They've all shown me nothing but encouragement, and some special mentions are necessary. Massive thanks to Ben Kennedy, who took time out of his crazy schedule to give legal advice and support with the contracts related to this project. Thanks to Alex Criado, who has been a sweetheart as always and went out of his way to rally our friends with *Spaceships* hype. Thanks also to Peej Moloney, who never stopped pushing me to get this thing published.

From Italy to America, from Barcelona to Kildare, I have family members rooting for me all over the world. I can only hope I have succeeded in producing a good book for their shelves. Rachel, the best sister a guy could ask for, you gave me crucial tips on the first few chapters early in the process. To Dad, you were the biggest and only fan of my fantasy writings as a teenager. To Mum, sorry for the midnight disco music as I wrote these stories in the early days.

Massive thanks to Tuyen, who weathered all the late-night edits, headaches and doubts that came with this journey. You also celebrated and contributed to every victory. I'm eternally grateful that you're my dancing partner.

Finally, thank you for reading this book. I hope you have enjoyed this adventure. Until the next time, there is plenty of music to discover and friends to be made. Go and have some fun!